Out of the Shadows

Jennifer Gipp, OD

Barrett Gipp, JD

Joe,

Thank you for making this book possible with your endless knowledge of Oregon!

Jennifer Gipp
Barrett

Jennifer & Barrett Gipp

First Published in 2018 by Jennifer Gipp & Barrett Gipp. Copyright 2018. All rights reserved in accordance with the U.S. Copyright Act of 1976. No part of this publication may be reproduced, including scanning, photocopying, and distributing in any form or by any means, electronic or mechanical, or stored in a database or retrieval system without prior written permission from the publisher. Thank you for your support of the author's rights.

ISBN-13: 978-1533641137

ISBN-10: 1533641137

Editing: Janis K. Weier

Life Less Ordinary Publishing

Disclaimer: This book is a work of fiction. All of the characters, incidents, and dialogue (except for incidental references to public figures, products, publications, and services) are imaginary and not intended to refer to any living persons or to disparage any company's products or services. The publisher has put forth an effort in preparing and arranging this book. The information provided herein by the author is provided "as is." The publisher and author disclaim any liabilities for any loss of profit or commercial or personal damages resultant from the information contained in this book.

Dedication by Jennifer Gipp:

For my Mom. Thanks for always being a shoulder to lean on and a wonderful listener. You have taught me so much. I hope I can be the rock for my family that you have been for me.

Dedication by Barrett Gipp:

For my wife and son, who consistently and relentlessly see the best in people. Thank you for collaborating on this story and in everything else we've shared together.

Chapter 1

Kayla

Sweat dripped from Kayla McCullen's brow as she delicately placed the final touches on the painting she had been working on for several weeks. Her shoulders were tense from hunching over her canvas and her back was beginning to ache. Satisfied that the painting was complete, she straightened her shoulders and arched her back. She stepped back to observe her work.

The canvas portrayed a breathtaking landscape capturing the drama of the Oregon coastline near Cannon Beach. The rugged cliffs towering above the pounding surf were set in the brilliant, but fading light of sunset. It was her best work yet, she decided. She breathed a sigh of relief.

The Plaza Hotel, the oldest and most celebrated hotel in Portland, had commissioned the painting. The hotel's board sought a masterpiece to serve as the focal point of the main lobby and wanted a local artist to create their vision. Their instructions were specific. They wanted a landscape and told her the exact size that the painting needed to be. Kayla had listened to their requests patiently. She then thrust herself into her work, balancing their requirements with her own creative style. They had put a lot of pressure on her to produce the perfect piece, and she knew that their opinion carried a lot of weight. This project could very well make or break her career.

Kayla glanced at the clock and realized it was nearly 3:00 AM. She had completely lost track of time. Carefully setting her paintbrush down and removing her smock, she grimaced realizing she'd promised her friends she would meet them for a drink earlier that evening. Having turned off her cell phone when she started to paint earlier that afternoon, she was oblivious to the time as hours passed like minutes. She washed her hands in her sink and then padded barefoot across her studio in search of her cell phone. She finally found it wedged between an unused canvas and a bottle of paint thinner. She turned it on and wondered if her friends would have even noticed she was missing. Her cell phone started to buzz with missed calls and voicemail messages, which reminded her that her friends had indeed missed her and had called her nonstop throughout the evening.

She sighed, wishing she were a better friend. Although she loved getting together with the gang for nights out, she often got caught up in her work and completely forgot about her social life. It was too late now to return any of the missed calls, so she sent out a series of text messages, apologizing for her unexplained absence and reassuring everyone she was safe at home in her studio. She promised she would make the next gathering and vowed to be a better friend in the future.

Kayla grabbed a bottle of water from her fridge and headed upstairs. She pulled off her work clothes on her way to her bedroom and left them lying in a heap on her floor. Then she pulled on her satin pajamas, crawled beneath her down comforter, and fell into a deep sleep wrapped up in her cocoon of feather pillows and Egyptian cotton sheets.

Her slumber ended abruptly when she jolted awake at 6:00 AM the following morning. She sat straight up in bed, her gaze scanning her room. Her breaths were coming in short gasps and sweat poured from her forehead. She stifled a scream.

"Calm down. It's not real. You are perfectly safe. There's no one here but you." Kayla told herself the same mantra every time she awoke with the feeling of terror that so often pulled her from a peaceful sleep. She glanced at her bedroom door to make sure the deadbolt was still in place. Then she checked the window to make sure it was locked securely. She'd made sure to pick out a bed that didn't have any hiding spots underneath and there were no closets in her bedroom, only a dresser with drawers too small for any human to hide in. Kayla had carefully designed her bedroom to ensure there were no hiding places and she could view every inch of the room from her bed. She felt her heart rate settle into a regular rhythm, and forced herself to calm down and accept the realization she was safe.

    Kayla glanced at her clock and felt disappointed that she'd only managed to get three hours of sleep. Now she was wide-awake and it was useless to try to get back to sleep. Memories had already started flooding back into her mind, and the only way to force them out was to get back to work. Grudgingly, she pried herself out from under her luxurious sheets, stumbled into her bathroom, and started a steaming shower.

Out of the Shadows

Chapter 2

<u>Hunter</u>

 Hunter Erickson braced himself for the series of massive moguls he was about to carve. He shifted his body weight with precision and allowed his knees to absorb the shock as he courageously met the challenging obstacles. The ease with which he was able to traverse the black diamond courses was awe-inspiring. He made the sharpest of turns look easy and seemed to glide over moguls that gave even the most experienced skiers trouble. With smooth movements, Hunter was able to build speed toward the finish line at the bottom of the hill and then maneuver his skis slightly so he came to a clean stop sending loose snow blasting into the air. The applause from the crowds was deafening. He gave them one of his trademark grins before stepping out of his skis and hurrying back to watch the rest of the races. He was clearly the favorite, and his performance today made it nearly impossible for anyone to catch up with him. He was the golden boy of extreme skiing, and the judges loved him. He was a true daredevil who never failed to impress. On top of that, he was extremely gracious and kind to both his rivals and his fans. He never let his ego get the better of him.

 Although he exhibited extreme confidence on the slopes, very little was known about his personal life. Women flocked near the locker rooms after every competition, but their hours of waiting to catch a glimpse of him were always in vain. Hunter was an escape artist. He always exited the competitions quietly and avoided the locker rooms. He preferred to stay at inexpensive motels far from the glamour and luxury of his rivals' hotels. This allowed him the opportunity to make a quick getaway before the crowds descended after races.

 On this particular day, when there were still two days left, Hunter craved solitude and rest. He quietly slipped out the back of the resort and into his rented hybrid. No one would expect him to be driving a small compact, which was by design. He drove the thirty minutes back to his tiny motel in Bellingham, WA, unlocked his door, threw off his coat, and collapsed on the bed. The other elite skiers might crave the company of glamorous women, expensive restaurants, and trendy bars, but for Hunter, the most important thing during a week of intense competition was sleep. He drifted off with nothing on his mind other than the feel of the snow rushing past his face as he flew down the mountain, cloaked in the peaceful silence that only the mountains could provide.

When he awoke an hour later, he realized that he hadn't even bothered to take off his shoes before he'd fallen into bed and drifted off. He rubbed his neck as he sat up and pulled off his shoes, tossing them unceremoniously onto the ground near the door. He stood up, walked to the bathroom, and splashed some water on his face. After changing into lounge pants and a faded T-shirt, he checked the alarm clock near his bed. It was only 7:00 PM. He felt his stomach start to growl, and called the nearest pizza delivery place.

"I'll take a large sausage and mushroom, thin crust with extra sauce, please." Hunter rattled off his hotel's name and room number and sat down at the small desk that was crammed in the corner and littered with brochures about tourist activities offered in the North Cascades. Although there were endless things to do near Mt. Baker and in Seattle, his schedule didn't allow time for sightseeing, so he opened a desk drawer and pushed all of the brochures and paperwork inside. He took out his laptop and booted it up. He struggled to find the Wi-Fi connection the hotel had advertised, but eventually picked up a signal and opened a browser. He quickly typed in the address for Chatham Online University. He signed into his account and let out a groan when he realized how many assignments were due within the next week. He shook his head slowly, rubbed the sleep from of his eyes, and began typing. It was going to be a very long night.

Chapter 3

Me

It was well past midnight, and there was stillness in the air that was rare for Fisherman's Wharf on a Saturday night. The place was usually thriving with people in their early twenties taking advantage of the nightlife or tourists strolling along the waterfront, stopping in to grab a glass of wine or a cup of coffee before ending their long day of sightseeing. Tonight was different. The clouds that made Seattle famous had rolled in during the late afternoon and the sheets of rain that had been mercilessly pounding the city were finally beginning to let up. Now the wharf was slick with moisture and a musty haze filled the air. The rain had slowed, but it was only a brief reprieve. I sit tucked away in an alley, out of view from any of the usual passersby. I like my position. It allows me to see without being seen. I like to be the observer and watch people at my leisure while avoiding the attention and judgment of others. I used to make the effort to be more social and carry on conversations with others. I tried to fit into their world, but no one seemed to understand me, nor I, them. People would always be laughing and discussing the most mundane topics. Whenever I offered something interesting to say, everyone reacted with a mixture of horror and disbelief. It was truly curious how these people saw fit to think me odd. They should have been thanking me for tolerating their idle chitchat when none of them could string together two consecutive sentences of interesting thought.

    I finally gave up the facade. What was the point of trying? People don't connect with me, and I've never wanted them to. I'm better off on my own. You see, my life actually has a purpose. I have a reason for being on this Earth. I'm not just here to live in the indentured servitude of society. I have no interest in grinding away at some 8:00-5:00 job just so I can see my money dissipate away to taxes, a mortgage for a cookie-cutter house in the suburbs or trendy loft in some generic hipster haven neighborhood, or tuition for entitled little selfish snobs. No, I won't be fooled into buying into the system. I don't want a family, a house, a boring, mind-numbing job, or any other presence on their grid. None of those things matter to me, nor have they ever.

Currently, the only thing that really consumes me in this life is making *her* suffer; to punish her for her ignorance and ungratefulness and make her realize that she can never escape me. I ache to watch her die a slow and painful death. That is my ultimate purpose, and I will not stop until I see it accomplished.

Out of the Shadows

Chapter 4

Kayla

    Kayla closed her eyes and let the steam roll over her body. She forced the tension out of her shoulders. She made a promise to herself that tonight would be the night that she would start sleeping more than three hours at a time. Tonight she would finally start living her life.
    Kayla stepped out of the shower, toweled off, and wrapped herself in a fluffy white robe. She ran a comb through her long chestnut hair, applied some moisturizer to her fair skin, and added a dab of sheer gloss to her full lips. She hummed softly to herself as she padded onto the soft carpet in her bedroom. The chime of her doorbell startled her. She glanced at herself in her full-length mirror. Her hair was still damp from her shower, and she was hardly presentable in her robe. She remembered that she'd ordered something online, and figured it was probably just the deliveryman. She dismissed the doorbell and focused her attention on getting dressed. She selected a soft coral-colored Maxi dress that accentuated her slim waist and added a long gold chain, which brought out the gold flecks in her almond eyes.
    Feeling presentable, she walked down the winding staircase in her 1920s Craftsman home. The floorboards creaked softly below her feet. The noise added to the charm of her house. When she reached the bottom step, she glanced through the peephole in her door. The porch was empty, so she unfastened the deadbolt and chain locks, and cautiously opened the door. Instead of the package that she was expecting, there was a white envelope sticking out from under her doormat. She reached down and snatched it. It looked innocent enough, but as she flipped it over, her heart skipped a beat. There was one world neatly printed on the envelope and it stopped her dead in her tracks. *Elizabeth.*

Kayla quickly stepped back inside, locked the door behind her, and leaned against the wall. She forced her breaths to remain even despite the fact that her heart was racing. The envelope was addressed to "Elizabeth". That was her former name, the one she'd used before her entire life crashed down around her. She hadn't gone by that name since she'd entered the witness protection program and been forced to relocate from her hometown of Chicago to Seattle three years before. She had fled from her cozy apartment in Wrigleyville. The only possessions she took with her were the clothes on her back, her camera, and a few photographs of close friends that she knew she may never see again. A federal agent had escorted her to the US Marshal Services Headquarters where she spent hours working with agents learning her new identity.

During her orientation, she was reassured that 8,500 people had been forced to enter the Witness Security Program. Never once had the security system been breached or any of the witnesses harmed. As long as she played by the rules, she would be safe. A team met with her and coached her on how to look and act like a different person. It didn't take long for Elizabeth Bronson with stick-straight blonde hair, minimal make-up, and unkempt eyebrows to be erased completely and replaced by a much more sophisticated looking woman with radiant chestnut hair, arched eyebrows, and prominent cheekbones. She soon learned that this new woman, this alter ego, was named Kayla McCullen. To make things official, she even had to turn in her old driver's license, passport, and credit cards.

The new driver's license and credit cards that she received stated that her new name was Kayla Catherine McCullen and she lived in Seattle. The carefully made-up face smiling back at her from her ID was a wavy-haired brunette who looked nothing like her former self. The agents did their best to explain why Elizabeth Bronson needed to disappear and why she couldn't contact her friends and family about her whereabouts right away, but it didn't make the reality of the situation any easier. She had been born and raised in Chicago. She had majored in Fine Arts at The Art Institute and had established herself as a free-lance photographer. She had recently started doing a lot of commercial photography for various businesses and kept busy shooting weddings and portraits in her spare time. Her studio apartment was on the 20th floor of a building with a gorgeous view of Lakeshore Drive.

Despite her love of photography, the Witness Security Program cautioned her not to pursue her photography career until things settled down. It had been a long, uphill battle for her to reclaim her life over the past three years. The new Kayla McCullen had decided to enroll in a Master's program focused on painting. She had hoped that the whole situation would resolve within weeks, but the weeks had turned into months and the months to years. Before she knew it, she had completed her Master's degree and started a new career as a painter. It had taken her months to become comfortable with a new medium. Photography had always been her passion. It was a clean, defined art. As long as she followed the rules of lighting and composition, she had a quality product. Painting was much different. She started with a blank canvas and had to make her own design. Every painting had to make its own statement, and she had to guide it into creation.

At first, the task was daunting, but over time she started to find comfort in her new art form. Creating a painting from a blank canvas reminded her of starting her new life from nothing. She found peace in the process and the strength she needed to put one foot in front of the other and carry on. She made new friends in grad school. Most of them were younger than she was and were from the greater Seattle area. They didn't seem to mind her need for privacy or her hesitancy to talk about herself. They accepted that she had moved to Seattle to start over when she ran into trouble in her old life. They all assumed she'd been in a bad relationship, got wrapped up with drugs, or perhaps both. She was beautiful, talented, and a great listener, so they accepted her for who she was and didn't pressure her to share more than she wanted.

Of course, all of that changed with that one single word typed on the envelope she was clutching. Someone had figured out who and where she was, and she was no longer safe. She carefully opened the envelope and took out a single sheet of paper. She slid it out and caught her breath when she read the short message. "Ezekiel 18:20 states that wicked people will be punished for their own wickedness. You were a fool to think you could escape, my dear Elizabeth."

Out of the Shadows

Chapter 5

<u>Hunter</u>

    Hunter woke up to a very loud beeping at 5:00 AM the next morning. He groaned and slammed his alarm clock with his open palm before rolling back over. Five minutes later, his phone rang in an ear-piercing noise that made him cringe. He picked up the phone and heard the front desk announcing his requested wake-up call.

    He groaned. Coach Sullivan knew him too well. He had been training with Coach Sullivan for years, and his coach knew better than anyone that Hunter was not a morning person. He'd lived through too many occasions where Hunter had turned off his alarm clock and nearly missed his competition. Coach Sullivan was used to hunting him down at his hotel and banging on the door until Hunter rolled out of bed. He had finally gotten smart and started ordering wake-up calls. Hunter rolled out of bed and sat with his head in the palms of his hands for a while, letting his head clear. He had been up until 2:00 AM finishing his assignments. He knew Coach Sullivan wouldn't approve, but then again, it wasn't Coach Sullivan's life. Hunter had dropped out of high school in order to pursue a career as a professional skier. He'd been happy with his decision for a long time, especially when he was winning world championships and qualifying for the Olympics. His speed, precision, and technical mastery had earned him two gold medals and three silvers. He was one of the best skiers in the world.

    The only problem was that he knew he wouldn't be able to maintain this level of competition forever. There were already younger skiers with impressive talent entering the competitions. He was beginning to feel like the old veteran. He knew that he had to think about the future. He'd started taking classes and completed his GED online a year ago. He hadn't told anyone about it because he was afraid he might fail. His reward to himself after he passed his test was to apply to online universities. He'd been thrilled when he received an acceptance letter from Chatham and had enrolled for their fall semester. He was pursuing a major in business and had successfully completed two semesters. It was tough for him to keep up with his classes when he was on the road, but he knew that he didn't stand a chance in the real world without a degree, so he made time to study while his competitors were out partying.

What he sacrificed in sleep, he gained in confidence. He found that the more he focused on his course work, the more focused he was on the slopes. His performance had improved from where it had been at the last Olympics, and he was already a favorite for the next Winter Games in two years.

When Hunter's head finally cleared, he stood up and stepped into the lukewarm shower. Hotels never seemed to have decent water pressure or hot water, but it was something to which he'd grown accustomed. He wanted to save all the money he could in order to cover his tuition and save up for a house whenever his life settled down. The sacrifice of staying in cheap hotels was worth it.

Hunter stepped out of the shower and wrapped a towel around his hips. He quickly shaved and was about to head into the bedroom to get dressed when he heard a pounding at his door.

"Open up, Hunter. I'm not letting you arrive late. You're in first place, and I'm not letting you blow this!"

Hunter opened the door after waiting a good thirty seconds in order to make his coach sweat. He had a sideways smirk on his face as he came face to face with his red-faced, pacing mentor.

"Good morning yourself, sunshine; you seem to have woken up on the wrong side of the bed this morning."

Coach Sullivan took one look at his towel-clad athlete and let out a low groan. "Could you at least put some clothes on? We should have left 15 minutes ago, and you're not even dressed."

Hunter grinned at his coach and stepped aside for him to enter. Part of his strategy was to show up just before he was scheduled to compete in order to avoid letting his competitors' fear and anxiety rub off on him. His Coach was a believer in punctuality and mental preparation, so he would never be able to understand why Hunter was perpetually late. Regardless of their differences, the pair seemed to have an unspoken understanding of one another. After working together for the better part of ten years, they knew just how to push each other's buttons.

Hunter decided that he'd messed with his coach enough for one day, and obediently gathered his things. Coach Sullivan looked around the room and took in the empty pizza box and the half-full coffee pot. "Looks like you've been eating the diet of champions."

"Give it a rest, Coach. You should be happy that I didn't down a bottle of tequila and smoke a pack of cigarettes like most of my competition did last night."

Coach Sullivan nodded. Hunter had a point. The ski circuit had a reputation for wild parties, and that was one area that he and Hunter had never had to argue about. Hunter may have had a few less than desirable habits, but when push came to shove, he was a good kid with admirable work ethic and a strong desire to succeed. So what if he had a few vices like greasy pizza and sleeping late. There were worse things in the world.

Hunter was ready within minutes. Coach Sullivan had to hand it to him. When he put his mind to it, he could move mountains, and the speed with which Hunter had managed to get dressed and get his gear in order was impressive. Coach Sullivan insisted on driving because the small compact Hunter had rented wasn't big enough for two people and all the gear. Hunter settled himself into the passenger seat and pulled out a bag of beef jerky. He waved the bag in front of his coach's nose, but Coach Sullivan shook his head. "I already had a real breakfast at my hotel. Please tell me that's not all you're planning to eat for breakfast."

"Trust me, this is what I eat before every competition," Hunter said with his mouth full.

Coach Sullivan just shook his head and smiled. Who was he to judge the habits of a champion?

Chapter 6

Me

We all get what's coming to us. Elizabeth Bronson deserves everything I have in store for her. That little snitch has been trying to ruin my life for the past three years. She may have information that could put me away for a very long time, but it's never going to come to that. I'll show her. I know who will have the last laugh in this little game of cat and mouse.

She really thought that she could escape me, but the joke is on her. She was a fool to think she could hide. It took me a while to track her down. She did a good job of transforming herself from a blonde hippie into a sultry brunette, but there are only so many things a person can change. I have to hand it to her, she did everything someone in hiding is supposed to do. She didn't contact her family or friends, not even once. I know because I've tracked everyone listed in her address book. I bugged the phone of every one of her family members. I even monitored their mail, but there wasn't a trace of their little Elizabeth. Not even a note explaining that she had left town. She truly just vanished.

Fortunately, she's an artist and the drug scene among artists in Seattle is strong. One of her classmates was fed up with her mysterious persona and inability to follow through on social plans. He started digging and found out why she'd moved to Seattle. He owed a dealer I know and turned over the information in exchange for drugs. I laugh at the simplicity of it all.

Elizabeth may have been able to evade me for the past three years, but I'm the master of this game. She'll die long before she ever gets the chance to testify against me on the witness stand.

Chapter 7

<u>Kayla</u>

    Kayla's hands shook as she held the letter. It occurred to her that she may be disturbing evidence by touching it. She dropped the note as if it was on fire and slumped down to the floor. She sat with her head in her hands and sobbed for several minutes before her survival instincts kicked in. She hadn't come this far just to give up. She needed to be strong if she wanted the chance to lead a real life. She got to her feet and grabbed her cell phone from her end table. She called the US Martial Service and dialed the extension for the Witness Security Program.

    "Please identify yourself," said the no-nonsense voice across the line.

    "Hello. This is number 57621 calling to report an incident." Kayla stated her birth date and social security number. She then proceeded to answer an endless list of questions ranging from what street she grew up on to the name of her childhood best friend.

    Satisfied that the actual Kayla McCullen/Elizabeth Bronson was on the line, the agent listened carefully to her account of the morning's events. The agent identified herself as Kari and stated that she was sorry to hear that there was a potential breach of security. The agency members prided themselves on all of the precautions they took to avoid situations like these.

    "Don't leave your house. Stay put, and lock your doors. We'll send agents over immediately. They will identify themselves by using the names of your favorite childhood celebrities. Do not; I repeat, DO NOT open your door unless the people asking to enter follow protocol."

    Kayla stated that she understood. Her voice felt small and weak without any of the usual confidence she exuded when she spoke. She silently cursed this man for stalking her and refusing to let her move on. Kayla reached into her footstool and pulled out her 25-caliber handgun. She sat in her recliner, facing the door. The only sound in the room was the ticking of her clock. After what seemed like an eternity, she heard a knock.

"Who's there?" Kayla asked cautiously.

"Jordan Knight and Jason Priestley," a voice responded.

Kayla flushed with embarrassment. She'd been asked to answer pages of odd questions that seemed unrelated to her case when she entered the Witness Security Program. Now she understood why. No one else in their right mind could possibly have known the answer to that question.

Kayla slowly stood up, went to the door, and peered through the peephole. She saw two agents dressed in plain clothes. The only thing that distinguished them was the badges they were discreetly holding up. She undid a series of locks and opened the door just wide enough to let them enter. As soon as they stepped into the foyer, she closed the door and refastened all of the bolts. Her hands were still shaking from the shock of the letter.

The agents quickly introduced themselves as Agent Jeffrey Franklin and Agent Harry Olson. They appeared to be in their mid-fifties and seemed kind, but austere. They obviously took their jobs very seriously. She relaxed ever so slightly when she realized they were both carrying guns that were loaded. She had a 25-caliber of her own to scare away potential intruders, but the truth was that the gun wasn't loaded. She couldn't stand the thought of a loaded gun in her house and was positive that she could never actually shoot someone, even if her life depended on it. Being with trained professionals who were not afraid to use force when needed made her feel more secure.

"Let's start from the beginning," Agent Olson began. He was a slightly rotund, balding man. He peered at her through his wire-rim spectacles that sat slightly too low on his nose. "You were upstairs getting out of the shower when you heard the doorbell ring."

Kayla nodded. Agent Olson continued, "You didn't answer the

door right away due to the fact that you were, shall we say, not dressed to receive company. When you did come downstairs and opened your door, you found an envelope taped to your front door?"

"That's correct." Something about Agent Olson's mannerisms made Kayla feel slightly uncomfortable. He seemed to be picking her case apart, rather than focusing on the letter.

"And this letter…do you still have it?"

"Of course, I do," Kayla was a little put off that he would even ask her the question. It seemed obvious that she would have the letter considering that it was the reason she had called the US Marshall's office in the first place.

Kayla walked over to the floor where she had dropped the letter and gestured to it. "I didn't want to ruin any evidence, so I haven't moved it from the place it was when I first read it."

Fortunately, Agent Franklin was a bit more personable and walked over to her. He pulled out rubber gloves and carefully picked up the letter, being sure not to disturb anything. He examined the note, and then slipped it and the envelope into a plastic bag. "We'll take it to the lab to search for evidence. It certainly looks as if the person sending it may have a clue to your real identity."

"That's what I was afraid of. I don't know what to do now. I've reinvented my life and my career over the past three years. I don't know if I have the strength to do it again." Kayla was terrified that she would have to relocate to a new city, with a new name, and begin a new career. She'd had to do it once already, and it had nearly killed her. She had grown to love Seattle and couldn't imagine having to adjust to life in another city. What if, after all that, he found her again? Living like a nomad didn't exactly sound like an ideal existence.

"We called the lead agent in on your case before we came over. Up until now, all of the leads we've had on the Kazimir case have been dead ends. We're no closer to finding him than we were three years ago. If we move you he'll disappear again, and it's unlikely that we'll ever find him. If that happens, you'll have to remain in hiding indefinitely."

Kayla nodded. She knew the detectives were right, but she was starting to lose faith in the system. She had originally joined the program expecting to remain in hiding for a year at the very most. Three times that amount of time had passed and after all of the struggling she'd done to keep herself alive, she might end up dead anyway.

"So, what do you expect me to do?" Kayla was starting to feel herself panicking. She had learned how to control her anxiety attacks with weekly visits to a therapist, but she was finding that even the breathing exercises and mental games she learned were ineffective.

"We expect you to carry on with your life. We're going to have agents posted at your house around the clock. You'll never be alone. It's likely that Kazimir or one of his accomplices will reappear. When they do, we'll finally get some information that will lead us to him."

"So basically, you're going to use me as bait?" Kayla's horror was evident by her expression.

"You could look at it that way," Agent Franklin began in a patient voice, "Or you could look at it from the perspective that the only way you're ever going to have control of your life again is if we close this case and put Kazimir behind bars."

Kayla sat looking pensive for a moment. She didn't have many options. She didn't want to create a new identity because he would very likely track her down again. The only way for her to take control was to bring him down for the violent crime he had committed, and she had mistakenly witnessed. It wasn't until he was in police custody that she would get her freedom back.

"Fine, I'll do whatever it takes to clean up this mess once and for all." Kayla let out a sigh, "What do you need me to do?"

Agents Olson and Franklin exchanged a glance. They were relieved that she was going to cooperate. This whole case would be a lot easier with her collaboration. "For starters, you're going to have to get used to us hanging around, listening in on every phone conversation in case he calls, and following you wherever you go. You might not be able to see us at all times, but we'll be able to see you. If we feel you're even in the slightest danger, we'll let you know."

"Great," Kayla stated in a less than enthusiastic voice. The one thing that she longed for in her life was privacy, and it didn't seem like she wasn't going to be getting any for a very long time.

Chapter 8

Hunter

 Hunter was introduced to downhill skiing when he was ten years old by his Uncle Jackson, who was a ski instructor. Growing up in Golden Colorado, just outside of Denver, Hunter's parents didn't have a lot of money. His father worked as a janitor during the night shift at a local elementary school and his mother worked in the checkout line at a local grocery store. They didn't have the money to go on large family vacations but made frequent trips into the mountains to visit his uncle in Breckinridge. His uncle worked at a ski resort and was able to organize for his nephew to get free ski passes. Hunter's parents didn't care for skiing and were content to sit around the fireplace in the lodge and read while Hunter and his uncle hit the slopes.

 Hunter's only formal training was from his uncle, who taught him the proper ski stance. He explained why it was important to lean forward with his chest directly above his toes and a slight bend in his waist rather than leaning backwards. He taught Hunter to control his speed and to angle his skis when he wanted to slow down. He instructed him to keep his chin and eyes up so he would be ready to anticipate turns and obstacles. Hunter followed his uncle's instructions, and within his first few hours of skiing, he had already graduated from green runs to blues and was begging his uncle to let him try a blue-black.

 Jackson couldn't believe how gifted Hunter was. He'd taught some children lessons for months, and they still couldn't ski with the skill that Hunter had on his first day. Jackson didn't tell Hunter what a natural he was at skiing. Instead, he continued to push him to see how far Hunter could go before he started to show fear. The joke was on Jackson. By the end of the short vacation to the mountains, Hunter was already skiing down black diamonds with the greatest of ease. On their last night in Breckinridge, Jackson waited for Hunter to go to bed, and then spoke in a low tone to his parents.

"Hunter is amazingly talented. I've truly never seen anyone pick up skiing the way he has. He's an absolute natural."

"That's wonderful to hear." Hunter's mother had said in a matter-of-fact voice. "We want him to enjoy the sport, so we can make trips to the mountains an annual event."

Jackson shifted slightly in his chair, looking uncomfortable. "I think Hunter should ski more frequently than once a year."

"In that case we could try to bring him up at least twice a year, if you don't mind finding him ski passes," Hunter's mother said, not fully grasping what Jackson was trying to say.

"With the right training and dedication, Hunter could be a champion. His skill is unlike anything I've ever seen before, and he loves being on the slopes."

Hunter's mother paused, taking in the full meaning of what her brother was trying to say. It was true that Hunter had been happier during his time in the mountains than she'd ever seen him. He was typically withdrawn and spent too much time by himself. She had always blamed it on the fact that he was an only child and didn't have siblings to keep him company. Now she realized that part of his moody demeanor could have been that she and her husband had pushed him into activities like piano lessons and soccer. He always protested about having to go to practice, and she thought it was because he was lazy and unmotivated. Now she realized that it may have been because he didn't have a true passion for any of those things. It was clear to her that Hunter did have passion and motivation after all. His passion was for skiing, and they would be wrong to hold him back from something he loved.

"What do you suggest we do?" She asked quietly.

"I suggest you have him spend winters with me in Breckinridge. I'll arrange for him to get a coach and will ski with him on my days off. He can attend school up here. Kids only go to class four long days per week and have Fridays off. He'll have plenty of opportunities to hone his skills. When he's old enough, he can start to enter competitions if he's still interested."

Hunter's mom was quiet. He was her only child. She had wanted to have more, but her second pregnancy had been ectopic. The complications had led to a miscarriage, and her doctors had informed her that she would never be able to have another child. She had always been grateful for the fact that God had given her at least one child and had made her peace with her small family. The thought of sending Hunter away for several months a year broke her heart.

"We'll talk to Hunter about it when we get home. It will have to be his decision. We certainly will support him in whatever he chooses, but it will be difficult for us if he decides he doesn't want to live with us in Golden full-time."

"I understand," Jackson said. "But I think you owe it to him to give him the choice."

Hunter's mom knew in her heart that he was right. Hunter had constant behavior problems in school over the last two years and seemed unhappy most of the time. It might be good for him to have a chance to make a new start. He would no doubt make friends in Breckinridge thanks to his passion for skiing.

It took Hunter all of fifteen minutes to decide later that week. "I want to go. I really want to live with Uncle Jackson and ski. Please let me go, Mom. You can come up and visit me every weekend, I promise."

After much deliberation, she and Hunter's father agreed to try out the arrangement for one year. Hunter thanked them profusely and soon proved that they had made the right decision. Hunter's grades went up, his behavior problems at school stopped completely, and he spent every free minute on the slopes. When he had spare time, he worked odd jobs at the resort, washing dishes or cleaning rooms in order to pay for his ski lessons.

Later that year, tragedy struck. Hunter's parents were killed in a terrorist attack while they were attending a football game in

Denver. The shooter was a young man with a long history of psychological problems. 27 people lost their lives, including Hunter's parents, and 32 others were injured. The news was devastating to Hunter. He couldn't get over the fact that if he hadn't chosen to live with his uncle, he would have been with them. He owed his life to his Uncle Jackson, who had agreed to be his legal guardian now that his parents were deceased. Hunter got through the funeral services and the months that followed by focusing on learning to snowboard. He cried whenever he thought of his parents and did his best to keep his mind busy. His Uncle Jackson, who was a lifelong bachelor by choice, stepped up to the responsibility of being Hunter's guardian. The bond between them grew strong. Hunter felt that he owed everything to his uncle and vowed to pay him back by becoming the best skier to have ever lived. It took him ten years, but in the last Winter Olympics, his amazing performance in the Alpine Ski events finally earned him that title. Jackson was proud of his nephew and never missed a competition. In fact, he was waiting at the slopes for Hunter and Coach Sullivan when they arrived at the base of the mountain.

Chapter 9

<u>Me</u>

She really thinks she's outsmarted me. It's hard to imagine that someone who is so talented is naive enough to think she stands a chance in this game. I could have killed Elizabeth outright as soon as I found where she was hiding, but that was just too easy. I want to toy with her, watch her suffer, and then ever so slowly and deliberately, end her life in the most painful and excruciating way imaginable.

Finding her wasn't as easy as I'd hoped. I had originally devised a plan to end her on her way home from work after she saw my destruction in the warehouse. My people staked out her apartment waiting for her, ready to move when she unlocked the door. If done right, it would have looked like she had run away, no forced entry, limited struggle, and no witness. We planned to make sure she was erased completely. The only problem was she never came home. We waited for hours, for days, and nothing, no sign of her. Her friends and family who had keys to her apartment came and went in search of her. They all appeared to be worried. Surely she would have shared her plan with one of them, but why would they be searching for her if they knew she was somewhere safe? It baffled me that she managed to disappear from Chicago without a trace.

With each passing day, my rage consumed me. I finally paid someone, a low level dealer I knew, to break into her place. I expected that she would have taken her things if she was going to leave, but my accomplice found that everything remained preserved like the ruins of Pompeii. Her coat was flung over the back of a chair. Unopened bills sat on her counter waiting in vain to be paid. There was even a half-eaten sandwich sitting on the table doing little but growing mold. The snitch had just up and vanished.

I'm no one's fool. I know she's not smart enough to skip town without professional help. To my core, I know that to be true. By the way her family was swarming her apartment, crying, and carrying on, I knew it wasn't them. They seemed too simple to participate in such a ruse.

I asked myself, "What would a little girl in her twenties do when she's witnessed a heinous crime and realized that she'd been spotted by the perpetrator?" To my chagrin, it's Occam's Razor. She called the police and told them her sob story. Despite their incompetence, they pieced it together and looked into probable cause for a dangerous and sought after criminal. They promised the girl protection and swept her off in the middle of the night. They gave her a new name, a new look, and deposited her in some far away city, hoping that she'd eventually be able to help them lock up their prize, me. It's almost comical how predictable they are using a trite, one-size-fits-all program like Witness Security.

They think they've got it all figured out. Well, they won't be the ones laughing when I finally get a hold of their precious little "Kayla" or "Elizabeth" or whatever the hell she's calling herself these days. At this point, it's about suppressing the impulsive part of my brain and being patient. It's about having the fortitude to allow the time necessary to see this plan to fruition and will be worth the wait.

You might wonder why I hate her so much. So she spotted me doing something awful and ratted me out to the cops. Big deal. I was already a wanted man, so what difference does it make if there's another criminal act added to the ever-expanding file that started in my teens? Well, she didn't just see me messing someone up. She also screwed up the biggest move of my career. Had she never shown her bratty little face that night, I would have been filthy rich. I could have skipped the country and been off yachting around the world living like the freaking one percent, but no, she couldn't let that happen. I loathe her to the depths of my soul, hate her with a passion, and despise her with every fiber of my being.

Chapter 10

Kayla

    Kayla mulled over her situation that night while sipping a cup of jasmine green tea. She had hoped that she would be out having an uncharacteristically carefree and fun night with her friends, but instead, she was imprisoned in her own house feeling more isolated than she'd ever been. She knew that Agent Franklin was perched just up the hill and had a view through her kitchen window. He was probably watching her sip tea through his binoculars. She could wave at him if she wanted to, but she didn't. She preferred to pretend Big Brother wasn't there. She knew she should be grateful there were people so eager and willing to keep her alive. She should feel lucky, but the idea of spending the next few years under lock and key was horrifying. She had her painting to keep her busy, but how was she supposed to find inspiration if she was risking her life by stepping out onto her porch? How was she supposed to get groceries? She started to picture herself wasting away inside her home, subsisting on every last scrap of food she had. Before she knew it, she'd be rationing out stale crackers.

    Kayla shook her head to ward off the depressing thoughts. She reminded herself she would have to be optimistic if she was going to get through this new hurdle in her increasingly challenging life. She wasn't going to starve. Agent Franklin said she could still leave her house, but he would be tailing her. She chose not to because she was still so shaken by the fact that her tormentor had managed to find her.

    She fought back flashbacks of that horrifying night in Chicago. She'd been at a friend's party near Hyde Park. She meant to leave the party early to go home, but the wine was flowing, the crowd was lively, and time escaped her. When she finally realized that it was well after midnight, she reluctantly said her goodbyes and headed for the subway stop planning to go north on the Red Line. The train arrived within minutes of her stepping on the platform, and she took a seat. Fatigue set in and she briefly nodded off. She awoke to a screeching halt and a voice over the intercom apologized that the train was experiencing technical difficulties. It instructed everyone to get off at the current stop. She grudgingly got up and stepped off the train, annoyed at her luck. She walked off the platform and down the steps. The train was nearly empty, so there weren't many people who followed her. Most people waited on the platform with their cell phones in hand paying no attention to the others. Kayla had lived in Chicago her entire life and was savvy. She figured she could make her way to a bus stop and ride the bus home. She was trying to think where the nearest stop was when she turned and took in her surroundings. She blinked a few times, unfamiliar with the neighborhood. Then it hit her. She had walked right into Washington Square Park, one of the nation's most dangerous neighborhoods after dark. No one was around and there was an eeriness surrounding the park. Suddenly she saw a few shadows. They looked like they were coming towards her, so she turned and started to walk swiftly in the other direction. She saw an alleyway and disappeared into it just as the shadows ran past. She sat for a minute, hovering behind a trash bin, praying they wouldn't come back. After several moments, she gingerly stood up and tiptoed down the alley. She was sure that if she found a busier street, she'd be home free. She could hear traffic in the distance and headed towards the sound. Just before she turned the last corner, she heard voices. What happened next would change her life forever. The images she saw that night where burned into her brain. A part of her joyful innocence was shattered that night, and in a sense, she lost the only life she had ever known.

    Kayla rubbed her temples, pushing the images that were trying to surface into the far-off corners of her memory. Reliving the past was not going to help her feel better. She needed to stop thinking and just be Kayla or Elizabeth or whoever she was supposed to be, for a few hours. She finally decided to do the only thing that allowed her to clear her mind and lose herself completely. She picked up her paintbrush and headed to her studio. She had a lot of work to do, and this was as good a time as any to get started.

Chapter 11

<u>Hunter</u>

 The conditions on the slopes were perfect with the snow smoothly packed and the wind blowing in the right direction. Hunter could feel the first beads of sweat emerging from his pores as time slowed to a crawl. He forced his hands to stop shaking at the starting line. He took a few deep breaths. The silence seemed deafening. Finally, the starting signal sounded loud and clear. Hunter's adrenaline immediately took over. His body instinctively knew what to do. He rapidly gained speed out of the start. His skis propelled him forward. Soon he was flying down the mountain at break-neck speed. He carved around the flags with skill and precision, slicing through the snow and gaining momentum. He hugged each curve and delicately shifted his body ever so slightly to the right and the left. He was efficient and in control. Complete silence descended on the crowd of onlookers as they watched him gracefully maneuvering down the mountain. There was not a wasted movement as he rapidly gained speed. No one dared to utter a word, for fear of breaking the spell that Hunter wove as he flew around each and every obstacle. He whizzed past the finish line and slowed himself down, finally stopping with a sideways slice that sent snow flying in a high arc. Every face turned to the clock and the onlookers erupted in thunderous applause. Hunter had not only achieved the fastest time of the day, but he'd also set a course record. He allowed a slow smile to spread across his face as he unhooked his boots from his skis and stepped out onto the snow. He turned to look for his coach and spotted him smiling from the front of the crowd. He watched as Coach Sullivan took a step towards him with a look of pride on his face.

 Suddenly, as if in slow motion, the world around him went up in flames. He watched in disbelief as his Coach's face contorted in shock and then pain as soon as the sound of an explosion erupted over the sound of applause. Hunter felt himself being hurled backwards by an invisible force just as his vision blacked out. His last memory was the shock of the impact he felt when his body was propelled into a nearby snowdrift, followed by a deafening silence.

Out of the Shadows

Chapter 12

<u>Me</u>

<u>I</u> watched the news coverage from the safety of my dingy hotel room not far from the explosion. I couldn't help but feel a sense of pride at the hype that I'd created. My only regret was I couldn't call anyone to share my victory. I knew better than to gloat at this stage of the game. Every local station sent a reporter to cover the scene. They all had pale faces and a look of shock and terror that was almost comical. I laughed in spite of myself at their utter confusion as they stuttered through their coverage of the events that had taken place. The reporters stated a bomb had exploded just feet away from the finish line at the World Class Alpine Competition that was taking place at Mount Baker in the Cascade Mountains. The paramedics on hand for the athletes had rushed to the aid of the countless victims. The security personnel assigned to crowd control had evacuated the scene and surrounded the area with caution tape. The ski lodge had turned into an impromptu medical station. Bodies were laid out on the floor and paramedics were scrambling to attend to all of the injured victims. They madly applied tourniquets to the growing number of people who were brought in with gaping wounds. Their supplies were limited and a string of ambulances rushed in from nearby hospitals, bringing supplies and taking away the most gravely injured. It was a scene of absolute chaos.

I chuckled to myself as I took a sip of cheap scotch out of a plastic glass from the hotel's minibar. It was hardly a worthy way to celebrate the enormous sum of money that I had just earned for taking Hunter Erickson out of the running for the next Olympic Games. It had been a risky maneuver, and I was going to have to lay low for awhile, but the money I had coming should be more than enough to allow me to live the life I so richly deserve.

I was in the middle of my second scotch when my cell phone

buzzed. I answered when I saw Jared's number pop up on the screen. Why he called on his cell phone and not a burner confused me, but I figured he was calling to congratulate me on my victory and to arrange a drop off for the money he owed me.

"Are you crazy?! I asked you to take out Hunter, and you went and blew up half of Mt. Baker?" Jared's voice sounded panicked, and I quickly realized that he was not pleased with my antics. This made no sense to me, and I paused before answering this ungrateful flyspeck.

"Look, you asked me to do a job and gave no specifics of how you wanted it done. You just said to take the mark out of competition permanently. That's done. You're in no position to criticize me. The only thing that should be on your mind right now is fulfilling your end of our agreement and paying up. I want my money so I can get out of town before the authorities start sniffing around."

"What if they trace this back to me? Do you know what that will mean? I'll be locked up for the rest of my life and will never see another ski run." Again, I paused after this latest whining drivel.

I calmly replied, "ski runs?" You hired a criminal mastermind to eliminate your competitor because you couldn't beat him yourself, and you have the audacity to question how I choose to do it and whine about ski runs? Think about it. A massive explosion that kills and maims a crowd tends to cover a single target, doesn't it? Now I suggest you get me the cash within the next 60 minutes or ski runs will be the least of your worries.

The silence that followed was interminable and the tension was thick. I hung up and tossed my cell phone on the nightstand. The Great Jared Klaus was an arrogant, pompous degenerate. He called me all high and mighty a month ago, and told me that he got my name from one of "his people". He told me that he was tired of living in Hunter Erickson's shadow and asked me to eliminate Hunter from the skiing circuit. I don't usually dabble in that sort of thing, but he offered me a tidy sum of money, and I've been running a bit low on cash lately. I took the job on the condition that I could take care of business any way I saw fit.

It took me a full week and a half to craft my plan and another week to collect the necessary supplies. Then all that was left to do was wait for the right time. I planted the bomb in the snow early in the morning during security shift change before any spectators were around. I'd meant to do it the day before, but there was a fresh snow fall and my tracks would have made it obvious, so I patiently waited.

The conditions were right this morning, and I snuck out just before sunrise and buried the bomb near the finish line. For such a high profile event, security was remarkably lax and the cameras had a few dead spots. I planned to detonate by remote, so all I had to do was make myself scarce. I stayed far away from the finish for fear of cell phone cameras and other recordings. The last thing I wanted was to be identified in someone's snapshot as the one person unsurprised by the pillow of flame. It was easy enough to be incognito in my ski gear. I wore black ski pants and a matching jacket. I looked just like everyone else in the crowd. Just to be safe, I kept my tinted ski goggles and ski mask on all day. Not even the most discerning person could have recognized me.

I waited until Hunter's race. I smiled as he shattered Jared's time. I didn't know Hunter, but Jared is a contemptible waste of space. My resolve steeled as I saw a look of entitlement cross Hunter's face at the finish line. I simply can't abide smugness, even for a fleeting moment. I felt joy and release when I pressed that little button. The explosion was perfectly timed. I allowed myself a few moments of uninterrupted self-satisfaction and admiration. There was no way Hunter or his insufferable coach could have survived. All those pretentious onlookers were little more than collateral damage meant to camouflage the actual target. They served more of a purpose in that moment than they had during the entirety of their useless lives.

I only stayed around long enough to not rouse suspicion. As the paramedics and security descended, I slipped away and drove back to my hotel. My next stop will be Seattle to take care of unfinished business, but first I needed to collect what's owed to me. Jared may whine about my methods, but he can't be stupid enough to back out now. He has to realize he has no hope of walking away clean without upholding his end of our deal now that he's seen firsthand how I work.

Chapter 13

Kayla

    Kayla was finally forced to take a break from her work. Her stomach growled mightily, and she realized that she wouldn't be able to concentrate on her work until she ate something. She carefully scrubbed the paint from her hands and dried them on a nearby towel. Then she walked into her kitchen and opened her pantry, hoping to be inspired. She was running low on groceries and planned to make a trip to the store, but the events of the morning forced her to change her plans. She settled on making scrambled eggs and toast. She popped a few slices of rye toast into the toaster and turned on the television. She mindlessly flipped through the channels. She flipped past cartoons and infomercials until something on one of the news channels caught her attention.

    A TV reporter was covering a recent tragedy at Mt. Baker. Kayla became so engrossed in the coverage that her toast burned. She didn't realize it until she smelled smoke and quickly unplugged the toaster. She turned on the kitchen fan and returned her focus to the coverage. Someone had bombed the finish line at the biggest Alpine ski event of the year. Hunter Erickson, one of the premier US skiers, had been rushed to the hospital and was listed in critical condition. Nearly a hundred people had been injured or killed in the explosion. The survivors suffered from shrapnel wounds, lost limbs, and concussions. It was a horrific event and the police had no leads on the motive for the bombing or the person responsible for the tragedy.

    Kayla shook her head sadly as she watched. It seemed that no one was safe anymore. She felt guilty for feeling sorry for herself when other people were suffering from horrific injuries or the loss of loved ones. The event helped her to put her problems in perspective. Although her situation was scary and frustrating, she had the protection of federal agents. The people injured in the bombing hadn't even had a chance to react. She continued to stare at the TV, having temporarily forgotten about her growling stomach, when a recent update came across the screen. Hunter Erickson's longtime coach and mentor, Coach Karl Sullivan, had been pronounced dead at the scene. She shook her head, amazed by the hatred and evil that existed in the human race. How could someone senselessly kill innocent people? The world had cheered Hunter Erickson on for years, watching as his talent exploded, and he became the world's premier downhill skier. He had always given full credit for his accomplishments to his uncle and his coach, who had insisted that Hunter push himself to be the absolute best.

 Hunter and Coach Sullivan's story was an inspiration to an entire generation of children who learned about work ethic, dedication, and camaraderie. Hunter was a fantastic role model and had given an inordinate amount of money to charities that helped under-privileged children gain access to education and athletic opportunities they would not have otherwise had the means to experience. It wasn't uncommon to see Coach Sullivan and Hunter side-by-side at under-resourced schools talking with kids and encouraging them to pursue their dreams. Now the dream appeared to be over. Hunter was in critical condition and his coach was dead. Everyone was baffled by the event and it was unclear whether an international terrorist was involved.

 Kayla felt intense grief for the lives that had been shattered by the tragedy. She switched off the TV, poured herself a cup of tea, and settled on a meal consisting sadly of granola bars since she had lost her appetite and was in no mood to cook. She pulled out a sketchpad and carefully started to put her emotions down on paper. She outlined the grieving face of one of the paramedics that had been shown on the newscast. She infused the sorrow she was feeling into the images she sketched. She felt that she owed it to the people who were suffering to document their grief. She sat for several hours, sketching image after image that had been burned into her brain from the post-explosion scene. She sketched until her hand hurt and her tea had become ice cold. Tears fell from her eyes onto the pages as she let the fear and sadness she had felt all day finally manifest. The moment was cathartic, and she found that she gained courage from her sketches. Somehow, feeling the pain of others allowed her pain to lessen and gave her the strength that she'd been searching for to carry on with her life.

Chapter 14

Hunter

  The sound of steady beeping was the first thing that registered to Hunter when he opened his eyes and took in his surroundings. He looked at the sterile white walls in front of him and saw the IV lines sticking into his arms. He attempted to move, but his muscles screamed in protest when he tried to shift ever so slightly. He tried to remember where he was. His last memory had been the feeling of flying down the slopes, weaving between flags, focused only on maximizing his speed. He tried to register what had happened after that. It didn't take him long to decipher that he was in a hospital. Had he wiped out? Did he somehow lose his balance? No, certainly he would have remembered if he had. He could clearly picture the finish line in his head and remembered watching the incredible time that had flashed onto the race clock as he crossed the finish line. He had skied the race of his life and finished with his fastest time. If he had done so well, why was he hooked up to heart monitors in the hospital? He searched through his foggy memory before remembering the look of shock that had registered on Coach Sullivan's face as the world had gone up in flames. Something terrible had happened, and people had been hurt. Hunter's throat tightened, and he started to panic. He fumbled around until he found the call button nearby and pressed it rapidly.

  A nurse quickly entered the room and rushed to his side. She administered another dose of morphine as soon as she realized that Hunter was in a state of panic. She couldn't blame him, considering he had no idea where he was. He'd been through a horrifying ordeal. He had suffered a major concussion and broken several bones from the force of impact when the bomb had gone off. Fortunately, his goggles and face mask had protected him from some of the shrapnel, but he'd still been in bad shape when the paramedics

Out of the Shadows

got to him. The hospitals near Mt. Baker had quickly filled up with victims and the doctors in charge had advised the med-flight team to transfer Hunter to Seattle General. It was a larger hospital and had the providers and staff necessary to provide him with the best possible care. His Uncle Jackson was allowed to go on the helicopter with Hunter. He had been terribly worried about his nephew but had managed to hold himself together and stay out of the way of the nurses and doctors during the flight.

Two days had passed since the incident. Jackson remained at the hospital, checking in on him whenever the doctors would let him. He camped out in the hospital's waiting room and subsisted on stale coffee and prepackaged muffins. One doctor finally advised him to check into a hotel in order to get a shower and a decent night's rest. He promised that he would call the minute Hunter regained consciousness. Jackson was hesitant to leave but finally agreed to go when he was reassured that Hunter was out of the ICU and was listed in stable condition. He didn't want to admit that he needed rest, but finally gave in when he saw his reflection in the bathroom mirror and barely recognized the pale, gaunt face with greasy hair staring back.

The doctor made good on his promise to call Jackson the minute Hunter woke up. He was still sleeping when the phone rang, and he dove out of bed to answer it. "It's Dr. Davis. I called to let you know that Hunter is awake. He's groggy and disoriented, which is to be expected. We feel it would be beneficial if you could come over right away to be with him."

Jackson didn't hesitate. He threw on clothes and jogged across the street to Seattle General. He quickly made his way to the seventh floor and was relieved to see Hunter reclining in bed with his eyes open. Hunter looked frustrated with a nurse as she explained that he had to remain in bed because he had broken several bones, and they didn't want anything to shift out of place. The exasperated nurse looked relieved to see Jackson enter the room. As she walked passed him, she muttered "He's all yours. Just make sure he doesn't move a muscle."

Jackson nodded at her and took a seat next to Hunter's bed. "How are you feeling, Sport?"

Hunter looked at his uncle and a half grin crept onto his face. "I've been better, Uncle J. Right now, I feel like I just got hit by a train. What happened out there? Where is Coach?"

"Let's take one thing at a time, Hunter. You were a victim of a bombing. It happened just after you crossed the finish line. We don't know who's responsible or why Mt. Baker was targeted. All we know is over a hundred people are dead or injured. It's going to take a lot of investigating to track down whoever did this."

"And Coach Sullivan?" Hunter felt a twisting in his gut even as he mentioned his beloved Coach's name. He almost didn't want to ask the question because he was sure he didn't want to hear the answer.

"I'm so sorry, Hunter. He didn't make it." Jackson choked on his words. He wanted to wait to tell his nephew the devastating news until he was stronger but knew that Hunter would never forgive him if he didn't tell the truth. Coach Sullivan had been like a father to Hunter, and the loss was going to be devastating to him.

The look that had crossed Coach Sullivan's face came back into Hunter's memory, and he let out a low groan. "How can that be? Who would do such a thing? Why would anyone hurt Coach?" Hunter felt like someone had just ripped out his heart and twisted it into knots. His chest hurt terribly, and he struggled to sit up, only to fall back in pain. Jackson signaled a nurse, who came in and administered another dose of morphine. Within seconds, Hunter's body relaxed and the fight drained out of his face.

"It was a horrible thing, Hunter. Everyone was celebrating your incredible run one minute, and then all hell broke loose. I was sitting in the stands, just out of range of the blast, but I saw everything. The sound was intense and the explosion occurred right where Coach Sullivan was standing. Limbs went flying, blood was everywhere, and mass chaos erupted. You were thrown back by the blast and landed in a snow bank, which broke your fall somewhat. You broke your left arm and leg when you landed on your side. One of your vertebrae was fractured, but your spine is okay and the doctors have reassured me that you'll be able to walk again. You had some internal bleeding, which the doctors were able to stop. All in all, they expect you to recover, although your left ankle is shattered, so they will have to do reconstruction on it and are unsure if you'll be able to ski at the elite level again. The important thing to focus on right now is that you're alive. Many people who were standing near where you were when the blast went off were not so lucky."

    Hunter took a moment to process everything his uncle was telling him. He appreciated how direct Jackson was being. He knew that it would be tempting to tiptoe around the truth, but that wasn't Jackson's style. Hunter wanted the facts laid out for him so he could process them and then figure out how he was going to deal with them. Jackson had done him the courtesy of giving him all the information, no matter how painful it was. Now he was going to have to find a way to carry on. It was hard for him to absorb the full shock of losing his coach and his career, but Jackson was right to point out that many people had not survived the blast.

    Just then a nurse entered the room and signed into his chart. She informed them it was time for Hunter to get cleaned up and have his vitals checked. She kindly explained it would be best for Jackson to let Hunter get a little more sleep. He had been through a lot, and it was crucial for his body to get enough rest in order to make a full recovery. Jackson voiced his understanding and said goodbye to Hunter. He could tell by Hunter's expression that the news he shared had been extremely difficult for him to hear. He also knew his nephew well enough to know that he was mentally and physically tough and would be able to sort things out with time.

    Hunter was already starting to drift off when Jackson left the room and headed back to his hotel to get a bit more sleep. Jackson knew the next few days would be physically and emotionally taxing, and he needed to be strong for his nephew. He placed a few calls to his boss in Colorado and his neighbors to let them know that he wouldn't be coming home anytime soon. His boss had been following the news and was very understanding of the situation. Jackson's neighbor, Mary, agreed to keep an eye on his place and make sure to check in periodically to ensure that his affairs were in order. He also called the post-office and asked them to forward his mail before he finally fell back into bed exhausted. His final thought before he drifted off was that he was going to find the person responsible for this and make sure they answered for their sins.

Chapter 15

<u>Me</u>

<u>I</u> got my money. Jared, the little whelp, came through as instructed, but did so just before his deadline and my patience for him expired. He was anxious and sweating like he'd just run a marathon. He kept checking over his shoulder as if he thought someone might be watching him as he approached my door. He didn't seem to realize that the only people who came to this motel were people who rented rooms out by the hour and demanded discretion. No one was going to pay any attention to him although his pathetically laughable attempt at dressing incognito invited much more attention than it would deflect. Still, all that mattered to me at the moment was getting paid and getting out of town.

Jared nervously handed me a black suitcase, which made me groan. This guy was *so* cliché. He might as well have handcuffed it to his wrist since he appeared intent on following the Triteman's Guidebook to Murder for Hire. I threw it on the bed, flipped it open, and counted the cash. His eyes were bloodshot and looked like they were going to pop out of his head. There was white powder beneath his nose. He had a crazed expression on his face. I snorted audibly. This guy can't even cover up signs of simple drug use. There's no way he could have covered up his wish to eliminate Hunter without my larger distraction dimming the focus.

"Don't you ever rat me out, you understand. I gave you the money, and now I'm out. I want nothing to do with you ever again." Jared sounded panicked as he stammered out the words. If it wasn't such a hollow threat, I would have respected his gumption.

"As long as you keep my name from your thoughts and words, you'll have no problems from me. If all goes as planned, you'll never see me again. Now I suggest that you sober up, calm down, and get your act together. There is nothing about how you look right now that says innocent. If you keep it up, everyone's going to know you had something to do with this mess." I was stating the obvious. Jared looked like he was a step away from a mental breakdown and the only think keeping him alive now that he'd paid me is the knowledge that he's a perfect fall guy if this does go sideways. He generally failed at life, but his greatest success could be as my patsy. He didn't know my real name, and I always covered my face with a ski mask when we met. The only conceivable connection I have to the bombing is this coked out loser so long as I can cleanly escape tonight.

    I snapped back to reality as the sound of his voice pierced the beautiful silence.

    "Look, Man," Jared began and I began to hate him more with each word he spoke.

    "I asked you to do one thing," he continued to my dismay. "ONE THING! Just take out Hunter Erickson. That's all I asked, and you went and injured or killed half the crowd. You're a lunatic. A freaking sociopath. I didn't have anything to do with this. It was all your idea. I'm totally innocent, and you know it."

    That made me laugh. "First of all, keep your voice down. Anyone listening just became a witness, and everything you just said is admissible, you moron. Second, you asked me to eliminate your rival. The minute you asked, that was solicitation. After we agreed and took steps, it became conspiracy. You're in this as though you did everything yourself. I did what you asked. Also, this brought your sport to an audience beyond flannel-wearing stoners. Since you are choosing not to show common courtesy, I suggest you consider self-preservation instead. Leave now without another word. Don't look for me, don't think of me. If you see me again, cross the street."

    With that, I waved a gun at him. He wet himself immediately. It was a pathetic sight. I slammed the door and watched gleefully as he sprinted to his car and peeled out. I allowed myself a smile before loading the money and the rest of my things into my rental and returning to Seattle. I had unfinished business with a certain artist who ruined my life a few years ago. The timing was inopportune as I should keep as low a profile as possible, but it was her turn to pay.

Chapter 16

<u>Kayla</u>

    Engrossing herself in her art gave Kayla strength she had forgotten she possessed. She felt a fight returning that had fled from her the minute she'd read the note attached to her door. Her despair was replaced by determination. She suddenly felt purpose. Painting seemed like a better alternative than living in constant fear. She realized that there were only a few things that she had control of in her life. One was her attitude and the other was her art. She knew she couldn't control her past, and she wasn't able to predict the future. What she could do was use her talents and energy to create art. She may not be able to leave her house often, but painting would continue to give her an outlet until she got her freedom back.

    At some point in the day, Agent Franklin called to check in. She answered her phone begrudgingly. She still wasn't comfortable with the idea of someone monitoring her every move. It made her shiver to think of federal agents keeping a constant eye on her home and her whereabouts. She knew that part of the reason they were being so vigilant was to keep her safe. She was the only one that could identify the horrible man who had committed unthinkable crimes on the night that had changed her life forever. As much as she wanted to see him put behind bars, she also wanted to have her freedom back. If she went out of protective services, she wouldn't last more than a few days. If she stayed, she would never be fully free. She knew that no matter what, she would always be watching her back, wondering if someone was going to seek revenge on her someday. But there was no point in questioning her lot in life. Her fate had been written in stone three years before, and if she wanted to keep living, she had to cooperate with the feds. She felt a renewed desire to stay alive after watching the devastation of the people injured at Mt. Baker.

Her conversation with Agent Franklin was brief. "Good afternoon, Frank." She knew full well that Frank wasn't his first name, but he didn't seem like a Jeffrey, and Frank seemed like a good nickname. If she was going to have to spend endless amounts of time with this man, she had to come up with something better to call him than "Agent Franklin" day in and day out.

He didn't seem to be put off by her impromptu nickname. "Hey, Kayla. Mind if I stop in for a bit?"

"Suit yourself. I certainly won't be going anywhere for awhile."

"Have you eaten anything today?"

Kayla bit her lip, trying to remember. "I had two granola bars. Does that count?"

"That's not acceptable. How do you expect to keep up your strength with a diet like that?"

"To be honest, I wasn't really thinking about my diet when I got a note from a guy who threatened to kill me."

"Okay, I get it, but I still think you should eat. Can I bring you a pizza?"

Kayla started to retort but was interrupted by her growling stomach. She wasn't one to skip meals, and she was starting to feel light-headed. "Okay, fine, but I get to pick the toppings."

"You've got yourself a deal. Agent Olson is going to take over my shift in twenty minutes, so I'll stop by after that."

A half-hour later, Kayla watched Agent Franklin's reaction with amusement. "Anchovies and mushrooms? Really?" He had been looking forward to a juicy slice of pepperoni pizza. Surely this was Kayla's idea of a joke.

"Try it. What are you so afraid of?" Kayla laughed, grabbing a big, cheesy slice and stuffing it into her mouth. "It's delicious," she said with a full mouth, laughing for the first time all day.

"You don't understand. I'm the world's pickiest eater. I live off of hamburgers and pepperoni pizza. I consider crunchy peanut butter to be adventurous. I've never touched an anchovy, let alone allowed one to contaminate my pizza."

"Try it," Kayla said insistently, shoving a slice onto his plate.

The look of horror as Agent Franklin brought it to his mouth was comical. He sniffed at it hesitantly and finally gained the courage to take a small bite.

Kayla sat for a moment in silence, waiting for his reaction. Frank thoughtfully chewed for a moment and then swallowed. A smile slowly spread across his face. "Okay, you win. It's actually not that bad."

"Not bad?!" Kayla was indignant. "Oh, this is better than 'Not bad'. This is the best thing since sliced bread. Admit it! You've never had pizza that tasted as good as this."

Frank thought long and hard. She was right. The pizza was delicious. "Okay, I'll admit it. It's really good. I should thank you for forcing me to try something new. My wife would be impressed. I'm glad I tried it." His lopsided grin was enough to make Kayla smile in spite of herself.

She quickly finished off her half of the pizza. As she licked the sauce off her fingers, she looked at him and smiled. "I should thank you for coming over and making me eat. I was feeling pretty down after I found the note. I've worked so hard to reinvent my life, and it felt like it was all for nothing when I realized that I was located and am back in the same place I was when I first went into protective custody."

"That's where you're wrong, Kayla. You're in a totally different place. You have the upper hand. Kazimir wouldn't be coming after you if he wasn't desperate. He's hurting because he's had to lay low for the past three years. He's probably out of cash, but can't do any big gigs because he's already on our radar. He's a desperate man, and he's going to have to show his face eventually. When he does, we'll be there to nab him, and your testimony will put him away for life."

"I'm really glad that you're so confident," Kayla said, failing to mask her sarcasm.

"I am, Kayla. I've worked on plenty of cases like this before. Criminals can only stay in hiding for so long. They're used to living large and can't handle a low profile lifestyle. Kazimir is bound to make a misstep sooner or later."

"I think it's different when it's your life on the line. I mean, you and Olson tiptoe around collecting information for your files and interviewing witnesses. What if you actually had your life ruined by this man? What if you and your family had been threatened? Would you be so eager to believe that everything was going to work out? I mean, even if we do put him away for life, who's to say that one of his sidekicks isn't going to come after me for revenge?"

"I see your point, Kayla, but you don't really have a choice right now. You have to believe that you will survive and get your freedom back one of these days. What other option do you have?"

Kayla sat, lost in thought for a moment. She knew that Frank was right. As much as she hated to admit it, hope was the only thing that had kept her going through this whole mess. "You're a pretty wise man, Agent Frank."

Frank fought back a smile at her unexpected compliment.

"So how about if you give me the last slice of your pizza?" she asked.

Franklin laughed, realizing that she'd been buttering him up to take advantage of the only remaining slice of anchovy and mushroom pizza. "Alright, you win…but you'll have to fight me for it next time."

Kayla laughed for the second time that day.

Chapter 17

Hunter

Hunter groaned. His body still ached. He opened his eyes and saw Uncle Jackson staring at him. It felt weird to have someone watching him while he slept. He would have made a sarcastic comment about him finding better things to do with his time if it didn't feel like a woodpecker was drilling at his head the minute he tried to open his mouth. Instead, he moaned a little, and Jackson immediately jumped up and told him not to move.

"Just tell me what you need, and I'll get it for you."

"How about a time machine so I can go back to Mt. Baker and get myself and Coach out before that lunatic created a fireworks display at the base of the mountain." Hunter fought through the pain. He knew that all he had to do was press the button underneath his right thumb. It would give him get a hit of morphine that would take all of the pain away, but he didn't want to do that. He was tired of feeling like he was in a fog. He wanted to think clearly and be able to process everything that had happened.

Jackson shook his head sadly. "Trust me, if there was any way I could have prevented this from happening, I would have. I would have given my own life so Sully could have lived."

Hunter fought the pain that was piercing his heart. It was hard for him to imagine a life without Coach Sullivan around. The man had been like a father to him, and now he was gone.

"What about funeral arrangements?" Hunter couldn't bear the thought of watching his coach being buried, but he felt like he needed to be there.

"I know you'd like to go, but the wake was this morning and the funeral is this afternoon back in Colorado. I know you'd like to be there, but there's no way you could have made the trip in your condition. Everyone will understand."

Hunter rested his head on his pillow, cursing his luck. Not only had one of the most important people in his world been killed, but he wouldn't even be able to say a proper goodbye. This was quickly turning into a nightmare. His only comfort was the knowledge that his uncle was okay.

"And what about you, Uncle J? Don't you have to get back to work?"

"My boss said I could work remotely for awhile. You need someone here right now. It's going to take your bones a long time to heal. You're going to need a considerable amount of physical therapy when you get released from the hospital, and you're not going to be able to drive until your legs heal. You're like the son I never had, and there's nothing I'd rather do than stay here and get you through this. You can try to chase me away if you want, but it won't work. For better or worse, you're stuck with me."

Hunter grinned in spite of himself. His uncle was never one to walk away from a challenge. Not when he had been a young boy learning to ski, and not now when his nephew was lying broken and bruised in a hospital bed.

"What am I going to do with myself?" Hunter couldn't imagine spending day after day staring at the pathetically small television in the hospital room. He knew that watching sports would only depress him because he couldn't be out on the slopes competing. The news would just remind him of all the horrible things happening in the world, and the travel channel would just remind him of all the places that he wouldn't be able to go anytime soon.

Jackson looked at his nephew. "Is there anything that you've been wishing you had more time for?"

Hunter thought for a moment. "Well, I have been working on an online business degree, but I won't be able to do any typing for the foreseeable future."

Jackson was quiet for a moment. He was impressed by his nephew. He had no idea that Hunter had started taking classes. It couldn't have been easy, considering how much traveling and training Hunter had been doing. "What if I bring in my laptop, and we go through your assignments together? You can tell me what you want to say, and I'll type it out for you."

Hunter smiled. "Thanks for taking me seriously, Uncle J. I knew I could count on you. I'm getting closer to getting my degree, and it looks like I might need a backup plan in case I don't get back on the slopes as soon as I'd like."

Out of the Shadows

Chapter 18

<u>Me</u>

    I'd grown tired of dilapidated apartments and cheap motel rooms, so I decided to reward myself for my victory by renting a room at the Hyatt. As I walked across the marble floors in the foyer and passed all the suit-clad Wall Street rejects and their air of perceived superiority, I contemplated two things. 1) It's people just like these who've made me despise New York's Wall Street stock-traders for years. 2) If I had the time and inclination, they would suffer the same fate as those at Mt. Baker. They carry themselves as the most important people in the room, when each of them is utterly replaceable, both at work and in this world. If they had an ounce of self-awareness, they'd realize they are just as fungible as the commodities they peddle. As I didn't have the time, or currently, the ability to be that retribution, they would simply have to wait their turn.
    An annoyingly perky blonde interrupted my thoughts in order to check me in. She wasted fifteen minutes explaining every mundane detail about the hotel. All I really cared about was where the bar was located. I found my way to my room, dropped off my suitcase, locked the small fortune I had in the safe, and headed down to the bar to get drunk on top shelf liquor. For a nice hotel, the bar lacked character, but no doubt it had an 18-year old scotch.
    Finally, at 3:00 PM, the bartender poured me one with two ice cubes. My thoughts briefly drifted to those businessmen who order scotch to impress those around them but don't have the decency to hold the water, club soda or excessive ice that blunt the taste. You order with a splash of water or a cube or two to open the bouquet... I stopped myself from thinking of those fools any longer. I hated them all the more and adding the courage of liquor would surely steel my resolve to punish them, and I still didn't have the time. I

swirled the golden liquid around in my glass, admiring the color and the change in consistency as the melted ice slowly permeated throughout, and took a swig, savoring my triumph as the liquid burned a trail down my throat, and the hint of peat moss lingered in my nose.

"You from around here?" The bartender asked, making light conversation. I hated him already, but social convention required a response to this peddler of one of the few remaining legal mind-altering substances. I despise small talk, but we were alone, and a silent loner pounding expensive booze in the afternoon paying cash may arouse suspicion, so I decided to make an effort this time. He may prove interesting given the chance. At the very least, a modicum of courtesy on my part may earn a shift drink later.

"No, I'm not from anywhere in particular. I just kind of float."

"Fair enough. You a journalist or something?" The hope of him being interesting was waning, and I was starting to get annoyed.

"You could say that," What was it those pseudointellectuals say in the moment? "I'm a student and resident of the world. I go where the experiences are."

The bartender seemed to accept my answer and understand from my tone of voice that I was no longer interested in idle speed-dating banter. He backed off and only reappeared when I waved for another drink. I reevaluated after my sixth round. Perhaps he's not that intolerable. He knew to keep my glass from getting empty and did so quietly and expeditiously.

As I drank, I contemplated my next move. Time slowed, and the air went stale as I thought. I needed to deal with Kayla. I could have taken her off the board when I first found her in this wretched city, but I needed her to truly fear again. She made me wait to find her. She had to wait, in turn, for what I intend. She had to know my suffering and see all she knows, trusts, and loves crumble before her.

My need to toy with her, to make her feel my pain, was myopic though, as I'd failed to truly account for the federal marshals sure to be flanking her at all times. I knew they were there and must be eluded to accomplish what must happen. It's just annoying now, akin to being badly sunburned on the first day of a beach vacation. I've been planning this for some time, so her "body guards" can't really affect my plans anymore than a house cat can stop a tsunami.

I reassured myself with the fact that Kayla wouldn't be able to identify me in a line-up even if those lazy federal marshals did find me. I'd taken some precautions after that fateful night when she'd witnessed what was to be my crowning achievement. I knew my only hope to continue with my life and work in the US was to change my looks after that disaster. It cost a pretty penny, but I was able to buy a new face. I opted for a smaller nose, more defined cheekbones, and instead of keeping my head shaved, I'd grown out my black hair and kept it neatly cut. Dental records wouldn't even help due to obtaining porcelain veneers. I also dropped about fifty pounds. Instead of looking like the bald thug I used to be, I looked more like a cross between a male model and a Wall Street broker. I shuddered at the assumed life I've lived as a result. Any confusion with me and a broker was enough to induce nausea and bring the taste of bile to the back of my throat.

Kayla had no chance of identifying me, and the cops had no leads other than her story. I simply needed to find a time when she would be out of her house. Once she's not in her safe haven, she's all mine. I'll be able to make a clean escape and leave the country until things settle down.

I signaled the bartender to refill my glass a final time. I had much work to do, but I wasn't ready to begin yet. Today, I just wanted to get drunk, temporarily ignore what's ahead, and enjoy something simple like the 1200-thread count Egyptian cotton sheets in my room.

Chapter 19

Kayla

Kayla was engrossed in her painting when her cell phone buzzed. It was a text message from Agent Franklin. She rolled her eyes, wishing he would leave her alone, but quickly reminded herself he was one of the only people in the world she could trust to keep her safe. She stepped back to admire the progress she was making on her painting. She was pleased with how it was taking shape but knew she had a long way to go.

She wiped off her hands and grabbed her cell phone to read the text. "Time to get out of the house. I've got a job for you."

She stifled a moan. Although she didn't want to be bothered, she had been shut in her house for the past thirty-six hours. She knew she needed to get out for her own sanity. Besides, she might be able to give him a list and convince him to do some grocery shopping for her if she buttered him up enough. She was completely out of any form of chocolate and was starting to go into withdrawal.

She picked up her phone and responded. "What do you have in mind?" Kayla was fully aware that she wasn't going to be able to go out into any crowded public places.

"How about volunteering at the hospital? Seattle General is in need of volunteers to visit patients who don't have a lot of friends or family in the area. They need volunteers who can keep patients company, play cards with them, and help them send emails or write letters to friends or family."

Kayla thought for a moment. Hospitals weren't really her thing. She didn't like the sterile white walls or the smell of bleach, and she was afraid of needles. At the same time, she was desperate for any excuse to get out of her house.

She sighed before replying. "Alright, I'll do it on the condition that you will buy me groceries when you get off your shift."

Frank texted back, "Deal, see you in 15 minutes."

Kayla glanced at herself in the mirror. Her face was smeared with paint, and she was dressed in her grubby paint-splattered sweatpants. She was going to have to clean herself up, but she didn't have much time. She took a quick shower to rinse off the paint, dried off, and slipped into a white cotton sundress. She towel-dried her hair and put a little gel in it to bring out the waves. She applied some lip gloss, grabbed her purse, and made it down the stairs just in time to hear Agent Franklin knocking on her door. She answered with a smile on her face. He was dressed in street clothes. His gun was concealed under his black fleece. He wore blue jeans and sneakers. It was nice to see him looking casual. It was bad enough to be under constant watch, but it would have been worse to be escorted by federal agents in their uniforms anytime she needed to go somewhere.

Kayla ducked into the passenger seat of Franklin's unmarked car. He reassured her that the windows were bulletproof, so there was nothing to worry about. The fact he felt the need to point out that bulletproof windows were necessary made Kayla even more nervous. She reminded herself she needed to do this for her own sanity. If she refused to leave, she'd become an out-of-touch shut-in. She needed personal interaction just like everyone else, even if it meant spending time in a scary hospital where lots of people were suffering.

Agent Franklin pulled into an empty spot in the parking garage and walked around the car to hold the door open for her. It seemed unnecessary, but a little bit chivalrous at the same time. Kayla fought back a grin and thanked him. Then she followed him into the entrance of Seattle General. To her surprise, the hospital was anything but scary. The entrance had high ceilings and skylights. Intricate blown glass sculptures hung from the ceiling and brightly colored paintings lined the walls. The nurses were all wearing colorful scrubs and had smiles on their faces. Kayla was instantly at ease and grateful her outdated stereotype about hospitals had been wrong. Frank had already signed Kayla up as a volunteer. He assumed she would agree to do it, even if it took a lot of coaxing. Fortunately, she agreed without a fight, and he could tell that getting out of her house was already starting to do her good.

Kayla was led into an orientation room where a comely nurse named Sheila walked her through her responsibilities. She would be required to spend two four-hour shifts per week at the hospital if she wanted to be part of the program. She would have to wear a name badge and royal blue scrubs. She'd be assigned to eight different patients and would spend a half hour with each of them. She could play games, watch TV, bring DVDs, and send emails to the patients. She could brush their hair, paint their nails, and do crafts with them. She wasn't allowed to bring food or beverages of any kind from outside the hospital no matter how much the patients insisted or how nicely they asked. She'd also have to keep a log of what activities she did with each patient as well as any of their likes and dislikes to help the nursing staff out.

It sounded straightforward to Kayla. She wasn't always great at meeting new people, but she figured it couldn't be all that hard. She could always just watch TV with them if the conversation started to lag. Sheila disappeared and came back a moment later holding a set of scrubs for Kayla. She quickly changed and smiled at herself in the mirror. She looked like a dedicated nurse, rather than a haunted artist. She decided it was nice to step into a different role for a while.

Kayla's first patient was an eighty-year-old man named Gus. He had lymphoma and was undergoing treatments. His prognosis was good, but he was still required to spend several days in the hospital. He was a kindly older man who could have been her grandfather. He enjoyed cribbage and was happy she knew how to play the game. He directed her to one of his dresser drawers, where she found an antique cribbage board. She quickly set it up and lost herself in the game for the next half-hour. Gus turned out to be a talented card player, but so was Kayla. The game was close, but Gus pulled out a win in the end. Kayla congratulated him and told him she needed to go. He clutched her hand, looked her in the eyes, and thanked her for taking the time to come by. It was the highlight of his week, and he hoped she would be coming back. Kayla reassured him that she would and gave him a kiss on the cheek before she headed to the next room.

Kayla knocked softly before she entered. She hadn't been given the patient's name, but her information sheet said she would be visiting a 25-year-old male who was injured in a bombing. She entered the room, introduced herself, and immediately recognized Hunter as the well-known downhill skier. "Wow, Hunter Erickson! It's a pleasure to meet you in person."

Hunter gave her a lopsided grin. "I'm sorry I won't be able to impress you on the slopes today. I'm feeling a little bit under the weather."

Kayla smiled back at him. "You don't need to worry about impressing me today. I'm just here to keep you company until you can break out of this joint."

Hunter gave a wry grin. "Considering I've got a shattered ankle and a broken leg, I'd say that it's a safe bet that I won't be busting out of here anytime soon. What are you in for?"

"To be honest, I'm under house arrest right now, and part of my deal with the feds was to do some volunteer work." She said it like she was joking, and it made Hunter laugh. If only it wasn't as true as it sounded. She scolded herself for her joke knowing Franklin would pull the plug if he heard it.

"No really, why do you volunteer here?"

"It's pretty simple really. I'm a tortured artist and don't get out of my house very often. I thought that it might be good to get out and meet people who know real suffering."

"Well, you came to the right place." Hunter couldn't disguise the haunted feeling that engulfed him whenever he thought about the bombing.

Kayla remembered seeing his picture on TV. "I'm so sorry you were in the wrong place at the wrong time."

"I had just finished one of the best runs of my life when the bomb went off. I was far enough away that I didn't get burned, but the blast sent me flying. I broke some bones, injured my spine, and got a pretty serious concussion from the force of impact. I thought I had it bad, but my coach wasn't as lucky as I was. He was killed instantly. The nearby hospitals were overwhelmed with victims, so they transported me here. My uncle came out to spend time with me, but he's all the family I've got."

"I'm so sorry." Kayla felt awful for him. She couldn't imagine what it would be like to lose a mentor and be injured too badly to continue doing the one thing that she loved most in the world.

"I am, too. It's been hard not to feel pretty low, but I've been working on a business degree and have been saving for the future since my career started. I'm confident I can keep my head above water whether I go back to skiing or not. I'm just having trouble understanding why anyone would want to hurt so many people. The bomber really destroyed a lot of peoples' lives. Who could possibly do something so evil?"

Kayla's mind flashed back to the night that ended the life she had known. She could still hear the screams and see the blood splattering. "I don't know, Hunter, but I hope they find out who it was and make that person pay."

Hunter decided right then and there he liked Kayla. She was kind and had a soft voice, but she also had a determination and intensity that he admired.

"You have the pleasure of my company for a half an hour. Is there anything you'd like to do? I just finished getting beaten badly at cribbage by an elderly gentleman, so I'm not up for cards, but I'd be happy to do anything else. I can paint your fingernails, bring you DVDs, or braid your hair. The one thing that I'm not allowed to do is bring you junk food of any kind, so don't even try."

"Let me think. I know this sounds ridiculous, but I have a paper due in two days for one of my classes. Would you mind helping me with my homework?"

Kayla smiled. "I'm an artist, so my ability to write a paper about business is limited; however, I can type fairly quickly, so I think I can manage."

Hunter directed her to his laptop. She flipped it open and brought up a blank document. "And what is the topic of this business paper of yours?"

"It's for my Social Media Marketing Class. I had my uncle do some research for me, so I'm ready to write the paper. I'm comparing and contrasting various social media websites and the advantages of advertising on each one."

"Did you consider asking your professor for an extension? I think that being a victim of a bombing would qualify you for an exception."

Hunter grinned at her. He knew she was right, but he'd put off getting his college degree long enough, and he had nothing better to do while he was stranded in the hospital. "I considered it, but you'd have to know my professor. She's pretty tough. Her nickname is the Rottweiler with Lipstick. She might even move my deadline up if she senses any weakness."

Kayla laughed out loud. She decided she was going to like this job.

Chapter 20

Hunter

    Kayla was the first good thing to happen to Hunter since the bombing. She was funny, smart, and a great companion. Before she left, she wrote down his top five favorite movies and promised to rent them from the local library and bring them the next time she visited. She noticed he was in desperate need of a haircut and promised to bring a pair of clippers with her to cut his hair, too. She was also one hell of a typist. Within a half-hour, they had been able to crank out a three-page paper that was of reasonable quality. She managed to keep him on track, while still joking around with him as they worked. He shared a good deal about himself with her, but she only spoke vaguely about her past. She often answered his questions with a sly grin and a witty retort or subtly shifted the subject back to him. He knew there was more to Kayla than she was letting on. He decided that as long as he was stuck in this hospital room, he was going to make it his mission to get to know her better.

    Hunter was sorry when their time was up and Kayla had to move on to her next room, but he was also starting to tire. His doctors warned him that he had to rest his brain due to his concussion and not push himself too hard. He decided to take their advice and rest. He closed his eyes and dozed off for an hour until one of the nurses came in to check his vitals and change his bandages.

    "I think you have some more visitors," She said as she finished adding notes to his chart on the computer.

    Hunter looked surprised. Uncle Jackson wasn't due to come back to the hospital until later that afternoon because he had some odds and ends that he needed to tie up with work. Fortunately, he was able to do it over the phone and email and didn't need to fly back to Colorado. He wished it was Kayla, stopping in to say goodbye before she left, but he knew she was only allowed to spend a half-hour with each person and wouldn't want to break the rules on her first day. He was baffled about who it could be.

Just then, two agents dressed in uniform entered the room. They introduced themselves and apologized for dropping by unannounced. They explained that they were investigating the bombing at Mt. Baker. They hadn't wanted to bother him but needed to find out if he had seen or heard anything on the day of the attack that would lead them to the person responsible. They had waited until he was out of the ICU and resting comfortably before disturbing him. They knew he was likely stilled devastated by the loss of his coach and expressed their sympathies as genuinely as they could.

Hunter reassured them he would cooperate in any way possible. He wanted to catch the person behind the heinous crime more than anyone. Unfortunately, his memory of the day was foggy. He'd been so focused on his race that he hadn't taken the time to notice much going on around him. His eyes were on the time clock when he crossed the finish line. He barely had time to react when the whole world exploded around him.

The officers keenly listened to Hunter's recollection and explained that many people had taken photos near the finish line leading up to and after his finish. They asked if he would look through them to see if he noticed anything odd. Hunter nodded his head and agreed to take a look. They spent the next hour going through photo after photo of the mountain, the lodge, and the finish line taken by various cell phones and digital cameras. There had been so many people milling around. Most were dressed in ski clothes, making it extremely difficult to identify anyone in particular. There were a few photos that included a man that had his ski mask pulled down so his face wasn't recognizable. It wouldn't have seemed out of the ordinary, except a few of the photos were taken in the lodge, where it was warm, and everyone else around him had removed their masks and goggles, but his mask was on in every picture.

They couldn't find any other clues in the photos about the identity of the attacker or attackers. Most of the people in the photos were carrying purses, backpacks, or bags, so it was nearly impossible to tell if anyone had been toting explosives. Hunter apologized to the officers for not being able to provide more feedback. They thanked him for his time and told him they would stop by again when they had more information. There were still more pictures coming in, and they would bring them as soon as they assembled the next batch. Hunter liked their determination and focus. For some reason, he felt confident they would find the responsible party, no matter the degree of difficulty. The stakes for this particular case were high. People needed answers to explain why their loved ones had been injured or killed. No one was going to sleep at night until the guilty party was taken into custody and faced the consequences of committing such an evil act.

It wasn't long after they left, that his uncle returned. Jackson walked into the room, took one look at the expression on his nephew's face, and grinned. "I have a feeling something good happened to you today. You have the same look on your face that you get when you've just won a big race. Why don't you fill me in on what I've missed, but please tell me that you haven't been hitting on any of the nurses."

Hunter grinned mischievously in spite of himself. "What? Don't you trust me to behave myself? Here I am, lying in bed, battered and broken, with several lovely nurses taking care of me, and you expect I'm going to let an opportunity for some female companionship pass me by?"

Jackson grinned back. He knew his nephew well enough to know when he was joking. "As romantic as it is to have a woman change your bedpan and feed you jello, I'm having trouble imagining you having any romantic forays while you're in this condition."

"Alright, alright, I'll tell you the truth." Hunter proceeded to

Out of the Shadows

tell Jackson about his visit from Kayla, the hospital volunteer. He explained how helpful and kind she'd been. He was grateful for her companionship and excited about the prospect of getting to watch good movies instead of daytime television.

Jackson nodded his understanding. He was glad to see Hunter grinning again after everything he had gone through. He knew it was going to be a long road to recovery for his nephew and was grateful to anyone who was able to make Hunter's life a bit more enjoyable along the way.

Jackson noticed a business card on Hunter's nightstand and picked it up. He turned it over in his hands. "What's this?"

"Some agents in charge of investigating the bombing visited me. They showed me a bunch of pictures that people had taken on their cell phones and digital cameras during the morning of the bombing. They asked me to look through the photos and tell them if I noticed anyone or anything that looked suspicious."

Jackson studied his nephew's face closely. He knew how stressful the subject of the bombing was for Hunter and wanted to make sure that no one caused any setbacks in his recovery. He was afraid that the agents' inquiries might have brought back unwanted memories from the tragedy. "Did they interrogate you?"

"Oh no, it was nothing like that. They were very kind and mostly just wanted to know if I had seen or heard anything. I told them I was so focused on the race that I hadn't paid attention to anything else going on around me. When we looked through the images, we saw one guy in several photos who was wearing a black ski mask. The weird thing is that he didn't take the mask off, even when he was inside the lodge. They are going to follow up on him. Nothing else looked remarkable. Apparently, they still don't know much about the explosives and couldn't say anything about a motive. No one has claimed responsibility yet either. They didn't share any other information with me."

Jackson nodded. He could hear the tone of conviction in his nephew's voice and was glad to know that instead of getting depressed about the tragedy, Hunter seemed determined to help locate the killer, no matter how long it took.

"We'll, I'm glad to hear that you cooperated with them and didn't throw them out for interrupting your rest."

Hunter laughed, "I wasn't going to sleep after my visit from Kayla anyway. I was already starting to miss her, so they were a welcome distraction."

Jackson laughed. He'd never known Hunter to fall for a girl after only one encounter. His nephew was typically wary of girls and their attention, but this seemed different. Hunter seemed truly happy to discuss Kayla and was eager for her to return.

Chapter 21

<u>Me</u>

<u>I</u> woke up with an intense hangover as my head throbbed and my mouth was devoid of any moisture. I knew I'd earned it and scolded myself for overindulging. Yes, it was sloppy and would cost me precious time I really didn't have, but I opted for a temporary revelry and wouldn't look back. A fleeting moment of panic gripped me as I thought of the consequences of my actions at Mt. Baker, but I dismissed them just as quickly. I'd hurt and killed many people, but I wasn't responsible for their choice to attend. My target was Hunter and the others were simply victims of circumstance. Their sacrifice helped create the artifice of mass chaos as opposed to a distinct mark. For that, I was ultimately grateful but can't help smiling at the knowledge that their decision to see Hunter in person bore as much responsibility as my talent with explosives.

At any rate, I'm fairly certain that I didn't leave any incriminating evidence, but those agents appear annoyingly thorough and determined. They swarmed the scene within minutes and don't appear to be giving up any time soon. When I turned on the news for the latest updates, the reporters said that a lead had turned up, but didn't provide any specifics. They suspected terrorism, but no one had claimed responsibility yet. Certainly, I'd like to receive credit, but my desire for affirmation is checked by a greater need to avoid any sort of penal consequences. I had hoped that some international terrorist organization might step forward to gain notoriety for the tragedy in my silence, but no such luck. The lack of any semblance of a public agenda appeared to render the pundits quizzical. Surely, they posited an incident of this grandeur warranted a very public grab for attention. The press's befuddlement delighted me all the more, as did the predictably slow and bureaucratic response of the FBI-led investigation. Surely, they wouldn't rest, nor could I, but

I'll take my chances with those half-wits who I've managed to elude for the past three years.

My wry smile faded when a photo of me in a black ski mask flashed across on the screen. The reporter smugly stated there was a suspicion that the unidentified man in the black ski mask might have some association with the bombing. They asked anyone with any additional photos or information to contact law enforcement immediately. Finally, they posted the phone number for the 24/7 hotline where anyone could call with information pertaining to the investigation. The number seared onto my retinas as though it signaled the harbinger of my capture. I felt a sudden chill with the realization. I knew there was a possibility they would find the guy in the ski mask, but the inability to identify the person underneath was my protection. Still, this brought them a step closer sooner than I'd like. It was excruciating knowing Kayla was still within my grasp, but the incident loomed over me. It was going to be difficult to eliminate her and escape the country before the feds caught up to me.

I allowed myself a temporary moment to peruse the situation and in that time, I struggled to move beyond my moderated hatred of Kayla. For a moment the walls shifted, the lights dimmed red, and time itself slowed to a crawl. I felt underwater as I agonizingly swam to the surface of my consciousness.

In that moment, nostalgia washed over me and my choice was made clear. I longed for a return to the dichotomy of a familiar place from my youth. I sought refuge in a city whose beauty was masked in equal parts vice and apathy. With a few clicks on my laptop, I was booked and headed to Amsterdam.

My flight didn't leave for 36 hours. I'd checked several flight options prior to finalizing my purchase. There were flights that left earlier, but they all had connections in other countries. I ultimately decided that a direct flight was my best option. I'd been careful to seek the best for red documents but was aware that the fewer times I had to deal with airport security, the better. This was especially true after my most recent work of art. Alas, my time in purgatory would continue for now.

In the interim, I had 36 hours to eliminate any evidence that could link me to the bombing. I still had the clothes I wore on the mountain. If I tried to take them with me and my luggage was searched, only the most incompetent TSA agent wouldn't figure it out. Of course, I can't just leave them here since a DNA test would surely identify me.

After some debate, I shoved them in a duffel bag and decided I would soak them in ammonia and dump them in the Puget Sound. I needed something heavy that would make the bag sink quickly. I scanned the room and noticed a clear vase filled with decorative rocks. I grabbed it and dumped half of the stones into the bag. I zipped it closed and tested its weight. It was definitely heavy enough to sink. Satisfied, I replaced the vase and tried to make it look as if it had never been moved. I finished just as room service knocked on my door. I went to the door and opened it enough to let the staff push the cart inside. I abruptly shoved money at them before they could follow the cart in and slammed the door closed. I could hear muffled protests from outside but then saw the two young men shrug at each other through the peephole when they saw the tip I'd given. They turned and walked away without any further filibuster. I grabbed the Bloody Mary I'd ordered and gulped it down in a few swallows. The vodka calmed my nerves, and I could feel my heart rate start to slow. I forced myself to eat the omelet, too. I couldn't really taste it from all the hot sauce in the Bloody Mary, but I didn't really care. I was eating both out of necessity and to pass some time while finalizing my plan to destroy the evidence.

I jumped in the shower, shaved, and dressed in pressed khakis and a white button down shirt. I grabbed my black leather jacket and glanced at myself in the mirror. No one would ever suspect that I was anything other than a high-class tourist. I checked out at the front desk and paid my bill in cash. I'd checked in under a phony name and used a ghost credit card that couldn't be traced back to me.

Fortunately, I'd had the foresight to purchase several fake IDs before completing my task, so I could rotate through any of several aliases to keep the feds off my trail.

"Thank you, Mr. Jones. We hope you enjoyed your stay and will come back to visit us again soon."

I smiled at the same perky blonde who had checked me in. Little did she know that within forty-eight hours I hoped to be higher than a kite near the red-light district in Amsterdam. Returning to Seattle was the last thing on my mind.

I made my way on foot to Pike's Place Market stopping at a corner shop along the way to get ammonia. I kept my head low and walked directly through the aisles, discretely choosing the bottle, paying cash, and leaving as quickly as I entered. Upon arrival at the Market, the place was swarming with tourists who were all marveling at the men throwing dead fish around. Everyone was too busy watching a man chasing a woman around waving a giant bloody salmon to notice me. I bought a ticket for the Bainbridge Ferry and boarded. The ferry left the terminal ten minutes later. I walked around until I found myself on a quiet deck without anyone else to observe me. Then I pulled the duffel bag out of my larger travel pack opened the ammonia, poured it in the duffle, and lowered the bag slowly over the railing. When I was certain we were at the deepest part of the Puget Sound, I let it go and watched it hover on the surface for a few seconds before slowly being pulled down into the black abyss. I breathed a sigh of relief as I watched it go. I wanted no part in the investigation of the bombing. Without any evidence, I would be home free.

The only remaining task was eliminating that little snitch, Kayla, before retreating to the city of tulips, wooden shoes, endless varieties of pot, and the infamous Red Light District. If I played my cards right, I would be living the good life in just a few short days.

Chapter 22

<u>Kayla</u>

Kayla was deeply affected by her first day at the hospital. She was amazed at the strength of the people she met who were facing huge obstacles. Some of the patients were dealing with terminal cancer, career ending injuries, and severe rheumatologic disorders. Many were suffering from chronic pain, yet they were still beacons of hope. Their optimism and admirable attitudes were astounding. A young girl who had been fighting cancer for over half of her life played dolls with Kayla and giggled with her. Even though the little girl spent more time within the walls of the hospital than in the real world, she still seemed delighted by the little things in life. Even her parents were very kind and gracious, which was even more amazing considering the fact that their only daughter was losing a battle with cancer.

Kayla could not imagine being in their place. She knew she would have been angry and bitter about the injustice of it all if she were in their position, yet they were committed to treasuring every moment they had left with their daughter. Even thinking about it broke Kayla's heart, but it also gave her courage. She may have lost her innocence when she witnessed the horrifying murders in Chicago, but she was still alive and had a future ahead of her. She was still able to pursue her dreams. She was not going to be losing her only child or die before she ever even had the chance to live.

Kayla felt selfish for feeling sorry for herself after seeing the battles other people were courageously facing. She found herself immensely moved by those she met in the hospital. She lost herself in her painting that night. Her paintbrush seemed to have a mind of its own. As she painted, her thoughts drifted back to Hunter. He was an amazingly charismatic man. Even bandaged up and dressed in a hospital gown, she could tell how incredibly handsome he was.

He had made her laugh and forget her own pain. She could not believe how gracious he was after watching his career crumble before his eyes in such a tragic manner. Yet, instead of focusing on what he had lost, he seemed focused on his future. She knew that part of it was self-preservation for him, but she also knew that part of it was because he was an incredibly strong and dedicated man who was not about to give up on life because of someone's evil actions. He seemed to feel that the best way to fight terrorism was to rise above the tragedy and carry on with his life. She admired him for that. When her life was threatened, she retreated into her safety zone and refused to leave her house. The only reason she had left today was that Agent Franklin would not take no for an answer.

Regardless, she was grateful she met Hunter. He made her feel a human connection that she had not felt in three years. She found herself eagerly anticipating their next encounter. She'd already sent Agent Olson out to pick up the movies that Hunter requested. Olson begrudgingly agreed, and she promised to throw in a batch of homemade cookies to sweeten the deal. She hadn't made the cookies yet but was planning to start baking as soon as she tired of painting.

Kayla was so engrossed in her work that several hours melted away. She finally glanced at her watch and decided it was time to start mixing up the batter. She knew she was going to be relying on Agents Olson and Franklin to run errands for her, so she wanted to make sure she stayed in their good graces. She'd promised Olson cookies, and she wanted to make sure that they were the best cookies he'd ever tasted. She started pulling out the ingredients, only to realize she was missing a few things. She was out of chocolate chips but had a chocolate bar, so she chopped it up into chunks to use in the batter. She was also out of eggs, but she had a banana that she used instead. She sighed in frustration when she measured out butter and realized she only had half the required amount, so she used peanut butter to make up for the rest. She realized that her cookies were not going to be the same as her grandmother's famous chocolate chip cookie recipe, but she was confident they would still taste good. She would just have to call them Kayla's Creation, she decided.

She sampled the dough and sighed at the combination of chocolate and peanut butter. She was surprised to find that the batter was delicious. She even wrote the recipe down so she could recreate it in the future. She was just pulling out the final batch when Agent Olson sent her a text message that he was on her front porch. He had instructed her not to open her door to anyone unless she was sure it was a trusted friend or agent. She made a list of the friends she had that she trusted beyond all doubt, but the list turned out to be very short. There were only two people on it. Agent Franklin and Agent Olson. Kayla's other friends were acquaintances that she met at graduate school. She didn't know if any of them were above ratting her out. They were all nice, but when it came down to it, she didn't know any of them well enough to trust with her life.

Other than the hospital, her only two trusted connections to the outside world were Frank and Olson. The three of them formed an odd type of family. Although the agents had their own families, they still treated Kayla almost as a daughter. Kayla wouldn't necessarily have picked Olson and Franklin as friends, but she was stuck with them, and the more she got to know them, the more she was finding to like about them. It seemed sad that she could only open her door to them if they texted her first, but these were the circumstances of her life, and there was no point in fighting it.

She crossed her living room and opened her door a crack after releasing the deadbolts. Agent Olson slipped through with a bag under his arm. He gave her a gruff hello and held out the bag. He wasn't thrilled about running her errands, but the smell of freshly baked cookies went a long way to soften him up.

"Come in, come in," Kayla motioned him into the kitchen. She gratefully accepted his bag and peered inside. All of the titles of the movies she had requested were neatly lined up. She smiled. "Thank you so much! This is perfect."

"It took them an hour and a half to assemble all of the movies you wanted. They had to dig one out of storage and had to track down someone who owed a lot of late fines to hand over another one, but they're all there."

Kayla gave him a hug. He didn't know how to respond at first but then forced himself to reach one of his hands around and pat her on the back. "I can't thank you enough! I'm extremely grateful."

"It was nothing, really. The librarian did all the work." Olson said, never one who was comfortable expressing emotion.

"The fact that you were willing to help me out means a lot. Now come over here and eat some cookies."

Kayla held out a tempting plate of her creation. The golden-brown cookies were still warm and gooey.

Olson couldn't help himself. He reached out and popped one into his mouth. His gruff expression turned to one of delight. "Wow, this is incredible! What kind of cookies are these?" He reached immediately for another.

"I call them Kayla's Creation. I had to doctor the recipe up a little bit because I was short on some ingredients, but I think it worked nicely."

"These are the best cookies I've ever tasted, and trust me," he motioned to his slightly rotund middle, "I've had my share over the years."

Kayla smiled. She started stacking some of the cookies that had already cooled into a plastic container. "You have to promise me that you'll take some of these to your family. I steal enough of your time, so the least I can do is make sure they get a few cookies in return."

Olson looked reluctant, already on his third cookie. "Alright, I think I can resist temptation and get them home without eating them first, but I'm not making any promises."

Kayla smiled. She had known that there must be a nice man under Olson's prickly exterior. It had just taken her awhile to find it. She poured them both some coffee and sat down at the table.

"How's the case coming? Have you had any leads?"

"We found out that Kazamir skipped town using an alias, which is why we haven't heard from him for a few days, but there aren't any good leads about his whereabouts."

Kayla nodded. "It's probably too much to hope that he's moved on to bigger and better things than hunting me down."

Olson gave her a sympathetic look. "Kazamir doesn't leave things unfinished. He may be keeping a low profile, but we'll hear from him again. Right now, the agency has been swamped dealing with the Mt. Baker Bombing, so we haven't made as much progress on the Kazamir case as we'd hoped."

"Do you think Mt. Baker was an act of terrorism?" Kayla asked, temporarily putting thoughts of Kazamir to the side.

Olson replied, "Our original suspicion was that a terrorist was behind the tragedy, but no one has come forward and taken credit for it. It doesn't add up. We're wondering if someone was paid to do it as a publicity stunt or if the bomber was just trying to take out Hunter Erickson, but botched it and ended up injuring a lot of other people in the process."

Kayla was silent for a moment. It seemed so pointless that someone would use explosives to injure an athlete and accidentally cause a massive blast that injured the spectators, too. Although it was unlikely, she knew that explosives could be unpredictable. A picture of Hunter flashed through her mind. What if the bomber had been targeting him? Could someone be so evil that he or she wanted to end not only his career but also his life? Who would be careless enough to miscalculate the amount of explosives and injure so many people? A few years before, Kayla would never have believed anyone was capable of such a horrible act, but now she wasn't so sure.

Chapter 23

<u>Hunter</u>

Hunter's face lit up when he looked into the bag that Kayla handed him. "You got them all!" He was going half-crazy watching sitcom reruns and daytime soap operas. Seeing the bag full of DVDs was one of the most welcome sights he had seen in days. "Thank you so much, Kayla!"

"Don't mention it. I just called in a favor from a friend. You can keep them for two weeks before I have to return them to the library."

It was Kayla's second visit to the hospital, and she didn't want to admit to herself how excited she was to see Hunter again. The color was starting to return to his face, and he appeared to have more energy. His smile came easier and she couldn't help but notice the dimple on his right cheek.

"I also broke some of the rules and brought you something else."

"Oh?" Hunter was really starting to like Kayla. He couldn't resist a woman who liked to live on the edge.

Kayla checked to make sure there were no nurses within viewing distance and flashed a small plate of her cookies.

Hunter's eyes lit up. "Wow, those look amazing. Are they for me?"

"Yes. I'm not supposed to bring you any junk food, but I don't classify these as junk food. I used a banana and some peanut butter in the dough, so they are at least a little bit healthy."

"I'm not going to argue with you." Hunter greedily reached for a cookie and bit into its doughy goodness. His eyes rolled back in his head as the flavor filled his mouth. He'd been living on gelatin, rice, and chicken soup for days. The taste of the cookies nearly sent him over the edge. "These are absolutely amazing. I think I must have died and gone to Heaven."

Kayla smiled. It felt good to make someone else's day a little better. She didn't want to admit it, but Agent Franklin had been right. She did need to get out of the house, and this had been the perfect way to do it.

Hunter devoured the cookies quickly, and Kayla stashed the plate with crumbs back in her bag to hide the evidence. Then she popped one of the discs into the DVD player and sat down next to him to watch a movie. A wave of contentment washed over Hunter that he hadn't felt in a very long time. He was amazed that in the midst of a career ending injury, he was able to find peace because of this incredible woman who had wandered into his life. He stole a glance at her, and she caught him looking. He grinned, and she grinned back. Then she reached over and arranged his pillows so he could comfortably see the TV.

The half hour went all too fast. Soon it was time for Kayla to head to the next room. Hunter protested when she said it was time for her to go, and agreed not to make a scene if she promised to stop by again when she was done with her rounds.

"You drive a tough bargain, Mr. Erickson," Kayla said, even though she was also feeling reluctant to leave. "But okay, I promise to stop by and visit again before I leave as long as you're not asleep. You need your rest, and I don't want to wake you."

"It's a deal," Hunter said, already feeling lonely as he watched her walk away. She stopped in his doorway, turned, and blew a quick kiss with a silly expression on her face. He wasn't sure if it was the ample amount of pain medication he was receiving, Kayla's adorable expression, or a combination of both, but his heart nearly melted then and there.

After she left, Hunter turned his attention to the news. The police were giving updates on the latest developments in the Mt. Baker case. The suspicious man in the black ski mask had shown up in other photos. He appeared to be carrying a dark gray backpack in security photos taken early in the morning on the day of the bombing but appeared without it around the time the bombing was about to take place. He could have loaded the bag with explosives and dropped it near the finish line. He could have used a timer or a remote control to detonate the bomb. At this point, the police just had theories. There was nothing concrete and no clear leads as to who the man in the mask might be. It didn't appear that the suspect had removed his mask from the time he'd arrived until after he'd left. Some witnesses recalled seeing him in the parking lot, but no one seemed to remember more about him than that. One of the employees thought they saw him with a backpack getting out of a silver sedan with rental plates before the resort opened. It had struck him as odd that someone would be there hours before the competition started, but he figured the man either wanted to get first tracks or make sure he had good seats for the competition. The police were searching nearby rental car companies to see if they could find out more information. The silver sedan wasn't a great lead, but it was better than anything else that had surfaced in the last few days.

  Hunter sighed in frustration. He had hoped they'd get to the bottom of the bombing quickly. He was glad they finally had a suspect but frustrated they hadn't established a motive or any solid leads yet. He knew things like this took time, but with the thousands of people that had been on the slopes to watch the competition, he'd have thought someone would have seen something that would incriminate the responsible party. The police still hadn't figured out if the act had been one of violence from an international terrorist or the horrible act of a crazed killer. At the very least, they had ruled out any possibility that it had been an accident. There was too much residue from explosives for it to have been a tragic accident.

  The brief wave of peace Hunter experienced during Kayla's visit faded and was replaced by frustration and anger. It was bad enough that he'd lost his parents to an act of terrorism, but now he'd lost his coach and his career. He wanted his coach's death avenged and wished he could be doing more to help the authorities.

Unfortunately, he was bound up in a hospital bed with broken limbs and a serious reliance on pain killers. He felt himself slipping back into the state of depression he'd been stuck in before Kayla had shown up when his Uncle Jackson walked in the door.

"Don't look so glum, kid." Jackson quickly crossed the room and clicked off the TV. "You don't need to be obsessing about the bombing. The authorities are doing everything they can to find the responsible party. There's nothing you're going to do to help them right now. Why don't you focus on getting yourself better instead of mulling over what's happening in the case?"

"Come on, Uncle J. You know as well as I do that's easier said than done."

"You're right, Hunter. I've been doing the same thing, and I'm beginning to realize what a waste of time and energy it is. I don't want you falling into the same trap. You really need to focus on your future right now, not the past."

Hunter sighed but had to admit that his uncle was right. "Okay, okay. I promise I'll avoid watching the news and focus on my studies and my rehab for now. You just have to promise you'll tell me if they catch the guy or figure out his motive."

"You've got yourself a deal. Now, how about some cribbage?" Jackson knew that Hunter had been borderline obsessed with the game since he was a kid.

They had just finished their second game, which Hunter easily won, when there was a knock on the door. Jackson and Hunter turned to see Kayla leaning on the doorframe, smiling at them. "You must be Hunter's Uncle J. Very nice to meet you. I'm Kayla. I'm a volunteer here."

Jackson shook her hand and grinned at her. "And you must be the reason that Hunter's been in a better mood recently. Thanks for turning him from a brooding and moody bore into a more tolerable guy."

Kayla laughed. "I'm not sure that I could ever call Hunter brooding or moody, but I have been doing my best to keep him company, bring him off-limits goodies, and provide him with entertainment whenever possible."

"I don't think you give yourself enough credit, but it's nice to meet you."

Kayla surveyed the room. "I can come back later if you two are in the middle of a heated game of cribbage."

"Oh, no. We finished our game. Hunter has humbled me one too many times. I swear he's learned a few tricks over the last few days. Either way, I don't think my pride can take another loss." Jackson pushed back his chair and stood. "I think I'll leave you both alone. I've got some calls I have to make to keep up with the office back home. It was a pleasure to meet you, Kayla. Hunter's fortunate to have a friend like you."

Kayla smiled shyly at the unexpected compliment. "And it was nice to meet you, too. Hunter has told me wonderful stories about what a cool uncle you were to him while he was growing up."

"We had a lot of fun, that's for sure." Jackson grinned. He understood why Hunter's mood had been improving. Kayla was extremely sweet *and* incredibly beautiful. "Keep him out of trouble for me."

With that, Jackson left the room, and Kayla turned to Hunter, "You weren't exaggerating. He's really great. I can only imagine all the fun you had with him while you were growing up."

"Yeah, he was always a bit of a free spirit, which was a refreshing change for me. He's always accepted me for the person I am and has never tried to turn me into anything I'm not. Even when it was obvious that I had a talent for skiing, he didn't push me. He let me make decisions on my own and was there for me 100% of the time. I feel a little guilty because he had to work really hard to pay for my coach while I was growing up and gave up a lot to travel with me to competitions, but he never complained. I worry that he's lonely now since he never had time to get married or have kids of his own, but he seems content with his life. I just hope that he does something for himself one of these days."

Out of the Shadows

"He seems very proud of you. Something tells me that you've been one of the bright spots in his life. He obviously adores you, and probably has been beside himself with worry these past few days."

"I'm just grateful that he wasn't at the finish line when the bomb went off. He watched me finish from the stands and was out of range when the bomb went off. It was hard enough to lose my coach. I couldn't imagine if Jackson had been injured, too."

Kayla nodded, infinitely impressed with how rational and logical Hunter was being in the face of such a huge tragedy and possible career ending injuries. She admired his strength and ability to take things in stride.

"Is there any chance that you have more of those cookies for me?" Hunter asked in a boyish voice, knowing it was probably too much to hope for.

"As a matter of fact, I do. I gave out a few to some of the younger patients but didn't want them to ruin their appetites and make the nurses suspicious, so I saved a few." Kayla produced what remained of her now-famous cookies. The look on Hunter's face was priceless as he reached out to grab one and devoured it in one bite.

"Thank you!" he said between mouthfuls, and Kayla giggled. It had been a long time since she'd taken so much pleasure in something as simple as baking cookies.

"You've heard enough about me. Tell me about how your painting is going." Jackson said, suddenly very interested in the woman whose presence was making his hospital stay bearable.

"Actually, it's going well. I've been able to put in a lot of time recently and have really gotten a good start on a big project. The subject matter is inspiring, and I'm making significant progress."

"Is it wrong to assume that there's no husband in your life since there is no ring on your left hand, and you're spending your free time at the hospital with dashing former skiers?"

Kayla gave him a warm smile. "Your assumption is correct,

Mr. Erickson."

"I'm relieved to hear it, but a little bit baffled why such a gorgeous, talented woman who bakes the world's most amazing cookies hasn't been swept off her feet by some charming young man."

Kayla looked at him, trying to decide if he was flirting with her or just trying to be friendly. It was hard not to get trapped in the depths of his piercing blue eyes. "You could say that my life has had a few twists and turns that have made relationships nearly impossible."

Hunter looked at her curiously. "I get it. You're a woman of mystery. Intriguing. Tell me more."

Kayla couldn't stop the laugh that erupted out of her. "Well, I guess that's one way to look at it. I was too busy feeling sorry for myself to think of it that way. Truth be told, I had to move away from my home and leave my friends and family because I witnessed a crime and there are certain people who would like nothing more than to see me dead." Kayla hadn't been so open with anyone in years. She wasn't sure what it was about Hunter that made her trust him. Perhaps it was the fact that their lives had both been altered by tragedy. Either way, she knew she could trust Hunter.

"Of course, if I told you any more, then I'd probably have to kill you, so I'd better stop. I took the job at the hospital to get out of the house because it's not safe for me to go anywhere in public right now. If you wouldn't mind, I'd appreciate it if you wouldn't mention this to anyone else. I'm not really sure who I can trust at this point."

Hunter was trying to absorb all of the weight of what she was telling him. Here was a beautiful woman who basically had to stay in hiding and limit her contact with the outside world because she had unintentionally witnessed a crime and now there were people who wanted her dead. He couldn't imagine what his life would be like if he had to pull a disappearing act and cut off contact with his friends and family.

"Wow, that's pretty heavy stuff, Kayla. I'm sorry I was teasing you about being single. I had no idea."

"Don't apologize! I'm at peace with it now. It's been tough for the past few years, but I have faith that they'll catch the guy sooner or later, and I'll be able to lead a more normal life. Until then, my social activities revolve around my hours at the hospital and my work. It's really not all bad."

Hunter knew she was being gracious about her troubles because he was facing such huge challenges of his own, but he was still aware of the huge sacrifices she had made in her life. She was young and beautiful. Most women her age would be out wining and dining with friends, going dancing, spending their Saturdays shopping, and dating. Instead, Kayla was spending her time holed up in her studio. Her only outings involved visiting the sterile halls of the hospital.

"I think you're an amazing woman, Kayla. If I could walk, I would offer to take you on a date." Hunter said, suddenly sounding serious.

"Well, I don't think we're going to be able to get more than hospital food and rented movies, but I'd still say yes if you asked me out."

"Then let's make it official. Kayla, will you stay in on a date with me? I can't offer you more than orange gelatin and stale coffee, but we could order dinner up and watch one of these movies tonight."

"You've got yourself a date!" Kayla grinned and quickly texted Agent Franklin to let him know her plans. She put one of his favorite movies in the DVD player and then settled into the chair right by his bed. It might not have been the most romantic of locations, but it was still the best date Kayla had ever had.

Chapter 24

<u>Me</u>

    <u>I</u> stayed on the ferry when it arrived at Bainbridge Island. I had no interest in visiting wineries, eating at cafes, or milling around boutiques. Instead, I watched as tourists disembarked with their fanny packs and guide books and felt a deep loathing for them. What a meaningless existence it would be to spend what little time you have off your crummy job being herded around, snapping pictures of everything you pass just so you have something to show off to your friends and talk about for the next year to make your life seem less dull. I rolled my eyes. I didn't feel bad about all the people I had killed. They were people just like these. They had nothing better to do with their lives than loaf around, oohing and aahing at everything because their lives were too boring to do anything meaningful. I was glad my fate wasn't going to end like theirs. Anyone stupid enough to stand in the freezing cold in order to watch someone hurl themselves down a mountain at 80 miles per hour deserved to die. Of course, I know society won't see it my way. I overheard plenty of people talking about "The Tragedy at Mt. Baker". It sounds like the wolves are howling for blood on this one. If they catch me, there will be no hope for a sympathetic jury, and the best thing for me to do is get out of town. My goal had been to get rid of the girl first, but time was running out. I was starting to feel anxious. If there's any hope to make it out of the country, I'll need to arrive at the airport at the last minute, sprint through security, and get on the plane right before takeoff. The less time I spend around TSA agents, the better.

    I pulled out my cell phone. I'd dropped a small chip into Kayla's purse when my inside source met her with a group of friends at a coffee shop a few weeks ago. She had no idea I was there. I just walked past and dropped the microchip right into her pretty coral bag. Fortunately for me, she takes the thing everywhere and never cleans it out. That's how I managed to figure out where she was living. My smartphone app indicated she was out and about at the moment. This was news to me because she had only left her house once since she received my letter. I looked up the address and realized she was at a hospital in the city. Maybe they made her go to counseling to deal with the stress I was placing on her life? If that was the case, it was good payback, because she put a lot of stress on my life when she blew my million-dollar deal.

I'd worked so hard to pull myself out of small-scale drug deals. A few grand here and there just wasn't worth it. I had bided my time until a really big score came along. It all started with a top medical research company that was working on a microchip containing living cells from all of the organs in the body. The chip could be injected with any type of drug in order to study the drug's side effects. Using the new technology, researchers could administer a new drug into the microchip, and it would travel through the gut cells, the liver, the blood stream, and the kidneys before the chip would excrete it. Then scientists could test for any toxicity the drug may have caused to the organs and measure the drug's efficacy. This new technology was intended to speed up the time it took for drugs to be approved by the FDA, eliminate the need for animal testing, and ultimately allow drug companies to get their medications on the market faster. The idea was worth millions and the researcher who invented it was desperate for cash. He had a coke habit and was in deep with some big time dealers. His life was on the line unless he paid them off immediately. He owed me some money and told me his little sob story. I'm an entrepreneur. When I see a good opportunity, I take it. I offered to take on his drug debts in exchange for his idea and the rights to the patent.

I didn't realize exactly how much this technology was worth until I started trying to line up buyers. Turns out ending animal testing is a pretty lucrative business and drug companies have a hell of a lot of money to burn. My contacts were jumping at the opportunity to get their hands on this invention, and I made a deal with the highest bidder. The deal was scheduled to go down on the night that Kayla barged into my life. I had met with the researcher and he had all the necessary information. The dealers he owed had agreed to keep him alive as long as they could come along and get their money. The researcher was supposed to hand over his data in exchange for my cash. I would pay his dealers, and he'd be on his way. I wasn't about to hang onto the information long though. It was his life's work, and I had a feeling he wasn't going to let it go that easily. He would give it up when everyone was at the meet, but it seemed just as likely that he'd think up some scheme to get it back from me once his dealers were off his back. The drug company representative was supposed to be waiting for me in the shadows, and come out as soon as the deal had gone down and the researcher and other dealers had left. Then I was going to make a quick exchange of the information and jump on the first plane out of the country to Barbados. Unfortunately, things didn't go as planned.

    When everyone arrived, the circle tightened and the exchange began. He gave me his research, and I gave his dealers my cash. The first one took it and turned to go, but the second one sensed there was more money to be made if he stuck around. The researcher started panicking. He knew he was in way over his head. He broke down and started whining like a wounded animal. His reaction pissed the dealer off. They started making a scene and the first dealer heard the chaos and came back to get in on the action. I turned to go, but guns came out, mouths opened, and brains powered down. I turned but kept walking away backwards to make some distance. The researcher pointed at me and said he had nothing else. If they wanted more, I had the only thing of value he's ever had or will have. As I saw them slightly lower their guns, I sensed they knew he was right and were thinking about killing both of us, taking the data and money, and disappearing into the night. Those thoughts turned to actions as they turned my way. I never hesitated or allowed them another move. I pulled a .45 I'd concealed behind my

Out of the Shadows

back as soon as the dealers went silent and started spraying bullets at them. Each caught two shots to the chest and fell where they stood. I heard the drug company rep crawl out of the shadows in disbelief at what had happened, panicking and contemplating running. We locked eyes, and I squeezed two shots his way, clipping him just below his left eye. He dropped his briefcase as his body hit the ground, lifeless. I turned toward the researcher and methodically walked towards him. He stood frozen, overwhelmed by everything he had just witnessed. I fired one more shot into each dealer, never losing eye contact with the researcher. My .45 had a 15 round clip, and I paused to think how many bullets I had left. I smiled as I computed the math, I'd always liked math, and deduced I had seven shots left. Perfect. I put one in each of his knees, paused as he fell whimpering to the ground and fired the last five into his chest once he finally looked up.

    As my blood cooled and my predilection for violence returned to my subconscious, I surveyed what lay before me and assessed my options. If I had the time, I'd likely pick up the shell casings, douse the blood with ammonia, pull all their teeth, and set the block ablaze. No DNA, no dental records. I didn't have the luxuries of time or a quiet, private location so bathing the scene in fire as quickly as possible would have to do. I dragged the bodies to one pile, ran back to my car to collect a gas can and a phosphorous grenade I had in the trunk (one must always be prepared after all) and scurried back to the pile to finish up. I found myself irritated at those corpses for making me rush. Manners... some people just lacked them completely... This was a location that law enforcement didn't regularly patrol or care about, but time was still of the essence as gunshots might be ubiquitous, but can't be ignored forever. I wiped my gun clean, threw it in with my quiet company, and poured the contents of the gas can over them.

    Of all the inopportune times to do so, my phone rang. I recognized the number as a contact I can't ignore in any situation, so I answered. While doing so, I pulled the pin from the grenade, lobbed it in the pile and briskly jogged away. The grenade exploded as phosphorous met gasoline in a remarkably beautiful marriage of light and heat that was sure to purge the bulk of any evidence of what happened and my involvement therein. It was the best I could hope for considering my truncated time allotment.

    In the flash, I saw a woman's figure duck around a corner. I quickly hung up and tiptoed over; catching a glimpse of her face. She thought she was trapped, but just as I got close to her, she darted to the side of a partition and disappeared through a doorway. I forgot about my money, the fire behind me, and time itself and became consumed in pursuing this potential witness. We played a game of cat and mouse around that warehouse. Every time I thought I had her cornered, she managed to find a staircase down to another level or a hidden room to cower in. The flames were growing and started to engulf the building. I could feel the heat against my skin. I knew that sooner or later, I was going to have to get out, but so was she. I just about had her backed into a room with no exit when a large, flaming beam fell right in front of me. I could feel the building start to sway and knew if I didn't get out, I wasn't going to see the light of day again. I abandoned my quest and ran for it. I managed to get out just as the building collapsed. I heard fire and police sirens coming closer, so I turned and ran through dark alleyways until I found the safety of my car. I looked down at myself and realized I was covered in sweat and blood. I couldn't show my face in public like this. Guilt was written all over me, and I had to leave. I was out of time and couldn't go back for the money I gave the dealers or the money the drug rep was set to pay me. Worse still, I suddenly realized I'd dropped the flash drive with the research somewhere in the chase, so I'd lost everything. She stole my future, my nest egg, my retirement. I escaped that night but in the moment our eyes locked, her features seared into my memory. She became a part of my consciousness. I saw her while awake, and she was featured in my dreams.

    It didn't take long to find her in Chicago, only to have her slip from my justice like the thief she is. She wouldn't escape again. I took all the time I could and found the "safe" house. Our game of cat and mouse has lasted three years, and I longed for it to end.

Chapter 25

Kayla

    Kayla left the hospital that night in a better mood than she'd been in for weeks. Hunter had a way of making her laugh at herself and accept her situation. Although she wished her life could be more normal, she also was grateful for her painting, her new friendships at the hospital, and the fact she had people who were watching out for her and committed to keeping her safe. She knew she had been lucky. Kazamir could have killed her in the warehouse all those years ago. She could easily have gone up in flames like the rest of the people he killed that night. She was fortunate the fire had bought her enough time to escape. Had the building not started to disintegrate, Kazamir would have surely tracked her down and ended her life in some unspeakable fashion. By some miracle, it hadn't happened like that. Beams had fallen, the building started to crumble, and she made a break for it. She didn't expect to make it out alive, but she did. She ran out into the dark Chicago night and panicked when she thought she heard his footsteps behind her. She expected him to shoot her, but the sirens had been her savior. She ran towards them, and he ran the other way. Within seconds, she collided with a police officer rushing to the scene and collapsed at his feet, sobbing, covered in soot, and in total shock about the events she witnessed.

    The police were kind to her. She didn't remember much about the drive to the station, but she remembered a kindly woman in a uniform handing her a paper cup filled with steaming tea. She'd accepted it gratefully and took deep breaths, but her attempts to calm down were futile.

    Handling violent situations was not something to which she was accustomed. She'd been raised in an affluent Chicago suburb, attended a Catholic High School, and graduated from Loyola

University. She'd grown up in a safe neighborhood, and her parents had shielded her from harm and danger her entire life. She as aware of the crime that happened in the metro, but for all intents and purposes, she'd been completely naive to danger up until that moment.

She realized she'd been leading the life of a privileged suburbanite. Her family always protected her and made her feel that the world was a safe and beautiful place, but the bubble of security she'd been shrouded in had been instantaneously shattered. At that moment, she no longer identified with her former naïve self. She'd seen the sadistic face of evil. It was burned into her brain, and she knew she could never forget the horrors she witnessed that night.

At the police station, she sat through hours of questioning. The police bombarded her with questions about what she had witnessed. It turned out that the police were familiar with the man she'd witnessed committing the horrible crimes. His name was Anton Viktor Kazamir, and he was what the police considered a "frequent flier" at their station. He'd been in and out of jail since he was a kid and was recently tied to drug deals and drive-by shootings. He'd been getting bolder for the past few months, and the police were eager to track him down. The trouble was that he was a master of camouflage. No two photos of him ever looked remotely similar, and he'd been known by several different aliases throughout his checkered past.

They had endless questions for her, most of which she hadn't been able to answer. She did her best to recall the details of the night, but everything happened so quickly. The warehouse was dark and she was too terrified to study her surroundings. She was afraid the information she recalled wasn't going to be of much use to the police. Eventually, they let her go home. She went straight to her bedroom and fell into bed in a state of total exhaustion. It crossed her mind to call her family, but she didn't want to disturb them at that hour. She figured it would be best if she called them when she was rested and calm, rather than frazzled and in shock.

She woke up the next morning, showered, and went to work. She didn't know how one was supposed to act after witnessing a heinous crime, so she moved as if on auto-pilot. She felt like a robot. She ate half of a breakfast sandwich while standing at her kitchen counter and watching the news. She turned it off when she caught a clip of the warehouse's charred foundation and remnants where she had been the night before. She didn't want to think about it and certainly didn't want the media to turn it into a donnybrook of pundits and sound bites.

The previous day, she had been a carefree, optimistic, young woman, but that day she felt much older and her optimism was replaced by knowledge of the evil that existed in human nature. She felt as if the weight of the world was on her shoulders. She walked to her studio without even a thought that someone might be watching. She spent the entire day alone and forced her brain to focus solely on editing photos. She put her cell phone on silent and cranked her radio up as she worked, still in a state of shock. She didn't want to think about the outside world. Her growling stomach finally forced her to look at the time. She gasped when she realized that it was nearly 7:00 pm. She put her things away, locked up the building, and walked outside. A hand immediately reached out and grabbed her shoulder when she reached into her pocket to pull out her keys. She stifled a scream and whipped around. She found herself staring into the piercing blue eyes of a fierce looking man. Her heart leapt into her throat.

How could she have been so stupid? She should have realized he would come after her. Just when she thought it was all over, the man flashed a badge. He quietly informed her that he was part of the WITSEC, or Witness Security Program. He explained there were concerns that Kazamir knew her identity and was going to come after her. It was in her best interest to come with him. Kayla knew she didn't have a choice. She nodded and followed the man to his unmarked car. She got in without asking any questions. She spent the next twenty-four hours listening to the authorities fill her in on the danger she was in. They informed her she was the only living person who had any tangible evidence to connect to Kazamir, which placed her squarely in his crosshairs. They informed her they had a duty to keep her alive and were the only ones who could do so. They told her Kazamir had already placed lookouts at her apartment and had likely already tried to place some tracking malware on her cell phone. They didn't have a full psych-profile on him, but he absolutely fits the textbook sociopathic stalker mold. He likely had no belief that what he did was wrong, felt no remorse, and honestly believed she had victimized him. He wouldn't stop until he was satisfied the score was settled. If she tried to go this alone, he would make sure she was never seen again.

    Kayla listened but had trouble absorbing all of the information. She agreed to enter the Witness Security Program without a fight, but it didn't occur to her until much later that she wouldn't be able to say goodbye to her friends and family or gather her favorite belongings. She was given a suitcase filled with clothes that were roughly her size, but nowhere near her taste. Her entire closet was filled with sundresses, strappy sandals, crocheted tops, faded blue jeans, and beaded jewelry.

    She looked up with a question on her face when she saw the clothes. The agent she was working with handed her a photoshopped picture of herself with dark, wavy hair dressed in tailored clothing. She had always had blonde hair, but the agent told her they would be dying it before the day was over. She cried when the hairdresser started applying color to her locks, but when they had finished drying her hair and spun her around to look in the mirror, she felt a small wave of relief hit her. She was no longer the naive girl whose innocence was shattered after witnessing a horrible crime. Instead, she was a new, tougher version of herself. She had an edge to her and a seriousness that her old self had never had.

    She spent a few weeks in a rural town in Utah, which was known as a transition period. The goal was to get her completely off the map. During the transition, she would focus on letting go of her old life and embracing her new one. She wanted to succeed and did her best to be brave and concentrate on everything she needed to know in order to start a new life and stay alive. During the intense training period, she memorized every detail about her new identity, Kayla McCullen. As far as the WITSEC Program was concerned, Elizabeth Bronson no longer existed.

Time seemed by creep by, but eventually, the feds provided her with new identification and instructed her to board a commercial flight using her new identity. No one who knew her would have been able to recognize her as she stepped into the airport. She was wearing a fitted sheath dress and delicate sandals. Her dark hair was flowing loosely down her back, and her blue eyes were shrouded with emerald green contact lenses. Her formerly tanned skin was pale and creamy. The stress of the past few weeks gave her a haunted, frail appearance that was a stark contrast to the relaxed artist she had been. She handed her license and boarding pass over to the TSA agent. He didn't give it so much as a second glance. Kayla didn't look back as she boarded the flight to Seattle where she would be starting her new life. She had truly become Kayla McCullen. It felt as if Elizabeth Bronson had never even existed.

She arrived in Seattle with the address of a place to stay. The Witness Security Program had agreed to provide her with housing and protection in exchange for her agreement to testify when they brought Kazamir into custody. She was under the impression the arrangement would only last a few weeks, and she would soon return to her old life in Chicago, but that hadn't happened. She'd been forced to carry on the lie of Kayla McCullen for three years. Now she didn't know if she knew how to be Elizabeth Bronson anymore. She was so comfortable with her new life that she sometimes questioned if she would even want to go back to Chicago when this whole thing ended. She had grown to love Seattle in all its artsy, foodie, overcast, rainy glory. She never stopped missing her family but didn't know if it would be easy for her to go back and pick up her old life. She had been so ridiculously blind back then. Now she was a more realistic, cultured, and savvy woman. Over the course of the last few years, she had grown more comfortable in her own skin and become a more self-aware person.

These were all thoughts that were floating through Kayla's mind as she dialed Agent Franklin's phone number. He had reluctantly agreed to let her stay later than scheduled because he was relieved she was finally getting out and getting her mind off Kazamir. He promised to pick her up from the hospital as soon as she was ready to go. Sometimes she felt as if he was an overprotective father. It was odd to negotiate a curfew with him, but she understood it was his duty to make sure she stayed safe. As much as she needed to have a little fun, he needed to make sure she remained alive and able to testify against Kazamir even more.

"I'll be there in five minutes and pick you up at the front entrance. And Kayla, don't even set foot out that door until I arrive."

Kayla rolled her eyes. He was *so* overprotective. But she heeded his advice and remained in the hospital's crowded entrance until she saw Frank pull up in his unmarked car. She gave a big wave and walked through the revolving doorway. She saw Franklin's smile turn to a look of panic just as she stepped outside into the fresh air. Franklin dove out of his car and tackled her just as the world around them exploded in gunfire. He had on a bulletproof vest and somehow managed to cover her body with his own as he forced her back through the revolving doorway and into the lobby. Gunfire pelted the glass wall at the hospital's entrance. Although the glass cracked into hundreds of cobwebs, it remained intact. He grabbed Kayla's hand and led her straight back to the hospital's security wing. He shoved her into a chair and reached for his cell phone. He dialed a few numbers and waited in impatient silence.

"It's Franklin. We have an active shooter with a semi-automatic outside of Seattle General. He tried to take out witness 5121. He did a number on the front of the building, but as far as I can tell, there weren't any casualties."

Franklin waited a moment. "Yes, it was likely Kazamir or one of his guys going in for the kill. I don't know if he's still around. That's why I'm calling you."

He sat in frustrated silence. He finally thanked the person on the other end and hung up. "They told us to stay put. They're going to comb the area for the shooter, but they don't want us to move until we get the all clear."

Kayla was near hysterics. She was finally regaining her confidence and at peace with her life, and then in a building where lives were constantly being saved, hers was almost taken. If it hadn't been for Agent Franklin's lightning fast reflexes, she would have been shot and killed before she had time to think about what hit her. As panicked as she was, she was also grateful to Agent Franklin. She expressed her deep gratitude in a shaky voice. "I can't thank you enough, Frank. You could have been killed, but you saved my life. I don't know how I'll ever be able to fully thank you."

"Save it, Kayla. You know as well as I do that I was only doing my job. I'm just sorry I wasn't able to track the shooter down. We're so close to getting him, but he keeps escaping. At this rate, I don't know if we'll ever be able to catch him."

Franklin was cut short by the sound of an explosion. Chaos broke out. People were screaming and running in all directions. The sound of sirens filled the air. Kayla jumped to her feet, but Agent Franklin threw his arm out and pushed her back down. "Don't move, Kayla. I'm going to go check it out, but I don't want you to leave this spot. I'll check in with you and give you updates, but you have to promise me that you will stay right here. He motioned to one of the security guards. "I need you to stay with this woman. Whatever you do, make sure she stays safe. The police will be coming in for questioning as soon as everything up front settles down." The guard nodded. With that, Franklin took off down the hallway towards the sound of the explosion. Kayla burst into sobs, shaking uncontrollably. The security agent was a bachelor in his mid-forties and had no idea how to comfort her. He finally gave her a pat on the back and asked her if she would like to go with him to watch security footage and find out what had just happened. It didn't take them long to find the cause of the explosion. The camera at the front entrance of the hospital had footage of the glass, already weakened from bullets, suddenly exploding into a million tiny pieces as a bomb came through the window.

Kayla stayed in the hospital that night. Agent Franklin didn't feel that it was safe for her to go home. Kazamir was desperate to find her and had risked a very public shooting in order to end her life for good. He was obviously crazed to make such a bold move. There was no telling what he would do next. He had somehow devised a way to track Kayla's whereabouts and there were no guarantees that he wouldn't come after her again, so Kayla made herself comfortable. She didn't want to bother Hunter again because she knew he needed his rest and was afraid the shooting would upset him and delay his progress. The hospital was kind enough to set up a cot for her in the security office. They provided blankets, pillows, and scrubs for her to sleep in.

There was so much running through her mind, that she wasn't able to fall asleep, so she sat with the security agent named Bill and watched the security video of the shooting over and over again. She saw her image walking towards Agent Franklin's car. Then she saw him throw himself out of the vehicle and tackle her at the same moment that a series of shots were fired. They had half-rolled, half-crawled into the revolving door and made it through just as a series of bullets assaulted the glass windows. She saw images of herself and Agent Franklin running for the safety of the security office. People around them were panicking and fleeing in all directions. Thankfully most had been smart enough to run away from the entrance. A few minutes passed before the entire entrance went up in a blaze as a bomb was hurled through a window. Glass flew everywhere in shards. The beautiful mobiles decorating the entrance where shattered and the artwork lining the walls burned instantly.

What remained was a charred, simmering mess. Fortunately, sprinklers had immediately been activated and the fire from the explosion hadn't spread any farther than the hospital's entrance. Everyone at the reception desk and in the waiting room evacuated the area the minute the bullets hit the window, so no one was seriously injured. There had been a few minor concussions from people who were working to clear everyone out, but no one had been close enough to the explosion to suffer any serious harm. It was almost as though the explosion was part of a subterfuge to mask his escape as much as it was a last ditch effort to kill Kayla. Police were swarming the area, taking pictures and samples of everything. Agent Franklin had called to say that the person responsible, who was presumably Kazamir, had escaped before anyone had spotted him. He sounded devastated. So far, they didn't have a witness or security footage that led anywhere other than dead ends.

The police had scoured the scene for any sign of the bomber. They had combed the area but hadn't been able to find any leads. A small victory occurred when one of the officers located a semi-automatic that used the same bullets that were found embedded in the glass at the hospital's entrance. If there were any prints, it would help them determine the identity of the shooter. Agent Franklin was certain it was Kazamir, but they would need to prove it.

Kayla was struggling with the emotional rollercoaster she was experiencing. One minute, she was with Hunter and all seemed right with the world. She felt safe and protected. The next minute, she was the target of a shooting. The assailant had been so determined to end her life that he or she had thrown a bomb at the building in order to finish the job. The plan had failed thanks to Agent Franklin's quick thinking, but only a desperate person would pull such a risky maneuver. If it was Kazamir, and he was willing to go that far to take her out, where would he stop? She did her best to cooperate with the police and answer their questions without sarcasm, but it was hard. She felt so broken and lost. There was no one she could trust other than the agents who were fighting to keep her alive. Her only confidant was Hunter, and he had so many issues of his own that she didn't want to add another burden to his life. She was scared and no longer felt safe in Seattle, but she didn't know where else she could go.

In the early hours of the morning, she finally felt exhaustion creep over her. She'd answered the agents' endless questions and had reviewed the security tapes so many times her eyes felt like they were crossing. There was nothing else left to do but escape into a dreamless sleep. She slept for six hours straight despite the lumpy cot and thin pillow. No one attempted to wake her. The police didn't want her to move until the entire scene was declared safe. No one knew if Kazamir was lurking in the window of a building somewhere, waiting for her to come out so he could take his shot. When Kayla finally woke up, she didn't know where she was. She stretched and reached up to rub her stiff neck. Only then did she realize she was still in a cot at the hospital dressed in borrowed scrubs. Agent Franklin was standing in the doorway holding two cups of steaming coffee in his hands. She let out a little shout of surprise, but then reached gratefully for the coffee that he was holding out to her.

"I didn't know if you liked cream or sugar in your coffee, so I brought packets of both."

"Thanks, Frank. I can always count on you to make sure my coffee is hot and to my liking…and oh yes, I can also count on you to save my life when a psycho killer comes after me with both a gun AND a bomb." Her statement made him grin. Kayla reached for the cream and sugar and dumped both into her cup. She'd have drunk anything with caffeine in it but preferred her coffee sweet and creamy. Franklin let her take a few sips before he started in with the details of the previous night. He pulled up a chair and watched her until her eyes became focused and the sleep vanished from her face.

"Fill me in. I imagine you had a pretty eventful night last night," she said.

"It was eventful, although we weren't able to catch Kazamir.

We're sure it was him though. There were fingerprints on the semi-automatic we found close to the scene. He'd wiped the outside pretty clean, but the techs pulled it apart and were able to lift enough partials on areas he'd touched when he cleaned it last. They matched the prints from the shell casings from the Chicago incident, so we're sure that it was our guy. We were able to locate a witness who saw someone run out of the alleyway. They gave a description of the man. He had a hat pulled low over his face, so he couldn't tell us what hair color he had or what his facial features looked like, but they could give specifics about his stature."

Kayla was listening intently. She was glad that the police had something to show for their long hours of searching.

"The unfortunate thing is that Kazamir is slippery, and we're not sure where he's headed. He's too smart to hang around Seattle and wait for us to catch him, although he seems to be getting pretty reckless and desperate. We're hoping he'll make a mistake and give himself away before he hurts anyone else."

"He definitely seems desperate. Anyone who's willing to gun someone down in a very public place and then follow it up with a bomb in order to try and finish the job has got to be a little desperate and a lot crazy."

"You're right on both counts. There was another interesting piece of evidence that surfaced."

"Oh? I'm listening."

"Preliminary field tests suggest the residue from the bomb matched the residue found at the Mt. Baker Bombing just a few days ago."

Kayla sat in stunned silence. She wasn't sure exactly what Franklin was trying to tell her. "Do you mean that the same manufacturer of the bomb was supplying both the Mt. Baker Bomber and Kazamir?"

"The bombs were homemade, Kayla. They certainly weren't made by a professional. We think that the bombers are one and the same."

Kayla was shocked. She understood why Kazamir wanted to take her out, but why had he injured so many innocent people at Mt. Baker?

"Why do you think he would have bombed Mt. Baker?" Kayla was confused.

"We don't think it has anything to do with you. Kazamir isn't the type to pull an act of terrorism just to make a point. He's a greedy sociopath who's running short on funds. You blew his shot at early retirement a few years ago and now he's got to make some quick cash to support his drug habit and other vices. We think someone paid him to commit the Mt. Baker bombing. Something tells me he didn't realize how big the blast was going to be. He made the bomb himself and probably thought he was going to be taking out one or two people. He ended up injuring or killing over a hundred. We suspect he's completely lost touch with reality. We're dealing with a dangerous man right now. He's obviously unstable and getting more reckless by the minute."

Kayla was shocked by the news Agent Franklin was telling her. She had always known that she was dealing with a dangerous criminal, but now she felt sure that he was a raging psychopath as well. If he was capable of hurting as many people as he had at Mt. Baker, there was no telling where he would stop.

"So, where does that leave me?" Kayla asked, wondering how she was ever going to pick up the pieces of her life and carry on.

Chapter 26

Hunter

Hunter watched Kayla walk out of his room and sighed. The date had been a huge success, but he hadn't been able to so much as kiss her goodnight thanks to all the casts and braces that his body was wrapped in. Despite the situation, it had still been the best date of his life. Hunter had never really fallen for a woman like he had for Kayla. The women he met usually threw themselves at him because they were interested in dating a high-profile athlete. They were after fame and fortune, not a real relationship. Before he started dating someone, he always tried to imagine what it would be like to date them if he were no longer an elite athlete. Would the woman be interested in settling down, having a family, staying in at night, and watching movies with him? More often than not, the answer was no. The women who chased after him wanted invitations to high profile parties, exciting awards shows, and attention from the media. None of those things interested him. He knew those women would be sorely disappointed when they realized he avoided parties as a general rule and had no interest in attending any premiers, award shows, or events that involved heavy media coverage. He decided long ago to focus solely on his career until he couldn't compete any longer. Then he would focus on starting a family. His crazy training schedule and constant travel weren't conducive to a real relationship, and he didn't want to end up hurting someone or getting hurt.

Somehow, Kayla seemed different. She was sweet, thoughtful, and seemed to want to spend time with him because of who he was, not who he had been. She had no interest in being at the center of a media frenzy. In fact, after what she'd shared, it sounded like she was much happier to lead a low-key existence. Even though they hadn't gone anywhere, she made him laugh, appreciated his favorite movie, and didn't complain about the horrible hospital food they shared. She was definitely a keeper. He wished he could take her out on a proper date, but he knew that it would likely be months before he could get around without crutches or braces. He had no choice but to accept his current state. If that meant watching DVDs in the hospital with her, then he was grateful for it.

Hunter was in the middle of replaying his date with Kayla when he heard loud voices coming from the floor below him followed by the sound of shattering glass. Suddenly everything went silent. He wondered what had caused the commotion and remembered Kayla was on her way out of the hospital. He hoped she was okay, and there was a harmless explanation for the sound of glass breaking. Perhaps they were replacing a window or using the Jaws of Life to get someone out of a vehicle. He tried to reassure himself there could be plenty of reasonable explanations for the sounds he had just heard. Just as he was starting to relax again, he heard a much louder sound. It sounded like an explosion. He shot upright in bed and cringed as pain seared through him. He hit the call button, signaling for a nurse. He felt a strong need to know what had happened and if Kayla was alright. He'd lost someone important to him in a bombing just a few days before, and he needed reassurance that he wasn't going to lose someone else. It was a long time before a nurse came to his room. She looked frazzled and worried when she entered.

"Can I help you, Mr. Erickson?" The nurse saw the pained expression on his face and wondered immediately if he needed more morphine.

"I heard an explosion. Can you tell me what happened?" Hunter asked, desperately looking for answers.

"I'm not sure of all the details." The nurse looked young. She couldn't have been older than twenty-two. It was obvious that she was deeply distraught by the recent events. "There was a shooting. A gunman shot at a woman who was exiting the hospital. From what I heard, she was able to escape back inside, but the gunman shot through the glass into the lobby. Apparently, he wasn't sure he had successfully shot her, so he threw a bomb through the window. Fortunately, everyone had cleared the reception desk and the waiting area, so no one was seriously injured, but the hospital is a mess. The entire entrance of the building was destroyed."

Hunter was panicking. "And the girl? How is she?"

The nurse looked exhausted from the commotion. "I've been told she escaped harm. They're keeping her in a safe area of the hospital until the situation settles down. I was asked to bring her a cot and a pillow. The authorities don't think it's safe for her to leave the building until the area can be completely secured.

Hunter breathed a sigh of relief. He hadn't realized he'd been holding his breath the entire time the nurse was talking. "Are you saying no one was killed in the shooting or the explosion?"

"Not to my knowledge. Police are swarming the area and taped off the site where the bomb exploded, but we haven't admitted anyone for injuries more severe than minor concussions.

Hunter let himself relax back in his bed for the first time since he heard the explosion. If Kayla was who the gunman was after, she was safe. He knew he wouldn't be able to reach her. The cops were probably running her through hundreds of questions and forcing her to stay in a secured area. At least he knew she was okay. He was certain she would contact him as soon as she was ready. He was grateful she escaped harm, but could only imagine the fear and anxiety she was facing.

Hunter tried to get some rest, but couldn't fall asleep, so he called his uncle. Jackson answered on the first ring. He never let his cell phone out of sight on the off chance Hunter would need to get ahold of him. He loved his nephew like a son and watching him suffer the way he had for the past few days had been excruciating.

"Hello, Champ. If you're calling me to bring you a cheeseburger and fries, you're out of luck. I made a vow to the hospital staff that I wouldn't sneak any food in. They promised me there would be serious consequences if I violated their rules."

"Well, that's not exactly why I'm calling, but I'm curious what sort of consequences they threatened you with?" Hunter was used to his uncle's antics by now and was happy to play along.

"For starters, they said they'd schedule me for a mandatory colonoscopy for every meal I brought in that wasn't allowed. I'm not sure if they'd follow through, but I'm not about to call that bluff."

"That seems like an appropriate punishment, so I won't hold it against you that my craving for a double bacon cheeseburger is going to go unsatisfied."

"It's a rough life, Sport, but I know you're tough. You'll survive."

"Only as long as a man can live on hospital food, Uncle J, and I can assure you that for me it won't be very long." Hunter grinned as he said it. "As much as I wish I was calling to complain about the food they're serving me, I'm calling with a bigger concern."

"And what might that be?" Jackson was suddenly very concerned about the somber tone of voice his nephew was using.

"There was another bombing, Uncle J. It happened just a few minutes after Kayla left my room. I was told there was a gunman who shot at a woman leaving the hospital. She escaped back inside, so he detonated a bomb at the hospital's entrance. Fortunately, no one was seriously injured, but I'm worried the target was Kayla."

"Do you want me to come over?" Jackson was ready to drop everything and dash out of his hotel to be there.

"No, no. I don't think it's safe yet. There was a lot of damage to the hospital's entrance and cops are swarming the place looking for signs of the shooter. I don't think they would let you in, even if you were the President of the United States. I just wanted to call and talk. I'm pretty worried about Kayla. A nurse told me the young woman was in a protected area of the hospital and won't be leaving until the area is considered safe, but I still can't imagine what she's going through if she actually was the target."

"That's some pretty heavy stuff, Hunter. Do you know why

he'd be going after her?"

"It's a long story, but she told me she had to leave her friends and family without so much as a goodbye and move to Seattle to get away from a man who had reasons for wanting her dead. I'm afraid he found her and tried to get rid of her once and for all tonight. Of course, I have no way of knowing if it was actually her, but the timing worries me. She would have been leaving the hospital just as this all went down."

Jackson sat lost in thought for a few moments. "What if you send her a note and have one of the nurses deliver it? Just let her know that you're thinking about her and would love to talk to her when it's safe. If it's not Kayla, then she'll have no idea what you're talking about, but if it is, she'll at least know you care about her and are concerned."

"Thanks, Uncle J. I knew I could count on you. I was feeling so helpless. I can't even sit up in bed without having pain shoot through my body, let alone run down and try to track down a lunatic sniper. It would make me feel better to let her know she's not alone in this."

After Hunter hung up with his uncle, he paged the nurse again. The same young woman stepped through his door. She was no taller than 5'0" and had thick brown hair. Her eyes were as big as almonds, and she looked pale from the unexpected events of the evening.

"Would you be so kind as to help me write a note and deliver it to the woman who was the target of the shooting? She's a friend of mine, and I can't imagine how alone she must be feeling right now. I'm worried about her and hope she's safe."

The nurse nodded sympathetically. She was grateful for an excuse to stay out of the hallways for a while. As far as she knew, the crazed gunman was still on the loose, and she wanted nothing to do with him. She pulled out a notepad and scribbled down the words as Hunter told her what to write. She was supposed to be dropping off a breakfast tray to the girl in a few hours and promised she would slip the note onto the tray. Hunter expressed his gratitude. He didn't have anything to give the nurse for her trouble, but she was well aware of who he was. Just a smile from Hunter Erickson was payment enough. He had a presence, even when he was laid up in a hospital bed surrounded by IVs and covered in bandages and braces.

Chapter 27

<u>Me</u>

Unbelievable. I had the perfect shot and would have had Kayla out of my life permanently had that empty suit not tackled her at the last second. I feel reasonably confident I'd hit him center mass, but he must have been wearing a vest. He'd covered her with his body as he forced her back inside, and what once was a clean shot became anything but. I squeezed off a few more rounds hoping I might get lucky, but I couldn't stick around long enough to confirm the kill. I panicked as I drove away. Killing Kayla had ceased to be about keeping her from testifying a long time ago. No doubt she'd written statements and recorded interviews for the investigation long ago, but that was all inadmissible and would only serve as a slap in the face to her protectors' collective incompetence once I finally take her off the board. No, my pursuit was purely personal; a gnawing at my psyche never allowing me a moment's peace. I needed her to know I'd never stop. I'd never quit. For now, I knew it was risky to go back to the scene, but my hatred for her over-ruled any rational thinking I had left. Poker players sometimes refer to this feeling as being on tilt. Without thinking, I banged a u-turn and pressed the accelerator on my rental to the floor. I reached behind my seat into my suitcase to retrieve the extra bomb I'd made. I used my teeth to grip the pull ring and yank out the safety pin. With no time to waste, I launched it at the hospital's entrance. I could hear sirens in the distance and knew the cops would be surrounding the place in seconds. I didn't wait around to see what happened. I just got out as fast as I could. It was a long shot, but when planning goes awry, sometimes calculated risks must rule the day.

I'd find out soon enough if Kayla was still alive. Surely the identities of any casualties would be all over the news, predictable click bait purveyors that they are, so I could confirm her death from anywhere in the known world with a reliable internet connection. I was sweating bullets the whole way to the airport, and my heart was racing like I was on a four-day bender. Thankfully, all the cops in the city had been called to the hospital so none of them were around to pull me over for speeding. I couldn't be bothered waiting for the rental car agency. I screeched into the parking place, threw the keys on the seat, grabbed my carry-on, and jumped on the airport shuttle. I'd used a fake ID to rent the car, so the add-ons for not filling the car up with gas and filling out the check-out paperwork would be sent to some poor sucker in Idaho.

The five-minute shuttle ride to the airport seemed interminable. I could feel my paranoia escalating and my palms felt clammy. My heart felt like it was beating a million miles an hour as I looked at the faces of the young carefree tourists sitting across from me and seethed with contempt at their entire entitled generation. I tried to force myself to relax and pretend like I was just another tourist, but I couldn't shake the feeling that I'd gone too far, too fast and too sloppy and I'd left a trail when all I wanted to do was sweep away the only connection I had to an old life before leaving for good. If they could follow that trail, it meant arrest, which would mean no bail and sitting in some musty cell awaiting trial and conviction… the only logical outcome for what I did in Chicago and Mt. Baker was a death sentence. I couldn't remember whether Illinois and Washington are Capital Punishment states, but I knew sure as I was breathing the Federal Government is.

Panic was mounting, so I forced myself to concentrate on the fact that I had finally managed to kill the tramp I'd been hunting down for the past three years. The more I thought about it, the more I convinced myself I was finally free of her and congratulated myself on my victory. I bounded off the shuttle without waiting for the driver to come around and unload my bag. All I had was my carry on, and I wanted no more personal contact than necessary until I was through security and safely on my flight. I was able to breeze through self check-in and the security guard didn't even look twice at my ID. The name might not have been mine, but the picture matched perfectly. He was at the end of a long shift and had a glazed look on his face. He sent me through without questions. I watched my bag clear the scanner and was relieved that I'd tossed my gun after the shooting. I also knew if anyone pulled that bag aside and checked it for residue, there would be no way it would pass. Thankfully, everyone seemed to have the same attitude as the guy who checked my ID. If I could just sidle past these fools and avoid any dogs in the terminal I'd be home free. If only…

 I raced to my gate and arrived with only ten minutes to spare before boarding. There was a large flat screen TV on the wall and everyone's eyes were glued to it. There was a reporter on the screen standing in front of Seattle General covering the bombing. She speculated the bombing may have been linked to the one that occurred at Mt. Baker just days before. No way that any competent law enforcement would release that to the public until they could confirm it, so someone was jumping the gun. Still, I cursed myself for being so desperate and reckless to help them connect the dots, but once again comforted myself with the knowledge that there was no way Kayla could still be alive. I had seen her roll through the revolving doors. She had to have been in the lobby when the explosion occurred. She was dead, and it wouldn't be long before I was out of the country. I just had to keep my cool for a little bit longer.

 The last thing I needed was to make a scene and give myself away moments before getting on a plane to freedom. I grimaced. I needed a cigarette like there was no tomorrow, but the airport regulations wouldn't even grant me that. I glanced at my watch and cursed because I didn't even have time to hit the bar for a shot to calm myself down. I stood up and started pacing until my loading zone was called, boarded the flight, and waited impatiently for beverage service to start. I missed the days when you could pay cash on planes. The service was much more prompt if you tipped well, and no one really checked if you paid with counterfeit bills. For now, I'd have to wait a few more minutes until I could rip through a few shots of whatever they had on hand.

I awoke several hours later and quickly ordered another round. I caught a glimpse of our location and breathed a sigh of relief when I realized that we were safely over international waters. I couldn't believe my lack of discipline after spending such an inordinate amount of time planning Mt. Baker and even longer tracking Kayla to Seattle. If I had spent another night in the US, I know I would have done something stupid to bring them to my doorstep. Fortunately, I'd gotten out in time, and she'd be little more than a memory I would forget within another month.

My thoughts changed to finding out if the feds were onto me yet. I pulled out my cell phone and connected to the onboard wifi. My browser opened up to a news site. The first thing to flash up was the latest from the incident at Seattle General. I clicked on a video link and felt a fleeting moment of pride as I realized I'd made the top headline, but that faded as I saw they were once again reporting the suspicion that Mt. Baker and Seattle General were linked. They mumbled something about terrorism and gave the same song and dance as the reports after Mt Baker that no one had claimed responsibility yet. The reporter relayed the belief of a single shooter and maybe another person involved in the bombing. Surely, the Feds wouldn't give up crucial details unless it was necessary, but I felt the agent they interviewed may have overstepped in referring to me as a crazed sociopath, even if he didn't specifically use my name. In the end, I decided I was proud of my new status. They could call me whatever they wanted. I was home free and those pathetic excuses for human beings were left scrambling to pick up the pieces. I'd be dining on champagne and caviar tonight while they smoked their cigarettes and drank stale coffee several thousand miles away.

Chapter 28

Kayla

There was a knock on the door, and Agent Franklin opened it a sliver to see who it was. He cautiously let a young nurse with a tray of food enter. "Compliments of the hospital," She said in a meek voice. "You need to keep your strength up." She wheeled in the cart and left without another word. Kayla wasn't particularly hungry, but she knew the nurse was right. She couldn't live off coffee alone. She saw a small square of white paper peeking out from under a plate. For a moment, her heart was in her throat, and she was afraid it was from Kazamir. She grabbed it with shaking fingers and unfolded it. She let out a sigh of relief when she saw it was signed by Hunter. The note was thoughtful and nonintrusive. It told her he was thinking of her and worried. He simply wanted her to know he was there for her if she needed anything. She smiled for the first time all night, and Agent Franklin was relieved to see her relax just a tiny bit.

She offered Franklin one of the muffins on the tray and bit into one herself. She was surprised to find that it was warm and freshly baked. She sighed a little as the sweetness of the muffin filled her mouth and for just a second, she forgot where she was. Franklin didn't take any time to enjoy his muffin. He stuffed it into his mouth and swallowed it in two bites before getting back to business.

"The authorities have cleared the area, so you'll be free to leave when you're ready. We've sent a bomb squad over to your house to sweep it for any explosives. We've had your house under 24-hour surveillance and haven't seen any mysterious characters, but we can't be too careful."

Kayla knew this information was meant to make her feel better, but it just put her more on edge. She lived in a historic home built mostly from wood. If a bomb went off, the whole thing would surely go up in flames within seconds. There were plenty of beautiful windows in the house and none were bulletproof like the hospital's windows. Kazamir had proven he wouldn't play it safe anymore. He wanted her dead, and she was sure he would stop at nothing to make it happen.

"What are my options, Frank? Don't worry about sparing my feelings. I'm well aware that I'm not safe if he knows where I'm living. He has plenty of connections in the drug trade and even if you catch him, my life could still be in danger. I also know it's not practical for you and Olson to watch out for me around-the-clock for the rest of my life."

"This leaves us in uncharted territory, Kayla. No witness has ever been located in the history of the Witness Security Program. The first thing we need to figure out is how Kazamir tracked you to the hospital. He must have put a tap on your cell phone or used some sort of tracking device. I'm going to take you down to the station for a full search. They'll issue you a new cell phone and ask you not to contact any of your friends in the area, as they might have been the ones that gave you away in the first place."

Kayla rolled her eyes. She had known that part was coming.

"I assume I won't be able to stay in Seattle. Do you have any idea where they plan on sending me?" She was afraid WITSEC would send her to some tiny town in the middle of nowhere.

"You'll be sent out of the country. We've worked out a deal for you to stay at an embassy for awhile. We don't think that Kazamir will be able to track you down if you're outside the US. In addition, embassies are completely secured so you'll be safe."

Kayla was stunned by this revelation. She couldn't imagine leaving the country but was intrigued at the same time. "What country do you have in mind?"

"You'll find out when you get there. We don't want to take any chances."

Kayla was intrigued, and life started to creep back into her eyes. At least she would be on an adventure and wouldn't be stranded in the suburbs somewhere.

"Can I at least say goodbye to a friend before I leave the hospital? I won't tell him any details about WITSEC's plans."

Franklin nodded. He supposed he could grant her that one request. "I'll come with you and wait outside in the hallway. When you're done, I'll take you down to the station so they can figure out how that lunatic managed to track you down."

Kayla excused herself to change out of her scrubs and back into her street clothes. She wasn't thrilled with her appearance when she looked in the mirror, but there wasn't much she could do about it. She found a small tube of toothpaste stashed in one of her pockets and used her finger to brush her teeth. She pulled out a small foldable hairbrush and combed out the tangles from her hair and added a touch of lip gloss. She gave her slightly disheveled reflection a lopsided grin and headed back out to meet Frank who walked with her to Hunter's room. She knocked on his door and saw that he was snuggled in bed watching one of the movies she'd brought him. He smiled when he saw her.

"You gave me quite a scare last night, Ms. McCullen. I bribed one of the nurses to find out if you were okay."

"Yes, I got your note. That was very kind of you. Thank you for that. It was a pretty long night, but I was lucky that someone was quick enough to get me out of harm's way. I'm okay, but unfortunately, the hospital has seen better days. The lobby area went up in smoke."

Hunter looked at her with concern, "They can rebuild all of that, I'm just glad you weren't injured."

"Me, too!" She sat down next to his bed and took his hand. "Look at the two of us. We've both been hunted down by a lunatic bomber in the last few days. It looks like it might even have been the same guy. Now that's a bond not many people share."

Hunter's eyes searched her face. He knew she was trying to be casual about the whole thing, but he was seriously worried about her. "What's your next move? You certainly can't hang around this joint any longer."

"I've put you all in danger long enough. I think I'll take my bad luck elsewhere."

Hunter looked concerned. He knew that Kayla had barely made it out alive last night. If the killer found her, he certainly wouldn't let her get away again.

"I'm going away for awhile. To be honest, I'm not even sure where, but I've been told I'll be safe. Before I go, I just wanted to thank you for being the best friend I've had in a very long time. I've had a great time with you and wish we had more time to get to know one another."

Hunter looked sad as she said it. "You know, you're the most amazing woman I've ever met, Kayla McCullen. I'm devastated that you have to go, but I'm grateful you're going to be safe. I want you to know I'm always going to be here. Whether you can contact me or not, please know you're never going to be far from my mind."

A few tears trickled down Kayla's cheek. She hadn't expected saying goodbye to Hunter to be so difficult. "Well, you know I'll be coming after you if you let late fees stack up on those movies I rented for you, so you'd better behave yourself."

Hunter chuckled a little at her attempt to lighten the mood. "You know I'm going to find you when this whole ordeal is over, and you get your life back, so I can get that cookie recipe from you."

Kayla let out a mock-gasp. "You'll never get it out of me, no matter how hard you try, but if you're *really* nice to me, I might make you another batch someday."

Hunter smiled. "I'm going to hold you to that promise."

With that, Kayla leaned in to kiss his cheek, but Hunter was quick and turned his face to connect with her lips. He gave her a breathtaking kiss. The kiss lasted for several seconds until she heard someone clearing his throat in the hallway. *Dammit, Frank*, she thought. He always had a way of sneaking up during inopportune times. She pulled away and gave Hunter a kiss on the forehead as she brushed his bangs back. He was smiling up at her with a boyish grin.

"Take care of yourself, Erickson. I expect you to be back on the slopes by the time I get back."

He gave her a mock salute, but his tone was serious. "I'll miss you, you know. Don't be a stranger."

"Same to you, Hunter. Thanks for everything."

With that, Kayla turned and joined Agent Franklin in the hallway. He was attempting to look like he was engrossed in a magazine but there was a smirk on his face. She gave him a little nudge on the shoulder, "You just have to go spoiling my moments, don't you?"

"Puppy love is such an adorable thing," he shot back in an equally playful voice. "Shall we head down to HQ? They have endless questions for you and there are a lot of preparations to make for your next adventure."

"I suppose I don't have a choice, so let's get this over with." Kayla followed Franklin down the hallway and out the back entrance of the hospital where a squad car was waiting. She ducked her head down and crawled into the back. She breathed a sigh of relief when Franklin closed her door for her, and she was safely inside the vehicle. She was half expecting the world to explode in gunfire and was relieved when they made a peaceful getaway.

Chapter 29

Hunter

Hunter lay in his hospital bed lost in thought after Kayla left. He had smiled and laughed with her and pretended to be strong, but the pain of losing his only friend in the hospital stung. Selfishly, he didn't want her to go, but he knew she didn't have a choice. He hoped she would stay true to her word and stay in touch. The hours at the hospital were going to pass by very slowly if he didn't have her visits to think about. He finally turned his attention to the news. Images of the demolished hospital entrance flashed across the screen. Everyone was speculating about who was responsible and where they might be hiding out. No one felt safe.

Jackson breezed into the room moments later. "It's a feeding frenzy of reporters and police out front, but I managed to charm them with my dashing good looks, and they let me through."

Hunter gave his uncle a half-hearted attempt at a smile. Jackson immediately realized something was very wrong. He walked across the room, shut off the TV, and pulled up a chair. "Wanna talk about it?"

Hunter smiled at his uncle. "Not really, but since you asked, I guess I might as well share. Kayla got my note and stopped by this morning. She was the target of the shooting and said she was going to have to disappear for awhile. She alluded to the fact that she's under the Witness Security Program but was discovered. The criminal responsible for the crime she witnessed came after her. She doesn't have a choice but to go away for awhile until things settle down."

Jackson nodded in sympathy. He knew Kayla had been a beacon of light to his nephew for the past few days. The fact that she was in danger and wasn't going to be able to come to the hospital anymore was a brutal blow. "I'm sorry, Hunter. I know this can't be easy for you. You've already been through so much. Now the one person who understands your situation isn't going to be able to be there for you."

Hunter nodded; wishing his heart didn't feel like it had shattered into a million pieces.

"This will all settle down at some point, and you'll be able to see her again."

Hunter wasn't as optimistic as his uncle, but he agreed with him anyway. "I guess this just means I'm going to have to get better so I can go and find her. In the meantime, I've got a degree I need to finish. Could you help me with a paper I have due next week?"

Jackson let out a small sigh of relief. He worried about Hunter getting depressed and was happy to see him turn his devastation into determination. "You've got yourself a deal." He pulled out Hunter's laptop and logged into his school account. "What are we going to be writing about today?"

Hunter smiled. "The topic of the paper is 'How Chapter 11 Saved the US Economy'. I haven't been able to do much research, so I'm going to have to rely on you to help me find some reputable sources to cite."

His uncle smiled. He had absolutely no knowledge about the topic Hunter needed to write about, but he had a feeling he was going to be an expert on Chapter 11 by the time the day was over.

They spent the day researching and writing Hunter's paper. It was an intriguing topic. Although it might not have been how either of them normally would have chosen to spend a day, they made the most of it and successfully wrote a solid paper by the time the nurses brought in Hunter's dinner. The food didn't look appetizing, but Hunter knew he needed to force it down. He started physical therapy the following day and wanted to build his strength back up as soon as possible. Jackson left shortly after dinner to go back to his hotel. He wanted to make sure Hunter was able to get the rest he needed and confessed that he had a date with a woman named Emily. He met her while she was working at the reception desk of the hotel where he was staying. He hadn't dated a woman in years but found himself spending a fair amount of time chatting with Emily when he passed by the front desk. He found out she was just a few years younger and had lost her husband in a car accident. They'd never been able to have children, and she was lonely. Her husband had been a successful businessman and left her enough money for her to live comfortably. She didn't need to work, but had taken a job at the hotel to socialize with people and get herself out of the house. It had taken Jackson several days to get up the courage to ask her to grab a drink with him, but he finally had, and she'd accepted his invitation with a smile. They agreed to go out to a quiet wine bar near the hotel when she got off her shift. He wanted to make sure he got back in time to take a shower and change into a pair of khakis before he met her. He chided himself for being nervous about a date at his age. She was a very kind, attractive woman, and he felt a boyish excitement when he thought about spending time with her.

Jackson hadn't intended to tell Hunter about the date, but he couldn't keep anything from his nephew.

"Wow, Uncle J! I've never heard you talk about going on a date in a long time. That's fantastic! Am I going to get to meet this mystery woman?"

"Slow down, Champ. We're only going out for a drink. I'm not even sure if you can call it a real date, considering that I'm not even officially picking her up. We're just meeting in the lobby when she gets off her shift."

"Oh, that's a date alright. All kidding aside, I'm happy for you. I expect to hear all the details tomorrow."

"It's a deal." Jackson gave Hunter an affectionate nudge on the shoulder and promised he'd be back after Hunter's first physical therapy session.

Hunter thanked his uncle profusely for all of his help before closing his eyes and falling into a deep and dreamless sleep.

Chapter 30

<u>Me</u>

I woke up when a stewardess shook my shoulder gently. She whispered that landing preparations had started, and I needed to move my seat into the upright position. I shook her off but did as she said. I didn't want to draw any more attention to myself than necessary on this flight. My head was pounding from the effects of alcohol. I wanted another drink badly, but the flight attendants were busy picking up everyone's trash and ignored me when I hit the call button. They knew by now what I was after, and they weren't going to indulge me in one more round. I rolled my eyes and tried to think about my plans when I arrived in Amsterdam. I'd have to pass through customs and hoped the news of the bombings hadn't reached Europe yet. Once I cleared customs, I would take the train to Amsterdam's Central Station. I'd booked a hotel within walking distance from the train station. All I had to do to get to my hotel after I left Central Station was cross the bridge over Open Havenfront and take a right on the Prins Hendrikkade.

I deplaned and headed to customs. I stood in line and started filling out my customs form. There were security agents everywhere and some of them had drug dogs with them. I was grateful I hadn't attempted to bring my stash of goodies with me. It had been tempting, but I knew that I'd be able to buy anything I wanted once I got to the Netherlands. I'd sold my stash to a dealer on the street for a bargain before I'd headed over to finish off Kayla.

As I stood in line, I watched the news on the television mounted on the wall. A few scenes from Mt. Baker and Seattle popped up, but I couldn't tell what the reporters were saying. I held my breath and hoped no one had caught a good enough glimpse of me to come up with a drawing that would allow people to identify me. A police sketch did flash up on the screen, but it was a picture of me from behind. It could have been anyone. Thankfully, whoever spotted me hadn't gotten a good view of my face. I could feel myself sweating as I approached the customs agents.

When I was at the front of the line, the customs agent waved me over to his cubicle. I handed him my fake passport. He asked me what the purpose of my visit was. I told him I was on a vacation. He flipped through my passport and saw that there weren't any other stamps. Then he looked at the date of issue and saw that the passport had only recently been issued. He scrutinized me very closely. I could feel sweat start to trickle down my forehead. He paused a moment and then asked me the length of my stay. I said I'd be visiting for a week, which seemed like a reasonable amount of time. He nodded and then looked over my customs form. I didn't have anything to declare. He seemed lost in thought for a moment; then glanced up at the large television screen just as it flashed a picture of the victims being carted off the mountain at Mt. Baker. My heart nearly stopped. "Damn shame, isn't it?" I felt like he was looking right through me, all the way down to my guilty soul.

"Terrible tragedy," I replied.

He shook his head sadly, stamped my passport, and wished me a good stay. I accepted it from him gratefully and got out of the customs area as quickly as my legs would carry me. I found my way to the commuter train that would take me to the city center and made my way out of the train station. As I stepped outside, the cacophonous cocktail of scents and sights that hit me was overwhelming. There was a mixture of hippies, bikers, drug dealers, and pot smokers crowding the polluted streets. I loved and hated it all at the same time. At first, my feelings alternated between sheer joy and overwhelming contempt. I ultimately settled on contentment as I knew these losers would provide my camouflage as I explored every curiosity I desired. This was a place where I could appreciate Van Gogh and smoke every variety of marijuana under the sun. This was my Eden.

Chapter 31

Kayla

Franklin hustled Kayla from the squad care into the police station. He directed her to a conference room where a kindly older officer, who reminded her of her grandfather, offered her a change of clothes. He recommended that she take a shower and put on the fresh garments. She had to turn over the rest of her possessions to be screened for a tracking device that could have alerted Kazamir to her location. She followed their instructions and handed over her purse and street clothes. It seemed unlikely that he'd planted a bug on her, but she supposed you could never be too cautious. She was grateful for the hot shower and obediently pulled on her new clothes. The style was far from what she was accustomed to wearing. This new outfit included a tight black skirt, a red cowl-neck cashmere top, and a pair of black peep-toed pumps. She had a little trouble walking at first, but found her balance eventually and went back to the conference room to wait. A young woman dressed in uniform was waiting for her. She smiled at Kayla. "I hope the new clothes fit. I picked them out myself. I'm Sheila, by the way. I'll be responsible for your new identity."

Kayla smiled back at her. "This is definitely a change from my usual style, but the clothes are incredibly sophisticated and stylish."

Sheila smiled back. "You look great in them. I hope you don't mind if we give you a new hairstyle to match your new image?"

"Of course not, I've been through all of this once before. I won't put up a fight."

Sheila looked serious for a moment. "We searched your belongings and found a tracking device hidden inside your purse. It was the size of a small button. We think that's how Kazamir was able to track you to the hospital last night."

Kayla's mouth dropped open. "How on earth did he manage to

sneak that into my bag?"

"It could have happened anywhere. He might have dropped it in when you weren't looking at a grocery store, a restaurant, or even on the street. It's impossible to determine how he knew that you were in Seattle, but once he found you, it appears he was on a mission to dispose of you."

Kayla shook her head slowly. She had naively led him around; unaware he had knowledge of every move she made. How could she have been so stupid?

"Don't beat yourself up over this. Kazamir is a master at disguise. We'll be lucky if we can find him. The important thing right now is to keep you safe. We've arranged for you to get your hair cut and colored. Then we'll create a new passport and driver's license for you." Kayla followed her to another room where a makeshift salon had been set up. A stylist greeted her with a smile and did an assessment of her long, chestnut-colored locks. She nodded and mumbled to herself before she picked up her scissors and started to cut. Inches of Kayla's hair fell to the floor, and she felt panicked. The stylist sensed her uneasiness and turned her away from the mirror so she couldn't watch the assault that was taking place on her head. When the stylist seemed satisfied with the length, she started adding color. Kayla wasn't sure what shade it was, but after it had set and the stylist rinsed it out, she saw it was a bright, coppery red. She gasped. The stylist didn't seem fazed. Instead, she turned Kayla away from the mirror again and got to work blow-drying and curling her hair until she was happy with the new look. Finally, she spun Kayla around dramatically to look in the mirror and pulled off the smock that was covering her outfit. Kayla couldn't believe the transformation. She looked incredibly chic with her shorter, angled, red locks streaked with lighter shades of copper. The color set off her porcelain skin tone and the new clothes made her look much more sophisticated then she felt. Sheila handed her a pair of large sunglasses to complete the look. Kayla had to admit that she looked every bit the part of a movie star. "Wow! You guys really did a good job. I don't even recognize myself."

"Good, I'm glad you like it. Your new name is Karina and you're from Montreal. I saw that you minored in French in College, so I think you'll be able to pull it off. We brought in a linguistics expert to help you with your accent and teach you any phrases that are common in the region you're supposedly from."

Kayla was shocked and excited by her new image. "Do you mind my asking where I'm headed?"

Sheila smiled. "Have patience, my dear. You'll find out soon enough."

Kayla nodded. She wasn't completely comfortable with the fact that she had no idea where they were shipping her, but not knowing took away any anxiety or fear she might otherwise have felt about her new assignment. All she had to do was make it through her linguistics course, memorize everything there was to know about her new identity, and figure out how she was going to walk in heels on a daily basis. All in all, it wasn't such a bad deal. She was just going to have to think of it like an extended vacation.

"Alright then, you've got your new look. Now it's time to immerse yourself in learning how to speak with a Quebec accent. I'm going to be sending you with Francois. He is a native of Quebec and will spend the rest of the day walking you through everything you need to know." Sheila pointed to a stunningly handsome man in his mid-thirties who had just entered the room.

"Francois, I would like you to meet your newest project, Karina Thibault. She minored in French in college, so she has a fairly good base to work from, but she's going to need to learn the appropriate accent for a woman who was born and raised in Montreal."

"Enchanté," Francois said, kissing the back of her hand.

Kayla couldn't keep herself from blushing. It was going to be hard to get used to her new name, but at least her new identity was exciting and intriguing. She liked Francois instantly. She knew he was the type of guy some girls couldn't resist, but she quickly looked past his charisma and focused on what he could teach her.

Out of the Shadows

Her life was at stake, and he was a trained professional. She smiled at him and said, "I'm looking forward to working with you, Francois. Thank you so much for transforming my hopelessly American accent into a French-Canadian one."

Sheila escorted Kayla and Francois back to the conference room. Francois had brought his laptop, speakers and a tape recorder. He had taught countless Federal Agents how to speak with any number of accents. He was an absolute wizard with language and could usually accomplish his goal within a few days. Of course, he pushed his subjects hard and didn't allow for many breaks, but he was focused, respectful, and always got the results he wanted. He walked over to fetch a pot of freshly brewed coffee. The welcome scent of a dark roast wafted through the room and made Kayla's mouth water. He brought her over a steaming mug, and she took a sip. Francois didn't waste any time getting down to business. He started by playing samples of speech that he wanted Kayla to imitate. He explained the emphasis he wanted to be placed on certain syllables and the intonations that were needed to sound authentic. Then he made Kayla repeat sentence after sentence. He didn't hesitate to correct her when she made a mistake. The hours flew by. Francois filled in the time between lessons by teaching her interesting historical facts about Quebec and Montreal. By the end of the day, Kayla almost believed she was a native of the region.

When at last Francois was satisfied with her progress, he handed her his business card. I want you to email me with any questions you have. I'm always just a phone call away if you need a little refresher. Remember to start practicing now. The more you use the dialect, the more authentic you'll sound. You don't have to speak French all the time, but you need to make sure that you're using a quality French-Canadian accent, even around your new friends. No one can know your real story. Trust me; I work with undercover agents all of the time. The more you believe that you are truly Karina Thibault from Montreal, the more others will believe it to. This isn't a game. This is your life. If you make a false move, you could endanger the lives of everyone at the Embassy, so be smart and be cautious. With that, Francois gathered his things and left the room. He said that he had an overnight flight to New York to catch. He had another intense training scheduled the following day.

    Kayla said goodbye and then waited for Sheila, who appeared a few minutes later with a tray of sandwiches. I figured you'd need some sustenance to get through the rest of the night.

    Kayla accepted a turkey, bacon, ranch sandwich gratefully, and sank her teeth into the soft bread. She inhaled the sandwich as quickly as possible, before focusing her attention back on the portfolio Sheila handed her. The first page contained a full-page picture of her that the stylist took when she completed her work. The next page had a freshly made passport with a smaller version of the picture inserted into it. There was also a driver's license from Montreal that showed her height, weight, hair color, eye color, and date of birth. These were all things that Kayla was going to have to memorize. The next pages detailed the story of her life

    The number of details that Kayla needed to memorize seemed overwhelming. She learned that her parents' names had been Claude and Annika. Claude was an accountant and his wife, Annika, stayed home with Karina. They enjoyed spending family holidays at a cabin that her grandparents owned. She spent lazy days horseback riding, canoeing, and fishing with her parents. She was an only child. Her high school boyfriend's name was Pierre. They had dated for four years but broke up when they started university. Pierre had chosen to go to school in the United States, but Karina had decided to attend the Université de Montréal to be close to her family. As an only child, she felt a responsibility to never abandon her parents and always be present at holidays, so her parents wouldn't feel lonely. Pierre hadn't understood, so they had decided it was best to go their separate ways.

    Karina was a journalist who was traveling abroad in order to write a series of articles highlighting the commitment that Spain and

Canada had made with each other to encourage tourism and student exchanges. She was also researching their commitment to support one another in the United Nations, NATO, and the World Trade Organization.

When Kayla read about her new 'profession', she glanced at Sheila. "Does this mean that you're sending me to Spain?"

"I think that's a safe assumption, but that is all I can tell you at this time. When you arrive at the airport, a Mercedes Benz with tinted windows will pick you up. Your driver's name is Leonard. He will introduce himself at baggage claim. If he fails to state his name directly, do not, I repeat, do not go with him. He will drive you to your new home. Everyone will be expecting you. They will welcome you and make you feel at home. Just stick to the story we rehearsed, and you'll be fine. If you have any questions, please notify me immediately."

Kayla nodded, letting it sink in that she would be living in Spain. She hadn't known what to expect. She was worried she'd be sent to a developing country that was politically unstable, but instead, they were sending her to a Spain! She was ecstatic but also anxious about her new identity. This would be a much harder sell than it had been for her to assume a new identity in Seattle. She had been living by herself in Seattle, so it didn't matter how she had acted in her free time, but at the Embassy, there would be people around all the time. Thankfully, Sheila and Francois had prepared her well. No one was going to be suspicious of her unless she gave them a reason. Journalists had flexible schedules, so it wouldn't seem overly suspicious if she stayed in her room a lot to "write".

Sheila had reassured her that her paintings would be stored safely until her return. She would still be able to paint in Spain, but she was going to have to tell people it was just a hobby and avoid selling anything recognizable until after Kazamir's arrest. She was frustrated by this because she'd spent the past three years building her reputation as a painter. Now she was going to have to put her career on hold, but she didn't have a choice. Sheila was adamant about her fully assuming her new identity and wasn't going to be swayed. She decided it would be to her advantage to obediently follow the Witness Security Program's instructions and ask as few questions as possible.

Sheila informed her she would be spending the night at the police station. They had a bunkroom for her to use. It wasn't very comfortable, but it would allow her to catch a few hours of sleep. She would have to answer one more round of questions surrounding the hospital shooting/bombing incident before she was flown to D.C. From there she would board a private flight to Spain.

When she got to her room, she spotted a suitcase with all the essentials inside. She found cotton pajama pants with a matching camisole and changed into them. Then she browsed through the rest of the contents. The clothes were beautiful. There were several dresses that were shorter than she normally wore. There were colorful scarves and long, elegant necklaces. She found a fitted leather jacket and some gorgeous snakeskin heals. Sheila had done an impressive job, she decided. Although it felt weird climbing into clothes that weren't her own, she decided she was going to like being Karina Thibault very much.

Exhaustion finally took hold of her, and Kayla closed the suitcase. She washed her face and brushed her teeth using items from a small bag of toiletries she'd been given. Then she crawled into bed and fell into a fitful sleep. She dreamed she was being chased around by crazed drug dealers and running through exploding buildings. She finally woke up in the middle of the night in a cold sweat. It took her several moments to realize she was safe and out of harm's way. She breathed deeply until her heart rate returned to normal. She spent the rest of the night staring at the ceiling, thinking about what Hunter was doing and wondering what her new life was going to be like.

Chapter 32

Hunter

The next day was brutal for Hunter. He expected his physical therapist to be a kindly doctor who would ease him into recovery. He was wrong, very wrong. His physical therapist was a woman in her fifties who took no mercy on him. He thought she would at least feel sorry for him, but apparently, sympathy wasn't her thing. After the first hour of therapy, he was nearly convinced she was a sadistic woman who thrived on inflicting pain. She forced him to use his muscles until they burned. She didn't listen when he complained and forced him to work harder when he told her he wanted a break. When the session was over, his nurse helped him back into his bed, and he fell asleep for several hours of uninterrupted sleep. His last thought as he drifted off was the depressing realization that only a week ago, he'd been capable of flying down the slopes at 80 miles-per-hour an hour. Now he was hardly even able to support his own body weight. His broken bones made it nearly impossible for him to get around. Thankfully, the doctors had told him that the hairline fracture in his vertebrae was healing remarkably fast, but he still wasn't allowed to make any big movements. It was frustrating. He wanted to will his body to heal, but he knew the only thing that would truly heal him was time. He'd always been one who could accomplish anything he put his mind to, but this situation was totally out of his control.

He was grateful when Jackson came by to visit later in the afternoon. One of the nurses told him to wait to visit until Hunter woke up. She explained the first few physical therapy sessions were usually pretty brutal and draining. It was best if patients had time to themselves to sleep and come to grips with the long road that lay ahead. When she saw Hunter was awake and seemed to be feeling better, she let Jackson know it was a good time for him to stop by.

Jackson came in and pulled up a chair. "How's it going today, buddy?"

"Not so good, Uncle J. I didn't realize how bad I was hurt until today. The morphine lulled me into a false sense of security. It's going to be a long time before I'm back on my feet."

"I know it's not easy, Hunter, but you've got to take the days one at a time. You're going to get through this. You can't let yourself get frustrated. If you do, it'll seem overwhelming. Let's just focus on your homework today." He flipped open Hunter's laptop and saw he had a reading assignment and a quiz due. "I'm going to read you this chapter, and we'll answer the questions together."

Hunter wasn't in the mood to focus on his course work, but he also realized he didn't have much of a choice. Jackson wasn't going to leave until his work was finished, and he didn't have anything else to do at the present moment. He reluctantly agreed and tried to stay focused on what Jackson was reading to him. He absorbed more information than he expected and managed to score 100% on the quiz at the end. He wasn't sure if it was because his uncle was screening his answers or if he actually was catching on. Either way, he was relieved he actually accomplished something that day.

"Have you thought about trying to work on the computer by yourself, Hunter?" It was an innocent question. Jackson thought it might give Hunter something to do if he could do his coursework when he had down time.

"It will take me forever to type with just one hand," Hunter answered with a look of frustration.

"That's where you're wrong. I installed a program on your computer that is voice activated. You can just talk to the computer, and it will type in what you want to say. That way you'll be able to type your own papers and complete your work if no one else is around." Jackson took the next half hour to explain the computer program to Hunter. It wasn't too complicated, and Hunter was able to "train" the program to know his voice and spell words it didn't already know. Hunter was impressed. It would give him a lot more freedom than he'd had before.

"Tell me about your date?" Hunter demanded. "Did you have a nice time?" He was anxious to hear the details.

"It was really nice. Emily is great. She's funny, smart, and beautiful. We shared wine and then decided to go to dinner. She was full of entertaining stories. We spent eight hours straight talking. Before I knew it, it was midnight and time to say goodbye. We're already planning a second date tomorrow."

"Way to go Uncle Jackson!" Hunter was happy to hear that even if his life wasn't headed in a great direction, at least his uncle's was. After all, Jackson had given up for him over the years, he was relieved that his uncle was finally doing something for himself.

Jackson stayed long enough to watch a movie with Hunter and play a few more rounds of cribbage before the nurses came in to take his vitals and get him ready for bed. Then he said goodnight and headed back to his hotel.

Hunter found himself feeling very alone when the nurses left. It was only a little after 8:00 PM, and he wasn't feeling tired. He decided to follow his uncle's suggestion and use his computer. He used the voice-activated software to scan the sports pages and then decided to reply to some of the emails he'd been neglecting.

When he opened up his account, he was surprised to see an email from an unknown address. There were several messages from various sports associations, but he rarely got any personal mail. He opened the message expecting it to be spam.

Dear Hunter,

I want to apologize for having to leave so abruptly under such dramatic circumstances. I know the last thing you needed after Mt. Baker was another tragedy. I regret endangering everyone's life at the hospital by leading the bomber to Seattle General. I'm extremely sorry that I put your life and everyone else's life at risk and am relieved no one was seriously injured. As hard as it was to leave, I find comfort in the fact that I won't be leading trouble anywhere near you. You have enough on your plate right now, and you don't need another tragedy in your life.

That being said, I wanted to tell you that meeting you was the best thing that's happened in my life over the past three years. You made me laugh and realize that there is life beyond my front door, which is something that took me a long time to figure out. I wish I could have had longer to get to know you. The date we shared at the hospital was the best date of my life, and kissing you goodbye broke my heart even though I've only known you for a short time.

I feel like I owe you this email to let you know I'm in a safe place. I'm out of harm's way and am starting a new life, even though in some ways, I will still long for my old one. I'm not allowed to tell you anything about where I am, for fear that someone may intercept my emails, but I wanted you to know that I'm safe.

I don't know if you will be able to email me back or not, but I hope your recovery is going smoothly, and you're getting to meet a lot of people at the hospital. I can only imagine how long the days must be for you there. I hope your uncle has been able to come by frequently. He seems like an incredible guy, and it's obvious how much he cares about you.

I don't have long, but I wanted to send you this email. If you ever want to write, please know that I am always here, even if I can't be around to talk to you in person. I hope to hear from you someday soon.

Yours,
   Kayla McCullen (one of my many aliases ☺)

P.S. I was serious about those late fees. Make sure you

get those movies back to the library. There's a very stern agent who will hunt me down if they aren't back on time.

Hunter smiled at Kayla's email. A wave of relief washed over him when he read she was safe. He felt a flicker of longing as he read the sentence that said how much their date and kiss had meant to her. He wished that he had been able to spend more time with her, but was grateful for the time they had together. He laughed as he read her closing. He knew she wasn't going by 'Kayla McCullen' anymore, and wondered what her new name was. He sincerely hoped he would be able to see her again one day soon. When that day came, he was determined that he would be healthy and would be able to take her out on a real date.

Hunter hit the reply button on his computer and turned on the voice-activated software. He checked his doorway to make sure no one was listening in the hallway and started to compose a response to Kayla's message. Dictating his thoughts felt weird at first and the computer misheard a few of his words, but he was able to go back and edit his writing. He reread the message several times and made small changes before he was finally satisfied with how it sounded. He hit the 'send' button and wondered where the email was heading to reach his precious Kayla.

Chapter 33

<u>Me</u>

　I strolled into The Plaza and smiled; my mouth agape at the lobby's marble floors and cavernous, high ceilings. The receptionist was efficient and got me checked in with minimal fanfare. I love the Dutch for their comfort with silence. Soon I'd found my room, dropped my bag, and stepped into the shower to wash away layers of travel funk before heading out and introducing myself to the creature comforts of this den of iniquity. I knew from the brief research I'd done online that I was close to the Pedestrian Mall area that led to Dam Square which would be a decent place to temporarily call home. I headed out into the warm evening air taking in the occasional waft of cannabis mixed with mildew and expectation. For once it wasn't raining in Amsterdam and the atmosphere was lively.
　　I walked on Damrak for a while. It used to be one of the main canals in the city but was filled in long ago. Now it was packed with tourists seeking out tobacco shops, souvenirs, and restaurants. I did my best to blend in with the crowd and eventually ducked onto a side street lined with hash bars. I stepped inside one that looked discreet and sat down. A young waitress painted with tattoos and piercings came over. She made some good recommendations and then disappeared to retrieve my cravings. When she returned, I pursed my lips into a smile I can best describe as appreciation mixed with anticipation. I carefully rolled my joint, and she gave me a light. I leaned back in my chair and let the mellow fumes envelope me, slowly exhaling not only the thick smoke that painted my lungs but also the weight of my desperation and hatred. It was the most relaxed I'd been in days. I'd been carrying an unnatural tension that had shortened every muscle in my body and seemed to wring my organs to a fraction of their functional size. That wasn't like me, but

the media portrayal of my work at Mt. Baker really drew me inward. It was supposed to be a job meant to eliminate the sport's top dog to clear the way for a sniveling weasel who couldn't measure up. Truthfully, I resented the client but found interest in the work. I wasn't a bomb maker by training but found a friend with some knowledge. As I had no concern about collateral damage, I thought it best to make it big and splashy to cover up the target and focus the attention on some sort of speculated motive such as terrorism or "making a statement." What a bunch of garbage. I killed them all because I could and because I was paid to do it. But Occam's razor doesn't fill a 24-hour news cycle.

With the benefit of time and distance, I still have no remorse for what I did, but I find myself pondering the consequences should I ever be caught. In those moments, I feel something I can only speculate is regret or possibly just worry. Whatever it is, I don't care for it. So, Amsterdam will be my new home. I can climb out of purgatory while temporarily enjoying the vice and creature comforts this wonderful testament to transience had to offer. I shouldn't have any trouble building a good client base around here.

Feeling sufficiently mellow, I turned my attention to discovering the news from home. Although, after some thought, I didn't even think of the U.S. as home anymore because I knew I wouldn't be going back ever again. After a brief internet search, one of the top stories indicated the police were certain there was a link between the Mt. Baker and Seattle bombings. I shook my head in disgust. I shouldn't have been so desperate with the bomb at the hospital. I needed to kill Kayla so badly that I had made a critical error. Even if the police had suspected I was the gunman, they may not have linked me to the Mt. Baker bombings. I chided myself for leading them to a trail they may never have found without my stupidity. Now I had heat. I took another long drag on my joint and told myself it didn't matter. Kayla was dead and there were no witnesses, but then something caught my eye.

It was a headline about the hospital, "Seattle General Suffered

Devastating Disaster, but Miraculously, No Deaths Occurred". Immediately, my pupils constricted, ambient noise silenced and the world around me seemed to slow as if in hibernation. No deaths? Certainly, there had to have been *one* death. I mean, *Kayla died.* She must have. As I read the article, I realized that she was still very much alive. There were no pictures of her, but the article stated that the gunman had been aiming at a key witness who could put one of America's most wanted criminals away for good. According to reports, the witness had escaped the gunfire and the explosion unscathed.

"That little tramp," I muttered. How had she managed to cheat me again? I threw my phone across the room and watched it shatter as it hit the brick wall. The people around me came back to life and turned in my direction, but I didn't care anymore. Kayla may still be alive, but it didn't matter. I was far away from any place where her testimony could hurt me. With that thought, I grabbed my wallet and decided to head down to the Red Light District where I was sure someone would be willing to help me forget my troubles.

Chapter 34

<u>Kayla</u>

Kayla's first flight went smoothly. She was feeling anxious but took a pill for motion sickness that helped her doze for most of the flight. She woke up in time to change planes but felt as though she was in a fog. She usually liked to be fully alert but knew from experience that her best shot to avoid jetlag was to sleep as much as possible. Everyone who traveled with her was very kind, and she was impressed by the comfort of the private plane that she boarded in Washington, DC. She tried not to think too hard about the future. She was excited about the prospect of living in Spain but nervous about pulling off her new identity. She did her best to practice a French-Canadian accent during the flight so it would seem more natural when she arrived at her final destination. She was a good student and had absorbed her linguistics lessons well. No one caught on to her ruse, except for the people from the Witness Security Program who were in the already know.

When the plane finally landed, the pilot welcomed the crew to Barcelona. Kayla's shock at her destination was quickly followed by elation. She had studied Antoni Gaudî in her Art History courses. He was one of the most famous architects of his time and had designed amazing architectural feats such as La Pedrera, a breathtakingly unique apartment building with a rooftop terrace that offered spectacular views of Barcelona's rooftops as well as chimneystacks shaped like bizarre alien creations. His most famous work was La Sagrada Familia, which has remained under construction since its inception in 1882. Kayla had always wanted to visit the city because of its Catalonian heritage and its festive markets along Las Ramblas. It was an exciting city filled with gothic architecture and colorful mosaics, not to mention the breathtaking scenery of mountains to the north and the

Mediterranean to the south. She was thrilled by her good fortune to be sent to such an amazing and lively city. Her exuberance faded slightly when she realized she would still be under the Witness Security Program's strict guidelines. It was unlikely she would be allowed to explore the city by herself, but perhaps if she asked very nicely she could convince some of the agents to take her out to experience a little bit of the culture.

Kayla stood up slowly and stretched her stiff legs. Her neck was sore from falling asleep with her head resting on the window. She gathered her bags and made her way down the aisle. She was dressed in a fitted black sheath dress and a pair of black heels. She carefully stepped through the door and took in her first view of Spain. There were snow-capped mountains in the distance and a brilliant cloudless blue sky. The air smelled clean and fresh and a soft breeze ruffled her sleek, coppery hair. For the first time in a very long time, she felt inspired. For just a moment, she felt as if her life were her own. The moment faded as soon as it came when a man named Leonard introduced himself, gripped her by the elbow, and led her to a black Mercedes Benz with tinted windows. He motioned for her to get into the back seat. She climbed in and sat quietly as he walked around the car and got in the driver's seat. She stared out the window, wishing she didn't have to be escorted around. She desperately wanted to jump on the metro and hop around the city, stopping to eat tapas and drink sangria whenever her heart desired. She knew she was being unrealistic, but for just a moment, it had almost felt real. She forced herself to accept the reality of her situation. She had fallen in love with Spain already. If living here meant that she was going to have to live by WITSEC rules, then she would follow them explicitly. It would be worth it if it kept her alive.

Kayla watched the countryside pass by as they drove from the airport into the city. She sat glued to the window as she watched the palm tree-lined streets pass. Women in chic clothes and high heels strolled next to well-dressed men on the sidewalks. No one seemed to be in a hurry. Groups of friends sat gathered along curbside cafes sipping small coffee and laughing. The sun was shining and everyone seemed to be outdoors enjoying life. Kayla smiled at the simplicity that seemed to embody life in Spain. No one was alone, even the elderly people she spotted were smiling as they walked their little dogs or strolled arm in arm with a loved one. Everyone seemed very at peace with life, and for a moment, Kayla was able to forget her inner turmoil.

The car eventually slowed down and turned into a gated driveway. The driver announced that they were at the Canadian Embassy. Kayla started to repeat the facts about her new identity to herself in her head so she would be prepared to introduce herself as Karina Thibault. She knew that it wouldn't be easy to pull off, but at this point, she really didn't have a choice. She had done everything by the book in the States, and Kazamir had still found her. She had barely escaped his attempts to kill her and knew if he found her again, he would make sure she didn't escape. She took a deep breath as the agent came around to her door and opened it. She smiled and stepped bravely out into the sunshine. She felt the warm rays caress her shoulders. She took in the sight of the gorgeous brick building that rose in front of her with its stone balconies and intricate spires. Things could be worse, she reminded herself. They could be much, much worse.

The housekeeper greeted Kayla with warmth and affection the minute she stepped into the door. The housekeeper's name was Marta. She was a robust woman with warm hands and a welcoming smile. To Kayla's relief, she didn't bombard her with any questions. Instead, she told Kayla they had been expecting her and were elated to have her as their guest for as long as she wished to stay. She explained that she was in charge of the day-to-day duties at the embassy. She cleaned, cooked, and attended to the needs of the guests. She reassured Kayla that while she was there, she was family. Kayla liked her instantly. Marta took Kayla's bags from the agent and carried them up the stairs to Kayla's room. It was a lovely, open space painted a soft, creamy yellow. There was a large queen-size canopy bed in the center of the room with a fluffy down comforter and endless pillows. An ornate desk along the wall served as a vanity. French doors led out to a balcony with a fabulous view of ornate gardens. Kayla thanked Marta profusely for her help. Marta brushed it off, saying she was just doing her job. She provided Kayla with the embassy's secured Wi-Fi password and explained that there was a business center, workout room, and casual and formal dining rooms in the embassy. She invited Kayla to dinner in the formal dining room that night. Everyone who was staying there would be gathering for dinner to celebrate her arrival. Kayla was nervous about meeting everyone all at once but grateful she would be able to get all of the introductions over with quickly.

Marta left her then, and Kayla stretched out on the bed, letting the soft down comforter swallow her. She rested for a half-hour but gave up when she couldn't fall asleep. She wasn't as tired as she'd expected to be after the long flight. She decided to open her computer and send a few emails from her new account. She knew she couldn't give away any information about her whereabouts, but wanted to reassure Hunter that she was okay. She thoughtfully constructed an email to him and reread it twice, making sure she hadn't made any obvious spelling errors or divulged any confidential information. She clicked the send button when she was satisfied with her wording. She tried to tell herself it didn't matter to her if he emailed back or not, but she knew it did. It mattered to her very much, and it would crush her if he forgot about her so soon. She knew it was unfair of her to expect that Hunter would be thinking about her during such a traumatic time in his life. She didn't want to be narcissistic and expect he would be pining for her after only knowing her for a few days, but she couldn't help but hope he might be a little curious about what became of her. If he was going to be laid up in the hospital for a while, she hoped he might at least have the time to send her a few quick sentences.

She closed her laptop, disgusted at herself for overanalyzing the situation. Her life was in danger, and Hunter's career was likely over. It seemed ridiculous that she would be concerning herself with a school-girl crush, but perhaps it was good for her to have something to focus on to help her forget that someone had recently done everything possible to end her life. A harmless crush was certainly the least of her worries right now.

Kayla picked up a binder one of the agents had left for her. It contained the names of each of the residents at the embassy as well as a brief description of where the person was from, what they did for a living, and their interests. Each caption was accompanied by a picture. Her assignment was to study it carefully so she was familiar with everyone at the embassy. Most of the residents were diplomats and ambassadors of Canada working in Spain to promote trade. They all looked stern in their photos, and she hoped that they would be friendlier in person. Simon Boucher, Laura Williams, David Smith, and Samantha Brown were all Canadians sent over by the Trade Commissioner Service to promote Canada's economic interests in Spain. According to her notes, they had lived in Spain for nearly a decade and divided their time between Madrid and Barcelona. Lawrence Anderson and Matthew Gauthier both worked with human rights and had been in the country for just over two years. She continued to memorize the names of the rest of the people at the embassy who worked for various organizations that defended global security and facilitated academic exchanges. Before long, her head was spinning. She finally collapsed into bed and let herself drift off to sleep. She awoke with a start two hours later and was surprised to see the sun dipping down in the sky. She glanced at the clock by her bedside table and realized it was getting close to 7:00 pm. Dinner was at 7:30 pm. She would have just enough time to shower and change before it was time for her to go downstairs. On a whim, she checked her email and was happy to see that Hunter had already sent a response.

Hello, You!

I'm trying to think of what your new name might be…perhaps you're referring to yourself as Vivianne or Candy these days. I can only hope you didn't get stuck with an old lady name like Beatrice. Either way, I'm going to keep referring to you as Kayla, because that's the girl who stole my heart, and I certainly don't want to forget about her. I was extremely excited to get an email from you. Believe it or not, I have been worried about you. I know you can take care of yourself, but that doesn't stop me from worrying. I'm sure you're just fine considering you simultaneously escaped a crazed gunman and a bombing, which makes me wonder if you have some sort of superpower. Somehow you managed to waltz into my life with freshly baked cookies, and before I knew it, you were battling the bad guys.

Seriously, Kayla, you are one incredible woman, and I hope I will be lucky enough to meet up with you again one day. In the meantime, I know you have your own battles to fight, so I'm going to make you a promise. I'm going to do everything I can to get better so I can sweep you off your feet and carry you off into the sunset like the hero you deserve when this is all over ;-) Okay, okay, I know I'm getting cheesy, but in all seriousness, I miss you. You really brightened up my days at the hospital. Without you, all I have to focus on is beating my uncle at cribbage, getting beat up by my physical therapists, and trying to get my homework done. It's not nearly as much fun as it sounds.

Anyway, enough about me, I hope you like your new home. You were probably worried about being stuck in some tiny town in the middle of nowhere. I hope that wherever you are, you like it. I suppose you don't have a lot of freedom, so my advice is to make sure you meet someone really cool who will pick up all of your favorite movies for you. I was lucky enough to have someone who did that for me and am really beginning to miss that person.

I'm sure you have places to go, people to see, and things to do in your new home, but I wanted to let you know how happy getting your email made me. I know you probably have limited time. The fact that you made the effort to let me know you're safe means a lot. Please know I'll be thinking of you and wishing you safety and happiness. Please keep in touch. I'm not going anywhere for awhile, and your friendship means a lot to me.

Keep it real, kid,
H.E. (that's right...my initials sort of spell something)

Kayla giggled as she read Hunter's email. He wrote the same way he talked. In fact, she could almost hear his voice as she read his message. His words gave her the courage to get up, change, and go downstairs to begin her life as Karina Thibaut. She knew it wasn't going to be easy, but Hunter's words had given her confidence. She felt at peace knowing she had someone she could confide in who understood how hard it was to face unexpected obstacles in life. If only he weren't an ocean away and her safety didn't rely on everyone, including Hunter, not knowing her current location.

Chapter 35

Hunter

Hunter felt the sunlight streaming across his face. For a moment, he couldn't remember where he was. He wracked his brain, trying to remember if he was traveling between competitions. Then he opened his eyes and looked around. The IV's and sterile walls sent him a grim reminder that he wasn't at an elite ski race. He was in the hospital and his career was in jeopardy. He felt a wave of depression wash over him but remembered he had one friend who was capable of understanding his frustration at having the only life he knew taken away from him. He opened his laptop and checked the inbox. His scowl turned into a grin when he saw Kayla had sent a response already. It had only been twelve hours since he'd sent her an email, and he was happy she hadn't felt the need to wait any length of time before responding.

Hunter,

My new life has officially begun. I sincerely hope this new persona of mine will only have to be temporary. I don't mean to sound ungrateful. My Big Brothers really outdid themselves. They put me up in a beautiful location with lots of things to do and see. They also spared no expense on my accommodations. I had fears of being stuck in a trailer court or a yurt, and I can assure you that my new home is very comfortable.

Your email made me smile. I miss you, too. I really looked forward to our talks and spending time with you. It's lonely here without having those visits to look forward to. I know I was still in hiding when I was in Seattle, but at least I had some freedom. I could go to art school and paint for a living. I have to be more careful now. It looks like I'm going to be spending a lot of my time staying in. I agree with you that I would be lucky if someone was kind enough to bring me movies to pass the time.

I hope you're cooperating with the physical therapists. I know that they can be tough and are probably forcing you to do things that cause you pain, but they know what they're doing. If I know anything about you, it's that you'll impress them beyond belief with your ability to heal and build your strength back up. I'm definitely going to hold you to your promise to sweep me off my feet one of these days.

Please tell your uncle hello for me. I hope he's still enjoying Seattle and that you're not beating him too badly in cribbage.

Thanks again for staying in touch. Getting your email made me smile for the first time in a while.

Be well, Hunter.
Kayla

Hunter slowly closed his laptop with a smile on his face that he couldn't seem to get rid of. Kayla had not only responded back right away, but she acknowledged that she missed him and wanted to see him again when this whole mess was over. That single thought gave him the motivation to get through his grueling physical therapy sessions and surpass his therapists' expectations. The thought of Kayla was all he needed to commit to his recovery with every fiber of his being. When he was first injured and thought his career was over, he struggled to find the motivation to make it through each day. Now all that had changed because of one amazing woman.

Chapter 36

<u>Me</u>

The days passed by in a blur of marijuana and prostitutes. One day dissolved into the next. I moved out of my ritzy hotel into a low key, dumpy apartment in the De Wallen Quarter because of my dwindling funds. I figured if I was going to be spending the majority of my time in the Red Light District, then I might as well be living close to it. My life had turned into a blissful, hedonistic stretch of doing whatever, whenever I pleased.

Everything good must eventually end, and my honeymoon came to a screeching halt when I reached into my mattress to pull out money to pay my dealer and realized there was nothing left. The endless supply of basic needs had left me completely broke. I should have been a little more concerned about my financial state, but given my surroundings and recent past, I wasn't really thinking pragmatically. Later that day, my landlord pounded on my apartment and screamed out something in Dutch. My rent was overdue, and I barely had a cent to my name. The Dutch are pretty relaxed about a lot of things, but prompt payment for goods and services are not among them. I couldn't go back to the States to my old gig because I'd be arrested the minute I landed. How was I supposed to get a job in a place where I couldn't speak the language?

I weighed my options as carefully as I could, which was difficult because I was still tripping from the box of mushrooms I'd consumed with a 6-foot tall blonde hooker a few hours ago. I finally decided to make my way down to the local coffee shop and ask around to see if someone with my qualifications might be of use to anyone. That's when providence smiled on me as I ran into another ex-pat like myself who made his living dealing the hard stuff. Soft drugs were legal in Amsterdam, but harder drugs were still difficult to get and, if you'll pardon what may appear to be a bad pun, in high demand.

Over the next few weeks, I built up a fair number of clients and got in good with some of the other dealers. Money was starting to pour in again, and I was able to pay my rent and resume my previous lifestyle, minus all the hookers. It turns out that legal prostitution is a drain on the wallet. The temptation is always there, but the prices are high. I decided to cool it for a while and focus on keeping my head above water. Rules still applied, and I didn't get high on my own supply, but I did frequent several hash bars.

I temporarily forgot about Kayla in the midst of binging on drugs and working to replenish my funds. Eventually, my head cleared enough to check with some of my contacts back in the States. All they could tell me was that she had escaped my attempt to end her life at the hospital before going back into protective custody. They didn't know where she was or what she was doing. They assumed that she was not only going by a new name but also had a new look that would make her difficult to recognize. Unfortunately for me, they stopped searching for her when I ran out of money to pay them, but I enticed them to resume their search when I wired more money.

Eventually, news came from one of my contacts that she was no longer in the country. The source had a contact with the feds, and was able to do some digging and find records of a private flight that had gone from D.C. to Seattle with several agents, and returned with one additional unidentified person. That same plane had left the country a day after landing back in D.C., but the destination hadn't been recorded. That greedy asshole had the nerve to demand more money if I wanted him to keep digging. I wired him everything I had in my account and kept only enough for living expenses. At this point, I was beginning to lose faith. If she wasn't in the United States, she could be anywhere. They could be hiding her on some obscure remote island without access to internet or telephones. They could have tucked her away in the mountains of Peru or a tiny village in Kenya. For all I knew, she could be sailing on an ocean liner in the middle of the Indian Ocean right now. I'm sure she was laughing the whole time, knowing she had eluded me twice and was living the good life, while I was excommunicated from the US and would likely have to scrape by for the rest of my days. Just thinking about her got me so worked up; I hastily screwed a j between my lips, lit it and drew in a breath heavy with the pungent smoke. I exhaled… she had not seen the last of me.

Chapter 37

Kayla

Kayla woke up the following morning with a mild headache. She had been nervous at dinner the previous night. The combination of using a French Canadian accent and answering in-depth questions about the life of Karina Thibault was stressful. She performed well under pressure and found the accent seemed to come more naturally if she drank wine. She was careful not to over-indulge, but the wine gave her confidence, and she slowly sipped from her constantly-refilled glass throughout the evening. She was accustomed to the occasional glass of wine with dinner, but last night the conversation had carried on well past midnight. She'd enjoyed everyone she met and was grateful for the company. Although the agents she worked with since she escaped the bombing were with her constantly, she still had felt very alone because she knew they were only temporary fixtures in her life. At least the people she was living with would be constants during her time in Barcelona.

The conversation had been lively and no one had questioned her presence in the embassy. Everyone was used to people coming and going and her accent seemed authentic enough. Lawrence and Matthew, who worked in human rights, were both single and grateful for the presence of a beautiful woman. Samantha and Laura were the only two females staying at the embassy and were excited to have a new friend. Simon had a boyfriend who lived in England and turned out to be the wittiest of the group. He kept everyone laughing with his tales of traveling throughout the world and seemed to have a talent for putting people at ease in his presence. David was quiet, but a keen observer. He kindly explained some of the tips he'd learned about how to get around in Barcelona, some of the cultural differences to be aware of, and which neighborhoods to avoid. He told her that she should be careful if she went to Las Ramblas.

There were endless booths selling colorful crafts and delicious foods, but the pickpockets were rampant, and she should make sure to hold on to her belongings.

 Kayla was grateful she had taken the time to memorize everyone's names and a little bit about them. She was able to deflect most conversations away from herself by asking questions about each person's occupation and their experiences while living in Spain. It seemed that everyone at the dinner had led an incredibly interesting life. Lawrence had lived all over Asia and Africa before coming to Barcelona. Matthew was in South America and the South Pacific before moving to Spain. He could speak five languages and had worked throughout Eastern and Western Europe. The rest had all traveled extensively because of their careers. Kayla realized quickly how sheltered her existence had been. She'd spent her whole life in Chicago before being sent to Seattle by WITSEC. This was her first time off the continent of North America. Of course, Karina Thibault, her alter ego, was supposed to be a very worldly and well-traveled woman, so Kayla kept her thoughts to herself. She did her best to smile and listen intently without discussing her personal life with her new friends. They seemed to accept her secretiveness as a part of her intriguing and mysterious personality. No one asked too many questions. They all had secrets and aspects of their lives they preferred to keep under wraps as well. No one pushed her for information for fear that they might be expected to share more than they wanted.

 The entire dinner was amazing. The meal started with tapas, or appetizers, that were impeccably prepared. The first course included large olives stuffed with anchovies and red peppers, chopitos, which were battered and fried squid, and patatas bravas, which were fried potatoes served with garlic mayonnaise and spicy tomato sauce. Next, the chef brought out a platter of cured meats, referred to as embutidos. David sat next to her and explained that all of these foods were very traditional Spanish foods. Barcelona was in the region that used to be the independent nation of Catalonia. Although

Catalonians spoke Spanish, they used a unique dialect referred to as Catalan. He explained that the region had French influences, and its food had its own particular flare. Although Catalonia had become a part of Spain, there were a number of residents who still hung Catalan flags and supported the idea of Catalonia becoming its own independent nation again. David was doubtful this would ever happen, but explained that this was just one of the many ways it was evident that the people of the Catalan Region of Spain were very proud of their heritage and unique traditions.

When the main course was finished, the chef passed around a tray of local cheeses. She particularly enjoyed a cheese with honey and preserves. David explained that it was a local cheese called Mato, which was sold by local cheese shops when it was only one or two days old.

The final course of the meal was a small tray of panellets, which were small round sweets made of almonds, sugar, and eggs. The sweets were rolled in pine nuts before they were served. Kayla enjoyed the sweets and thanked David for taking the time to explain the Catalan foods and traditions to her. She had a much better appreciation for the meal thanks to David's commentary.

The Rioja wine particularly impressed Kayla. According to David, the wine was made primarily out of Tempranillo grapes, which grew at relatively high altitudes in Spain. The grape was dark black in color with a thick skin. The advantage of growing the grape in Spain was that it could tolerate a much warmer climate than other varieties. It produced a wine that was ruby red in color and had aromas that varied from berries and plum to vanilla and leather. Kayla had to remind herself to sip the wine slowly because she didn't want to slip up and blow her cover.

When the night eventually ended, Kayla returned to her room, relieved that she'd managed to convince everyone that she actually was Karina Thibaut. After washing her face and brushing her teeth, she opened her computer and composed an email to Hunter. She reread it several times to make sure she wasn't giving away any information about her whereabouts. Satisfied that she was adequately discrete, she hit the send button. Then she curled up in a ball on her bed and drifted off into a deep sleep, feeling safe and happy for the first time in a very long time.

Chapter 38

Hunter

    For Hunter, the progress was slow but steady. He knew it would take a long time for his bones to heal fully, but he was becoming more mobile. Doctors assured him that the casts and braces could be removed sooner than expected, thanks to the fast rate at which his bones were repairing themselves. Eventually, he was released from the hospital with the understanding that he would stay in Seattle and continue to return for outpatient therapy sessions. His doctors didn't want to attempt a flight too quickly in order to avoid causing blood clots or any unintended injuries during the transfer. Although Jackson would eventually need to return to Colorado for work, he was able to telecommute for most things, so he could stay with Hunter.

    His relationship with Emily was progressing, and he was in no hurry to leave while things were going so well. They had started talking about a future together, and Jackson wanted to stick around long enough to figure out how they were going to make their relationship work. They had talked about trying a distance relationship, but they would eventually need to be in the same place if they were serious about staying together. Hunter felt guilty for monopolizing the majority of his uncle's time with his recovery process, but Jackson didn't seem to mind. He was happy to be there for his nephew and spent the rest of his time with Emily.

    Hunter divided his time between his coursework, physical therapy, and time with his uncle. Even with his grueling physical therapy schedule, he still had a significant amount of time to himself. Kayla was never far from his mind, and he looked forward to writing her emails and reading her responses. He couldn't help but worry about her. As long as Kazamir was alive, her life was in danger. Anyone who was willing to bomb an entire wing of a hospital was obviously desperate. Hunter feared he would stop at nothing to get rid of Kayla for good. He hated the idea that Kayla would have to be in hiding for the rest of her life. He knew she'd accepted her fate, but he couldn't imagine having a real shot at a relationship with her when she couldn't even leave the sanctuary of her guarded home for fear of being kidnapped or shot.

He decided to learn everything he could about the man who was making Kayla's life a living nightmare. Most of the information on him was classified, but he was able to find articles that detailed some of the crimes Kazamir had committed. The amount of information he was able to find by searching through public records surprised Hunter.

Anton Viktor Kazamir's life of crime had started at a young age. His father was suspected of killing his mother. No one ever knew what became of her, but his father had a history of abuse and a violent temper. One day when Kazamir was twelve and was away on a class trip, his parents had a major blowout. Neighbors reported hearing shouting and screaming coming from their apartment. His mother disappeared that night. Her body was never found, and the apartment had been wiped clean of prints and any evidence as to what really happened, but no one heard from her again. Kazamir's father insisted she ran away. He claimed that she couldn't handle the responsibilities of motherhood, but the police suspected otherwise. Shortly thereafter, his father was arrested in a major drug bust and sentenced to twenty years in prison. Kazamir had no extended family willing to raise him, so he entered foster care. His file indicated that from a young age he demonstrated an uncontrollable temper, extreme anger, and a tendency towards violence. He bounced from family to family but never stayed anywhere longer than a few months. His foster families couldn't control his rage and violent actions, and he was eventually sent to a juvenile detention center. He was smart enough to demonstrate remorse for his behavior and able to convince people that he was reformed, but when he was back on the streets, he would return to his misguided ways, getting involved in drug deals, theft, and violence.

He was in and out of jail from the time he turned 18. Each crime got bigger and more elaborate. Anyone who crossed him disappeared without a trace. There were rumors that he had connections to the mob and was in charge of a major operation when things went very bad one night. A deal he'd been working on went sour and the police had enough evidence to put him away for life without parole, but he managed to disappear. There was no information on him after that until he was suspected of orchestrating the Mt. Baker Bombing.

The job had been reckless. Kazamir, who was known for destroying any evidence of his crimes, had left a much larger trail than ever before. Police suspected that he was mentally troubled and burnt out on drugs. They were finally getting close to bringing him in when he bombed the Seattle hospital in an attempt to wipe out the witness he believed would put him away. Little did he know that the police had more than enough evidence to make sure he never walked free again, with or without a witness. Unfortunately, he had managed to flee the country directly after the bombing, and no one knew where he was hiding. There was a lot of speculation as to his whereabouts. Some reporters suspected that he had returned to the States and remained in hiding. Others thought he had left the country and never planned to return. No one could say for sure where he went and the authorities were open to hearing any leads that might point to his whereabouts.

Hunter was even more concerned about Kayla when he finished his research. Kazamir was a mentally unstable man who was under the influence of drugs. He was a desperate sociopath who had completely lost touch with reality. If he found Kayla, Hunter was sure he wouldn't allow her to get away again. This thought worried him, and he vowed to himself that he would figure out Kazamir's whereabouts before he had the chance to find Kayla. He knew it wasn't going to be easy, especially considering the fact that he was confined to his bed or a wheelchair thanks to his broken bones; however, he had nothing but time to devote to finding the man who had ruined both his and Kayla's lives. He'd already lost so much, and he couldn't bear the thought of losing her, too.

Kayla,

I smile every time I get a message from you, but it also makes me miss you even more. Every day that goes by, I worry more and more about your safety. I'm sure you're being careful and are in good hands, but it's still hard not to worry about you. You didn't tell me the whole story of what happened, but I've done a lot of reading about the Mt. Baker and Seattle General Bombings. It sounds like Kazamir has a major vendetta against you. I know you can take care of yourself, but I'm still concerned. Just know I'm always going to be here for you. Please call (or email) me if there's anything you need.

I wish I could come visit you, but unfortunately, my biggest adventure lately has been getting released from the hospital and returning on an outpatient basis. It's nice to be away from the sterile rooms, the hospital food, and the constant stream of IVs and medications. We rented a suite across from the hospital so it's easy for me to get back and forth. Uncle J seems content to stay with me, especially because he's been dating a great lady who seems to make him happy. I don't know that I've ever seen him in a relationship before, so I was surprised when he told me he had a date. He used to always be so restless, but he seems much more content and relaxed over the last few weeks. I think this woman might be a keeper.

I'm trying very hard to keep my grades up. Considering that I don't have much else to do, I've been pretty successful. I added a few more classes to my course load since I have more free time, and am on course to graduate sooner than expected. Knowing that my skiing career could be over has made me grateful I decided to pursue my degree. I knew that I needed a back-up plan, but I never imagined it would be so soon.

That's enough about me. I know you can't tell me much about your life right now, but I care about you and want to learn everything there is to know about you. I want to know what your parents were like, what your favorite subject was in school, and what you did for fun when you were growing up. I want to know what your favorite color is, what type of music you listen to, and what movie you rent when you're feeling down. Just because we can't talk about where you're living, doesn't mean that we can't get to know each other better.

Sweet dreams or good morning or whatever greeting is appropriate for the time of day it is where you live.

*Cheers,
Hunter*

Chapter 39

<u>Me</u>

My phone rang early in the morning, and I fumbled for it. I answered it on the final ring before it went to voicemail. I mumbled a semi-coherent greeting. My voice sounded gravelly even to my own ears.

"Look, Kaz, I think I've got a lead."

I sat up straight. It was my contact. He had information on Kayla. I felt a wave of adrenaline rush through me.

"Where is she?"

"Not so fast, Kaz. I was able to pay off a nurse at the hospital who was working the night you created a fireworks display at the hospital's entrance. It turns out that she was visiting a certain Hunter Erickson. I think you might be familiar with him considering you tried to end him, too."

"What's your point?" I was not amused.

"My point, if you'd wait for me to finish, is it turns out that your two bombing victims happened to have fallen for each other. Kayla was at the hospital that night visiting Hunter, and they were looking very cozy. That was, of course, until you messed up royally, demolished the hospital, and became Public Enemy Number One."

"Look, enough about me. I hired you to find Kayla, not for unconstructive criticism. Have you got anything else?"

"We were able to hack into Hunter's email account. It appears that the two of them are still keeping in touch, but she's being tight-lipped about where the feds have stashed her. She hasn't even given a hint about what country she's in or who she's with. On the other hand, they communicate every day, so she's bound to slip up at some point. It looks like the best chance we have of getting to her is through him."

"Got it. Keep up the good work. I want an address. I'm not

letting her get away again."

"Okay, but this isn't a blog. This subscription costs money."

"Let me worry about the cost. Just do your job." With that, I hung up the phone. My head was pounding from the bender I'd gone on last night. I rubbed my temples, downed some pain pills, and rolled back over. I couldn't bear to face the day just yet, but with some sleep and this new intel, I could feel a good day was on the horizon.

Chapter 40

Kayla

    Kayla awoke to her buzzing alarm clock. She rolled her eyes. She had a meeting with federal agents from the US who were stationed in Barcelona. They were more desperate than ever to track down Kazamir and arrest him. They seemed convinced that the information she had would lead them to him. The reality was she hadn't been face to face with Kazamir since that dreadful day in Chicago. Other than his threatening letter and his attempt to end her life once and for all in his very daring display at the hospital, they hadn't had any direct communication. She tried to tell the feds that, but they still insisted she come in for an interview. It turned out that they were sure that Kazamir had left the US. They assumed he used a fake passport to pass through security. He'd flown to Europe, but they had no idea where he went after arrival. He may have stayed in Europe, or he could have taken a connecting flight anywhere in the world. They hoped she might have some insight, but she assured them that she had no new information for them. They insisted on keeping her for the entire morning, asking her questions about the Chicago incident, the threatening letter, and the hospital attack in Seattle. She had been over all of the questions many times on multiple occasions, but he was a major international criminal, and they insisted on asking her the same questions over and over in case she had something else to add. She didn't, and they eventually let her go. A sedan with tinted windows drove her back to the embassy. The driver punched in a code at the gated drive and waited for the doors to swing open.

    Kayla looked out at the grounds of the embassy. The grass was green and the fountains in the yard were bubbling with fresh, clear water. Flowerbeds in full bloom dotted the premises. Bright reds, violets, and shades of yellow blanketed the gardens and expansive shade trees provided shelter from the hot sun. It was a breathtakingly beautiful place, but despite the gorgeous surroundings, Kayla felt as though she was in a serene and luxurious prison. She couldn't leave the premises without an escort and wasn't allowed to go to public places. She couldn't make any phone calls and had to be on guard at all times. The worst part was that she couldn't get close enough to anyone to risk revealing her true identity. Although emails were allowed, she knew they were being screened by the feds before being sent off into cyberspace. Anything that might give away the slightest hint about her whereabouts was deleted. She was allowed to paint if she desired, which helped, but it was hard to be inspired when she was under around-the-clock surveillance by the federal agents.

She let out a long sigh, knowing she should be grateful. She was living in an amazing city, enjoying gourmet food, and surrounded by interesting people. She was out of harm's way and lucky to be alive after everything that happened in Seattle, but she would have traded it all to have her freedom back.

Kayla thanked the driver as he parked at the top of the circular driveway. She stepped out of the car and surveyed her surroundings. The colorful flowers and brilliant sun sparked a desire for her to start painting. She decided to get to work after lunch. She had been away from art for too long, and it was taking a toll on her. If she ever wanted to feel complete again, she had to start painting. She made a decision to find out what supplies were available in the embassy and what things she would need to order. The idea of painting made her smile to herself as she headed back inside the embassy.

Kayla was pleasantly surprised to find a light lunch of delicious bread and cured meats waiting for her. She hadn't realized how hungry she was, but this morning's interrogation had left her with a ravenous appetite. She devoured her lunch and then began her quest to find painting supplies. One of the housekeepers was kind enough to lead her to a closet that contained canvases, oil paints, and an array of brushes. Apparently, they had received a request to have painting supplies delivered prior to her arrival. She was relieved that she could get started that very day. With the help of the housekeeper, she set up an easel in the garden and started to paint the scenery around her. She felt more like herself than she had in days. The hours drifted by, and before she knew it, the sun was dipping lower in the sky. She looked down at her work, which was nearly complete, with a look of satisfaction. She'd been able to capture the vibrant colors of the garden and the way the sunlight caressed the trees and the grass exactly as she'd hoped. She slowly started to clean up and take things back inside. David was just coming home and walked across the lawn. He paused to look at her painting and grinned at her.

"I didn't realize you had so many talents."

Kayla did her best to put on the persona of Karina Thibault when she answered. "I've always enjoyed painting and was feeling a bit homesick today. I thought it might help me pass the time and forget about being so far away."

David looked at her sympathetically. "I understand what it's like to miss home. I've spent most of my life traveling, but homesickness always has a way of creeping up at inopportune times. It seems to get easier with time." He said in a reassuring voice. With that, he picked up some of her supplies and helped her carry everything back inside. Kayla thanked him for his help and made a mental note to give him one of her paintings before she left. He had been so kind and helpful to her and the only thing she had to show him her appreciation was her art.

After they parted, she climbed up the stairs to her room and sat down on her soft comforter. She opened her laptop and grinned when she saw Hunter's email in her inbox. Her heart seemed to flutter every time she thought of him. She was glad he hadn't forgotten about her.

Chapter 41

<u>Hunter</u>

Hunter had been used to having his life entirely focused on skiing. He read every article on how to improve his aerodynamics as he flew down the mountain, researched the best skis for his build and technique, and trained tirelessly on the slopes. His intense focus had earned him the elite status in the world of skiing, and now that he was injured, he needed to find another focus. His business degree helped him pass the time, and he was grateful for the additional time he was able to spend with his uncle. For years, their relationship had revolved around skiing and competitions. Since the accident, he'd been able to spend quality time with Jackson watching movies, playing card games, and learning more about his adventurous uncle. It amazed him that even though his uncle had avoided relationships when he was younger, he hadn't hesitated to become the sole guardian of his nephew, even when it meant a drastic change in the lifestyle he had carefully cultivated.

Hunter was used to challenges. He had become accustomed to the intense adrenaline rush skiing provided. In a way, he'd become addicted to the endorphin-high he experienced flying down the slopes all day. Now that he was stuck in a hotel and unable to ski, he found a similar sort of adrenaline rush from pushing himself to the max during his physical therapy sessions. His doctors had never seen someone with so much willpower who pushed his physical limits quite the way Hunter did. It seemed that the more pain he experienced, the harder he pushed. The more fatigued his muscles felt, the more he demanded from them. Although he was still confined to a wheelchair, he could do many things for himself and was gaining confidence with each session. He was as aware as anyone that the road to recovery was going to be long and exhausting. His therapists and doctors all assumed that his determination came from his desire to get back on the slopes. Although Hunter loved skiing and hoped to return to competition, he was also a realist. He had been one of the oldest skiers in this year's competitions and was well aware that physical limitations would eventually make it impossible for him to continue performing at an elite level. His real motivation was to recover enough to visit Kayla. He knew she couldn't give out her location, and it would compromise her safety if he tried to find out. However, he also knew that Kazamir was getting more crazed and reckless by the day and was bound to end up in custody eventually. When this happened, Kayla would at least be able to regain some of her freedom, and he wanted to be there to help her celebrate when that day finally came.

 As Hunter sat lost in thought wondering where Kayla might be, his uncle knocked on the door to his room. He and Jackson had found a suite at a hotel across from the hospital that had two bedrooms, a small kitchen, and a living area. It wasn't fancy, but it provided them with their own space and a kitchen to cook basic meals. They weren't master chefs, but they combined their talents and made passable scrambled eggs and bacon for breakfast, grilled cheese sandwiches for lunch, and ordered pizza or got takeout for dinner. Jackson's knock brought Hunter back to reality.

 "What's up, Uncle J?" Hunter asked, taking in the contemplative look on Jackson's face.

 "I was doing a little research on the best rehab programs in the country for your type of injuries. There is a program at the Willamette Wellness Center in Portland, Oregon that has treated a number of elite athletes with serious injuries and gotten great results. You'll be getting out of your casts soon, and it might be worthwhile to think about transferring your care there to have the best possible chance at a full recovery."

 Hunter mulled over what his uncle was saying. "What about you? You have your job waiting for you in Colorado, and you just started dating Emily. I don't think I could go by myself at this point, and I don't want to ask you to give up more than you already have on my account."

Jackson smiled. "You're always worried about me, even when you're facing the biggest challenge of your life. I really appreciate it, but I've already thought things through. I can continue working remotely, so it doesn't matter where I am. I already talked with Emily, too. She thinks it's a great idea. In fact, she and her late husband bought a second home near Southeast Division Street in Portland. He used to do a lot of business there, and they loved the neighborhood. The house is all one level, so it will be easy for you to get around. She had been renting it out, but it's currently vacant. She offered to let us stay there and is willing to come with to help us get settled and keep me company. In fact, she's already put in her notice at the hotel that she'll be leaving."

Hunter grinned at his uncle. "It looks like you've already put a lot of thought into this, Uncle J. I think it's a great idea, and it's incredibly generous of Emily to allow us to stay at her home. It will be a lot more comfortable than an extended-stay hotel. We'll need to run it by my doctors at Seattle General first, though."

Jackson and Hunter agreed to discuss the transfer of care with his doctors and physical therapists at Seattle General the following day. The fact that Portland was only a three-hour drive from Seattle would make the move much easier than if he'd had to fly. The Willamette Wellness Center had state-of-the art facilities and was considered the nation's premier rehab institute. He knew that he owed it to his uncle and Coach Sullivan to do everything he could to make a full-recovery. Even though he often felt discouraged by his current limitations, and wondered if he'd ever return to skiing, he didn't want to give up on the years that his uncle and coach had dedicated to getting him to the elite level. If going to rehab in Portland would give him a better chance at a full recovery, then he knew he had no choice.

The following day, Hunter and Jackson met with his internists and physical therapists. After discussing his options, the consensus was that it would be best for Hunter to be referred to Willamette Wellness Center. The lead physical therapist on his team knew the Chief Medical Officer at the rehab center from Residency and agreed to make the referral. Everyone agreed that Seattle General had done all they could, and it was time for Hunter to enter a program that catered specifically to his injuries. The paperwork would be completed, and Hunter would be transferred the following week. In the meantime, Emily had agreed to go to Portland to get the house ready for their arrival. Hunter would start the intense rehab program immediately after arriving in the city. The rehab center was just blocks away from Southeast Division Street. He and Jackson would be able to walk there as soon as Hunter's casts came off, and he was out of a wheelchair.

Hunter sat down that evening and smiled when he opened up an email from Kayla. He had been so busy over the past 24 hours that he hadn't had a chance to check to see if she'd replied to his most recent message. He was happy to see that she had.

Hunter,

"Don't worry, I didn't forget about you! In fact, I've been thinking about you a lot and hope your rehab is going smoothly and your uncle is still dating that wonderful woman named Emily who seems to make him so happy.

I've been keeping myself as busy as possible. I've met some good friends where I live. I can't tell them much about myself, but they all have interesting stories to tell, which has helped pass the time. I've been able to do some painting as well, which is making me feel much more like myself. I'm surrounded by beautiful things where I live, so it hasn't been hard to find subject matter. Agent Franklin must have been watching out for me because they had all the supplies I needed to paint waiting for me when I arrived. I'm sad that I can't go exploring on my own, but the people where I'm living have graciously invited me to join in on some pretty amazing dinners. I've been able to try all the local foods. Although I'm not typically a very adventurous eater, I have to admit that everything I've tried has been incredible. I hope I'll learn how to make a few of the dishes before I come home. Maybe that will be my next project to keep myself busy since I have no idea how long I'll be here. I'm hopeful that something will surface soon.

I hope you are well and making progress in rehab. Thanks for keeping in touch. Your emails always bring a smile to my face and make this whole ordeal seem more bearable.

Always,
Me (I have too many names to choose from ☺)

Hunter smiled as he read her closing. He slowly closed his laptop before he climbed into bed and drifted off to sleep. He knew the next week was going to be extremely busy as he and Jackson prepared for their move. He didn't know much about Portland but was looking forward to exploring a new city. He knew it was famous for being bike friendly and had endless parks, gardens, and outdoor spaces, which would help him stay active during his recovery. He'd heard their new neighborhood was famous for its wide array of unique restaurants, food trucks, and coffee shops. After living off eggs, grilled cheese, and pizza for the past few weeks, he was looking forward to sampling Portland's wide variety of culinary delights.

Chapter 42

<u>Me</u>

    I can't believe it! All those emails, and not one clue as to Kayla's whereabouts. It was like the feds were screening and redacting them. Of course, they were! I should have known from the beginning. My time and money had been wasted. I took a long drag from the spliff between my teeth and tried to think about my next move, but my mind was cloudy from the mixing and matching of pot and Dutch gin. I was finally realizing how royally I'd compounded my errors into a lethal concoction of ineptitude. I'd advanced from being a drug dealer wanted for murder to being a terrorist responsible for two separate bombings. There was no way the feds were going to give up. They probably had authorities all over Europe hunting for me. I'd been crazy to think that I'd be able to disappear into thin air by getting out of the country. Every news program and newspaper had daily headlines about the Mt. Baker and Seattle General Bombings. The articles didn't give away how much information the feds had or if there was any new information, but it appeared that they weren't going to give up easily or soon. They knew the suspect had left the country, and they'd traced me to Europe. According to news reports, no one knew if I was still in Europe or had traveled elsewhere. Regardless, I was going to have to be careful.

    I decided to visit a salon and get my hair cut and colored. I'd cut it short and dye it light brown. I had been working on growing a mustache, but so far, my attempt at facial hair was pathetic. My cheekbones were starting to look more prominent from all the drugs and lack of food. I had been forgetting to eat, and it was starting to show. I looked in the mirror and cringed. I looked gaunt and pale. My eyes were sunken into their sockets, and there were dark bags under my eyes. I ran out of breath trying to climb up to my fifth floor walk-up due to all the smoking I'd been doing and my clothes seemed to hang from my emaciated frame. It suddenly occurred to me that Amsterdam might kill me before the feds did. I decided to get myself a cup of coffee and try to put myself back together.

Chapter 43

Hunter

Dear International Woman of Mystery,

I know neither your name nor your location, but I imagine that wherever you are, you're charming your new friends and learning all sorts of interesting things about your surroundings. Today was a big day for Uncle J and I. We met with my doctors at Seattle General in order to decide the next step in my recovery. We mutually agreed it would be best to transfer my care to the nation's top rehab facility in Portland. Jackson's girlfriend, Emily, is going to let us stay in her rental house while we're there. I'm excited to begin the next stage of rehab, but nervous because I've heard the therapists there take no prisoners (and I thought the physical therapists in Seattle were demanding!). I'm scheduled to get my casts off fairly soon, which will be a welcome relief considering they're getting hot and itchy.

All-round, I'm excited about the move. The fact that Uncle J will be able to work remotely, and Emily is coming, too, eases my guilt about him putting his life on hold for me. Emily has already made a list of places we need to visit and food we need to try. I guess she's tired of me moping around my hotel room and has taken it upon herself to make sure that I get a cultural experience while I'm in Portland. She's fairly insistent that I improve my diet. According to her, pizza and grilled cheese sandwiches aren't exactly the food of champions. She's excited to introduce me to the farm-to-table restaurants and organic grocery stores in her neighborhood. Apparently, she has a degree in dietetics from Oregon State and is anxious to put it to use again. I think it will be good for me that she's taken it upon herself to become my unofficial nutritionist. Between my new rehab team and Emily monitoring my diet, I anticipate that I'll have my strength back very soon.

That's all I've got for now. I'm going to finish my reading for one of my classes and then head to bed. I'm a little embarrassed to admit that I'm usually asleep by 9:00 pm these days. Thanks for staying in touch with such an old soul.

Adios,
Hunter (boring as it is, I only have one name)

Chapter 44

Kayla

The sun slanted through her window as Kayla slowly awoke. It took a few moments for her surroundings to come into focus as she opened her eyes and glanced around her room. She ran her hands through her short hair and let her current situation sink in. "You're Karina Thibaut from Montreal," she reminded herself. "You're a journalist researching trade between Canada and Spain." She realized that she was going to have to try a little harder to sell her career to her housemates. During her stay, she'd mostly hung around the embassy and painted. She reminded herself that she was going to have to work harder in order to make it look like she had interviews and writing to do.

Fortunately, she had a reason to leave the embassy today. Agent Franklin had flown over from the States to work on tracking down Kazamir. He had requested that she come down to the precinct for an update on both Kazamir's case and the outlook on her situation. She rolled herself out of bed, hopped in her tiny shower (she was quickly realizing that bathrooms in Europe were far smaller than in America), and dressed in a pair of wide-legged flowing trousers and a fitted sweater. She threw on a delicate scarf to complete the look and then headed downstairs to the dining room where Marta brought her a café con leche (a large cup of coffee with milk) and a fresh croissant. There was a vast amount of fruit set out on the table as well, and she helped herself to an array of brightly colored berries.

David was just finishing his own café con leche and explained to her that the fruit came from La Boqueria near Las Ramblas. "You really must visit it when you have time. It's like nothing you've ever experienced. La Boqueria is an enormous food market that features specialty stalls selling fruits, vegetables, meats, cheeses, olives, seafood, chocolates, and much more. It's a feast for your senses. As you walk around, you'll be mesmerized by the intense colors and smells of the displays. The vendors pride themselves on the incredible way they present their products. It will put every grocery store you've ever been in to shame."

Kayla thanked him for the explanation as she sipped her creamy coffee and smiled. "I feel as if I'm going to be an expert on Catalonian culture and cuisine by the time my stay in Barcelona is over thanks to you, David."

David just smiled and bid her good day. He was a natural teacher and couldn't help but provide the history and the background of anything he found interesting. He was glad she appreciated his commentary.

After Kayla finished her breakfast, she walked to the door and was greeted by none other than Agent Franklin himself. She launched herself into his arms and gave him a bear hug. He barely recognized her with chic, coppery hair and tailored clothing, but the second she smiled there was no mistaking the girl he'd known and helped in Seattle. He relaxed and returned her hug. Kayla's joy at seeing him was genuine. It had been a long time since she'd seen a familiar face, and she hoped that he might have good news for her regarding Kazamir.

"What are you doing here, Frank? Isn't this a little far for you to come?" Kayla couldn't help teasing him. It felt good to be around someone who she could be at ease with again.

He gave her a nudge, "Don't forget your accent, *Karina,*" He whispered, reminding her to stay in character.

She snapped quickly back into her role of Karina Thibaut, tossed her scarf over her shoulder, and followed him out to a black sedan that was waiting for them. They climbed into the back and settled in as their driver pulled away from the curb.

"So how have you been, Frank? How's your family?"

Agent Franklin smiled at Kayla. She was always trying to switch the focus away from herself. "We're all doing well. The kids are giving us a run for our money with sports, friends, and cell phones, but they're good kids and have made us proud."

Kayla smiled. It wasn't often that she could get any information about Franklin's personal life out of him. His willingness to share even a few details was a big step.

"You still haven't told me why you came all the way over here. I know for a fact that international travel isn't your favorite activity, considering you've never left the state of Washington since I've known you."

Agent Franklin glanced up to make sure the soundproof barrier in the car was up. Then he cleared his throat uncomfortably. "It turns out that Kazamir has a contact who works at Seattle General who's been supplying him with inside knowledge on your whereabouts. We placed a wire on the phones in the hospital and monitored emails, which clued us in. We took the employee in for questioning when we'd gathered enough evidence, and she broke down and admitted to informing a nosy individual about your relationship with Hunter Erickson. We suspect the individual was working for Kazamir. We think they might have even been able to hack Hunter's email account. Fortunately, there was nothing in your emails that gave up your location and the contact gave us valuable information after she realized that she was likely being paid by someone working for a terrorist.

Kayla sat in silence, taking in every word Agent Franklin was saying. The idea that Kazamir was monitoring the emails she sent to Hunter sent chills down her spine. Not only was she in danger, but so was Hunter. She slowly let out the breath she'd been holding. "What does this all mean for me?"

"That's a good question. Kazamir's elevated himself from a drug dealer and murderer to an international terrorist with the bombings at Mt. Baker and Seattle. We're gathering a lot of evidence that links him to both places, which means that at this point, he's got a lot more to fear than you ratting him out."

Kayla nodded slowly. Her testimony about the murders she'd

witnessed should be the least of Kazamir's concerns right now. In fact, it would be ludicrous for him to risk giving himself up by coming after her at this point. Regardless of whether she was dead or alive, he was still going to go to prison for life and facing death-row as soon as the feds caught up with him.

"Why do you think he's bothering to hack my email account and paying off people in order to track me down? Kazamir's got a lot bigger things to worry about right now?" Kayla looked quizzically at Franklin.

"That's just the thing, Kayla. Kazamir got desperate and reckless. Hunter's biggest rival, Jared Klaus, turned himself in yesterday, saying that he'd hired Kazamir to take out Hunter Erickson at Mt. Baker. Apparently, Klaus couldn't live with the guilt of what happened. The bombing that injured and killed so many people was supposed to be a small-scale explosion that just injured Hunter and ruined his chance at the Olympics. Apparently, Kazamir took the job because he was desperate for cash, but didn't do his research. He used an explosive that was far more powerful than he anticipated. Instead of just injuring Erickson as he intended, he blew up a good portion of the ski village. Jared said that he saw Kazamir the night after the bombing, and Kazamir had absolutely no remorse for what happened. In fact, according to Jared, he was proud of himself. I think we are dealing with a sociopath, Kayla. He's not relying on logic and reason. He's volatile, detached, and incredibly dangerous. We think he might have snapped, and that's why he not only tried to shoot you in Seattle but bombed the hospital to try and finish the job. You and Hunter have been his biggest failures, and we're worried he might seek vengeance on you both. He's got nothing to live for at this point, and revenge may be the only thing that's keeping him going."

Kayla was silent. She had known she was in danger, but it hadn't occurred to her that Hunter was, too. "Do you think he'll go after Hunter?"

"Good question. We know that Kazamir's not going to show

his face in the US for a very long time because he knows that we'll pick him up the moment he sets foot on American soil. There's the possibility that he could hire a hitman to take out Hunter, so we've posted agents around Hunter's house, and he will be under 24-7 surveillance."

Kayla breathed a sigh of relief. She was glad to know that Hunter would be safe. "What about me? Do you think he'll be able to track me down?"

"We certainly hope not, but Kazamir has connections everywhere. We're going to do the best we can to keep you safe, and will fill you in on any information we gather about his whereabouts."

"I'm starting to worry about blowing my cover at the embassy," Kayla looked pointedly at Agent Franklin. "I'm supposed to be a journalist researching trade agreements between Canada and Spain, but so far, this is the first time I've left the embassy. Everyone has been extremely kind to me, but I'm starting to worry that they'll doubt my story unless I start acting like a journalist."

Agent Franklin looked thoughtful. "You make a good point. I think it would be okay for you to leave the embassy from time to time, but you have to be accompanied by someone at all times. I'll be staying here for a few weeks and can take you anywhere you need to go. As long as Kazamir is not aware of your location, I can't see any harm in you leaving the embassy now and then."

"Good, I'm glad to hear you say that." Kayla looked relieved. "After all, you made me come all the way to Barcelona. I believe that I deserve to see at least a few sites and get a little bit of the local flavor while I'm here."

Agent Franklin looked skeptical, but eventually, his expression softened. "Very well, I promise to escort you around the city from time to time while I'm here. It will give us a chance to discuss the case."

Kayla didn't hesitate, "Perfect. Tomorrow I want to go to La Pedrera."

Agent Franklin gave her a pointed look. "Okay, but just remember, I'm still a Federal Agent and not a tour guide. Don't expect me to give you a history lesson or anything."

"Deal," Kayla grinned, relieved that she was no longer going to be under house arrest.

Chapter 45

<u>Me</u>

<u>I</u> slammed my cell phone down on the table and shouted out a plethora of expletives. I'd just hung up on my connection who had an in at Seattle General. Apparently, the feds were onto me. Somehow, they figured out that I fled to Europe and worse still, someone in the Red Light District had ratted me out. They were aware that I was hiding out in Amsterdam. I knew I should have been more careful. I'd gotten in over my head with drugs and dealing and must have let something slip when I was higher than a kite. Living large was apparently no longer an option, even in a huge, international hub like Amsterdam. I was compromised and needed an out before they tightened the noose.

I'd recovered financially after my initial binge, but was going to have to skip town and lose all the connections I'd made dealing. I hated to leave when the money was really starting to roll in, but I didn't have a choice. I looked around my crumby apartment. It would only take me 15 minutes to pack my things, and an hour or two to track down the people that still owed me for drugs. If I hustled, I could find a car and escape before the feds got to me first.

I had a half-formed plan of where I was headed. I didn't want to risk taking a train or a plane to travel. There were too many people on the lookout for me. I also couldn't spend much time in any one place. It would be best if I stayed on the move. I needed some time to think and plan my next moves, so driving was my best bet. I decided to drive south through Belgium and France in order to get to Spain. If I could make it to Spain, then I could take a ferry over to Northern Africa. I figured that Morocco would be a good place to disappear for a while. I could dress in a djellaba and blend in. Women still wear long, loose garments and cover their hair and faces with scarves and head coverings, which would be a perfect disguise in case the feds were looking for me. I could picture myself traveling to Marrakesh and hiding out in a riad amidst the winding alleys of the Medina. I'd be able to stretch my money there and lay low for a while. Road trips weren't usually my thing, but at this point, it was my best option. Despite my circumstances, I couldn't help but feel some regret over leaving the pleasures of Amsterdam in exchange for an Islamic culture that expected women to cover everything up and shunned drinking. Coastal cities like Casablanca were more liberal, but the further inland I would go, the more conservative it would get. My seemingly carefree days of prostitutes and endless drugs had waned and were about to be squarely in my rear-view.

Chapter 46

Hunter

It didn't take long for Hunter to realize that he was going to like living in southeast Portland. There were endless restaurants and food trucks lining Division Street. Parks like Laurelhurst and Mount Tabor were only minutes away. Although the weather was rainier than he preferred, he didn't find it any worse than Seattle. The sunny, vibrant days made up for the occasional gloom. He was surprised to find that the city felt more like a park than an urban area. Lush trees and brightly colored flowers lined the surrounding streets. Many of the original craftsman homes had been renovated and boasted large front porches for people to sit outside and enjoy the fresh air. He found himself instantly relaxing amidst the gorgeous scenery and friendly people. He was grateful to his uncle for suggesting a change of location. Getting away from Seattle and the memories it held, both good and bad, helped him fight the nagging depression he'd been feeling since his accident occurred.

No one seemed to know who he was in Portland, or if they did, they didn't seem to care. It was a relief to be just another person and not have to endure people whispering about the event that killed his coached and eliminated his chance of competing in the upcoming Olympics Games. He relished the fact that he was fairly anonymous in Portland.

Hunter continued to keep up with his business classes and particularly enjoyed studying investments and trading. One of his classes required him to complete a simulation that involved investing money in the stock market. He was required to research the stocks he purchased and make trades using the basic principles he learned. It felt like a game to him, and he quickly realized that he had a talent for picking lesser-known companies with solid reputations whose stocks quickly increased in value. He also had a good sense of when to trade stocks in order to get out while the price per share was high. He would then use his earnings to invest in stocks with lower prices and watch with satisfaction as their earnings per share increased. He ended up with an A+ in the class and realized he may have found his second calling. Even after he'd completed the class, he continued to repeat the simulation in order to hone his skills. As he gained confidence, he started to invest a small amount of the money he'd saved from his competitions and promotions. His small investments quickly yielded respectable returns. His days started to go more quickly now that he was living in a real home. He dedicated the majority of his time to his therapy sessions, business degree, and investments. However, the highlight of his day was always reading the emails he received from Kayla.

    He found himself checking his inbox on a regular basis, hoping that she'd sent him a new message. Her clever words and wit always seemed to make him feel better. He could almost hear her voice and picture her dimpled grin as she made interesting observations about her surroundings. He hadn't been able to figure out exactly where she was, but it sounded like she was making the most of her situation.

    Although he knew she was safely tucked away in protective custody, he still worried about her. She had eluded the criminal mind that plagued her for many years, but it seemed the longer this game of cat and mouse went on, the more desperate Kazamir was to find her. He was no longer the elusive, calculating criminal mastermind that he once had been. He was a desperate man who made impulsive decisions and was willing to risk anything to punish the people who got in his way, which he'd proven by bombing Mt. Baker and Seattle General within days of each other. Hunter could hardly believe the crazy lengths to which Kazamir was willing to go. He clearly had lost touch with reality and no longer took calculated risks. He was a madman who would set the world around him ablaze without remorse.

    The fact that Kazamir was laying low lulled both he and Kayla into a false sense of security. Hunter was aware that Kazamir could resurface at any time which concerned him. He doubted that he would be stupid enough to show his face in the US anytime soon. He must know that as soon as the feds caught wind of him, they would lock him up for life without chance of parole.

What little was known about his whereabouts pointed to the fact that he was hiding out abroad. If there was anyone he would try to hunt down, it would be Kayla. Hunter wanted to find Kayla more than anything and protect her from the evil that threatened her peace, but it was impossible. Even though his casts had come off and he had started walking, he was still recovering from the severe injuries he sustained. Plus, there was no way he'd be able to find out where the Witness Security Program was hiding her. He knew Kayla would tell him if he asked, but he didn't want to compromise her safety in any way. After all, Kazamir likely had contacts who would attempt to intercept any information about her current location. If he truly cared about her and wanted to keep her safe, he would need to respect her privacy and remain in Portland. If he focused his energy on gaining his strength back and finishing his studies, he'd have a lot more to offer her when this whole ordeal was over.

Uncle Jackson seemed to sense Hunter's frustrated, morose mood and decided to distract his nephew. He contacted Hunter's physical therapists and got them to agree to let him take Hunter on a field trip. Instead of doing physical therapy in the sterile rooms of the clinic, Jackson planned to take his nephew out to explore one of the Willamette Valley's most beautiful sights.

"Get out of bed, Erickson!" Jackson's voice came booming into Hunter's room at the crack of dawn.

Hunter groaned and covered his eyes with his pillow, peering out at his uncle with one eye barely cracked open.

"I'm not going to stand by and watch you mope around. Life is for the living. Now get out of bed and get dressed. We've got things to do today."

Hunter groaned. The light shining through the windows when

his uncle yanked the curtains open caused him physical pain. He fought back the urge to yank the covers over his head and burrow back into bed. He knew it would be childish to ignore his uncle, but he also wasn't in any shape to interact with other humans until he'd at least had some coffee.

Uncle Jackson knew him well and thrust a steaming mug of a dark roast under his nose. The smell immediately engulfed him and helped to sharpen his senses. "Why on earth are you barging in like this, Uncle J? I don't have physical therapy for another few hours."

"I talked to your doctors and they think it's time we added a little variety to your therapy. Today we're going hiking to Multnomah Falls."

Hunter scratched his head. He'd heard of Multnomah Falls. It was a famous tourist destination just outside of Portland. A massive waterfall spilled down the mountainside, and tourists loved to hike up to a bridge where they could feel the spray from the waterfall and take pictures. It sounded like a beautiful place, but he hadn't visited it due to his injuries. From what he'd heard, it was a steep climb.

"It's time you started challenging yourself again, Hunter. You've been holed up in your room ever since we got to Portland. You need to push yourself in order to build your strength back up. Your therapists have agreed that a hike outside in the sunlight will do your muscles and your attitude some good.

Hunter gulped down his coffee during Jackson's speech, and the caffeine started to work its magic by constricting his blood vessels and increasing the blood flow to his brain. He could feel his headache letting go of its binding grip and a feeling of alertness allowed him to take control.

"Alright Uncle J. I'm in," Hunter liked the idea of getting outside and getting his mind off the danger Kayla was in. He knew his uncle was right. If he sat around in his room, he'd just continue to worry. There wasn't anything he could do to change the situation, so he might as well work on getting his strength back.

He quickly showered and dressed before meeting Jackson

downstairs. They piled into his uncle's jeep, picked up his physical therapist from the clinic, and made the 30-minute drive through the Willamette Valley until they reached the turnoff to Multnomah Falls. It was still early and only a few parking spaces were taken. They stepped out of the car, and Hunter looked around taking in the steep hike he had ahead of him. He was excited to see the falls and be outside, but the intimidating ascent made him question his decision to come along.

The initial climb up to the bridge wasn't difficult. He enjoyed hiking through the woods and emerging on a bridge with mist from the falls spraying his face. The waterfall was stunning and so high he had to crane his neck to see the very top of it. Hunter enjoyed the view and was grateful for the opportunity to explore the gorgeous area surrounding Portland. Jackson and his physical therapist led him to the other side of the bridge, and they began hiking the path up to the very top of the waterfall. It started with a steep ascent and then leveled out. He had convinced himself that he could make it, but then he noticed the switchbacks leading up the mountain. He quickly realized that the trail was steep, narrow, and winding. He could feel his muscles straining as he courageously attempted the climb.

"Remember to take it one step at a time, Hunter," Jackson coached him, recognizing the look of defeat on Hunter's face. It was a look he'd never witnessed until the bombing but had recently become a frequent expression. It troubled him that Hunter was feeling so discouraged, and he had made it his mission to help his nephew get his confidence back.

Hunter shot his uncle a look. He grimaced as he rounded yet another curve and continued to climb. His lungs ached, his muscles felt like they weren't getting enough oxygen, and he was starting to feel lightheaded. He wanted nothing more than to turn around and never attempt this ridiculous climb again. Had he been hiking with anyone other than Jackson, he would have thrown in the towel and booked it back down the trail at record speed, but he couldn't let his uncle down. He saw a look of concern cross his uncle's face, which tugged at his heart. He couldn't handle showing weakness in front of Jackson or his physical therapist. He took a deep breath and vowed to give the climb his best effort. He silently counted down the number of switchbacks they rounded and focused on breathing. He concentrated on each step and didn't let himself look over the edge of the cliff. Finally, they rounded the last curve and came out at a clearing by the river feeding the waterfall. They followed it down to a platform that allowed them to look over the edge. A feeling of accomplishment overwhelmed Hunter. He'd been so focused on all the reasons he couldn't finish the climb that he'd forgotten to think about all the reasons he *needed* to reach the top.

Standing at the peak was a huge accomplishment in his recovery. It was the first time he realized all the progress he'd made over the past few months. He realized his body was capable of more than his mind believed, and he was finally regaining the confidence he lost the minute he learned Coach Sullivan was dead. Thinking about the loss still made him feel sick to his stomach, but he also didn't want his coach to have died in vain. He knew Sully wouldn't have wanted him to spend the rest of his life moping around. If anything, he would have wanted Hunter to get out and live his life with boldness and conviction.

He felt his coach's strength and memory surrounding him as he watched the water crash down the mountain, sending its mist spraying over the valley. It was at that moment he realized he was going to be okay and had no choice but to be resilient for himself, for Jackson, and for Kayla. Although he couldn't change the past, he knew his choices and attitude going forward would profoundly affect his future. He'd spent a lot of time feeling sorry for himself recently and for the first time in months, he decided he couldn't let the terrorism that killed his coach and so many innocent people him stop him from protecting the people he cared about.

Chapter 47

Kayla

Exploring Barcelona gave Kayla a true love for the city. She convinced Agent Franklin to take her everywhere she had read about. He was reluctant at first, but she slowly started to wear him down with her optimism and willingness to discuss her knowledge of Kazamir. Franklin had spent the better part of the past decade working with the Federal Government to hunt down Kazamir, and he wasn't about to allow him to harm Kayla and continue to elude justice. As long as he was with her, he knew she was safe, so he finally gave in and took her to the places she requested. He generally disliked traveling but had to admit that Barcelona was an extremely intriguing city. Each place they visited made him appreciate the culture and the history of Catalonia more and more.

First, Kayla demanded that they visit many of the buildings and structures designed by Antoni Gaudi, an architect who lived in the 19th and 20th centuries and designed many of Barcelona's most iconic buildings. One of his favorites was La Pedrera, an apartment building that looked more like a sculpture than a residential building. The rooftop in particular impressed Kayla. Gaudi had designed the roof with smoke stacks that resembled monsters. As they climbed between the tiers, admiring the sculptures, they passed under archways decorated in mosaic tiles which provided a stunning view of Barcelona's colorful rooftops. The most impressive view was of the Sagrada Familia cathedral in the distance. Kayla could almost imagine that she was on an exotic vacation as she watched the sunlight glinting off the streets of the city with the mountains in the background and the shimmering Mediterranean nearby. As she gazed out at the Barcelona rooftops, she reflected back over the past few years of her life.

She would have never imagined that her charmed Chicago life

would be dramatically changed the night she witnessed the murders. Uprooting herself and relocating to Seattle caused her a great deal of stress. Initially, she convinced herself she would return to her life in Chicago as soon as Kazamir was apprehended, but that hadn't happened. Instead, she had been uprooted again and shipped off to a foreign country. Her future seemed so uncertain, yet as she gazed out at the Barcelona skyline, she felt at peace with her destiny for the first time since the whole ordeal began. She hoped Kazamir was far away and would never come after her again. Certainly, he would lay low now that he had escaped the United States. She could almost imagine him becoming an expat in a place like Bali where he'd use the money he'd accumulated from his life of crime to lay around sipping cocktails and relaxing on beautiful beaches.

    She shook her head and snapped out of her daydream when Agent Franklin tapped her shoulder. "It's getting late. We should probably get you back to the embassy." Kayla nodded and gave him a sad smile. For just a moment, she believed that Kazamir was out of her life for good, and it felt wonderful. Yet even her eternal optimism wasn't enough to convince her that Kazamir would leave her alone. He was a sociopath without remorse. She had witnessed his biggest defeat, and he wasn't the type of person who could let things go. She took one last look at the ornate terraces and sculptures gracing the rooftop of La Pedrera before following Agent Franklin back into the building. They wound their way through the wooden arches that made up the top floor of the building before returning to the ground floor. They exited the building through the gift shop and slipped into a black car with tinted windows that was waiting to pick them up. Kayla took a mental picture of the unique architecture of the building as they drove away, and smiled at Agent Franklin.

    "Thanks for following through on your promise, Frank." She gave him a gentle nudge on the shoulder. "I'm impressed you kept your word and let me venture out into the world for a few hours."

    "A deal's a deal," he replied. "Besides, my kids would be

angry with me if I traveled all this way and didn't take the time to at least visit a few of the places their mother's been teaching them about."

"Can we be honest for a minute?" Kayla looked carefully at Agent Franklin.

"You know that I'm always as honest with you as I can be," he replied, truthfully.

"Do you think I'll get to stay here for a while or am I going to be uprooted again and shipped off to another location? Up until now, you've placed me in some intriguing cities. I worry that you'll hide me out on a sheep farm in the mountains somewhere next time."

Agent Franklin smiled at her. "We hope to have Kazamir in custody soon, so you'll be able to go back to your old life in Chicago."

It was an interesting thought. Kayla gave him a small smile. She tried to picture herself going back home and resuming the life she'd lead before this whole mess started. It was hard to imagine carrying on as if nothing had happened and Seattle and Barcelona had only been a dream. An image of Hunter flashed through her mind. She couldn't shake the thought that without all of this craziness, she would never have met him. If she went back to Chicago and acted as if nothing had happened, she'd be acting as if Hunter didn't exist. In that instant, she fully understood exactly how much he meant to her, and how much each email he sent brightened her day. Even if Kazamir went to prison for the rest of his life, she wouldn't go on with her life as if the whole thing never happened. She didn't want to forget what she'd been through because she was a stronger person for it. Most of all, she didn't want to forget Hunter.

Chapter 48

Me

 Driving through Belgium wasn't exactly inspiring. The cramped, European car has a persistent rattle of which I can't identify the origin. To make matters worse, it smells faintly of what I perceive to be cheese. Worse still, I'm alone with only my thoughts, which I truly loath. I have yet to see any good result from self-reflection and introspection. I am the logical sum of my actions and dwelling on possibilities lost seems wasteful, which makes it all the more unbearable that my subconscious seems determined to second guess every choice I'd made since Mt. Baker. This road trip has been painful. Low country, indeed.

 I had to stay focused on my route and this ridiculous car had no GPS, so I was stuck transposing what I could from a map written in French to the roadway before me. I constantly made wrong turns and spent the majority of my time frustratedly cursing out the other drivers. Thus far, Belgium's only redeeming quality was the waffles bought from a street vendor. They came wrapped in paper and covered in powdered sugar. The waffles melted in my mouth as I bit into the warm, soft dough. The powdered sugar taunted me as I bitterly wished it were a different white powder... I began to loath the vendor for that failing. I hate this country.

 Despite my issues with navigation, I made my way through the Netherlands and Belgium in a reasonable amount of time. I was grateful the Low Countries weren't very big and took only a few hours to drive through. Had I been driving in the States, I may not have even crossed through one state in a similar time period, but thanks to the fact that European countries are small, I was a few hours into France before nightfall. I found a tiny hole-in-the-wall hostel and paid cash for a room. It was shabby and didn't even have a TV. I wore my hat low over my eyes hoping no one would blow my cover. I didn't sleep well and woke up early the next morning. I downed a few shots of espresso, which only exacerbated my already skyrocketing anxiety, jumped back into my roller skate of a car, and began my journey across France. Where I a tourist, I might have enjoyed the countryside, but in reality, I couldn't stop checking my rearview mirror hoping the cars behind me weren't feds or Interpol. I forced the nagging image of federal prison from my mind and kept driving. The day stretched on painfully as minutes seemed like hours and hours crept by as stagnant as water on the verge of freezing.

    Finally, I could see the Spanish border and I smiled, knowing I was only a few hours away from my final destination in Europe and freedom from this suffocating vehicle. I breathed a sigh of relief upon noting the change in road signs from French to Spanish as a smile crept across my face. I knew they were on my trail, but I'd managed to keep them at bay thus far. That smile was short-lived when I realized I had resumed checking my mirror for the agents I knew were back there somewhere. My pulse raced and my hands slipped from the wheel a few times from the flop-sweat. Despite being within a few hours, my body began to fail, and I could drive no further. I found a place to stay and immediately washed down a few lorazepam with a bottle of Crianza Tempranillo from a corner market. I reaffirmed a well-known truth that mixing sedatives and alcohol is a bad idea when I woke up around 1:00 PM the following day in a puddle of drool with only a foggy recollection of events after last night's arrival. I cursed as I rolled out of bed and staggered into the communal shower. At least it was late enough that no one else in the hostel was around. My carelessness put me behind schedule again which cut in to any lead I had on the imbeciles at my back. I couldn't afford another mistake like this with the noose tightening every day.

    I pulled on my well-worn clothes from yesterday, ran my hands through my quickly graying hair, and allowed myself a quick bump of coke to jolt my brain awake before I jumped back into that infernal roller skate. I unfurled the new Spanish map I'd purchased along with the wine and made my way through Catalonia toward Barcelona. The weather became significantly warmer as I approached the Mediterranean. I wasn't sure if it was the hangover lifting or the improved climate, but I began to relax slightly as the kilometers clicked off the odometer. When I finally arrived in Barcelona, I checked the ferry schedule. To my disgust, I realized that the next available ferry to Morocco didn't depart for three days. I would have to spend more time in Spain before I could escape to Africa. I knew I could get there faster if I flew, but I didn't want to risk going through security at the airport. With nothing on my hands but time, I decided to make the most of the situation.

 A friend of mine had once mentioned Las Ramblas was a great place to pick-pocket because tourists were too engrossed in the colorful displays to pay attention to their belongings. I usually didn't reduce myself to such antics and worried I would only bring attention to myself, but was running low on cash and figured that swiping a few wallets and handbags would at least provide me with some funds to keep me on my feet until I found a new cash flow in Morocco.

 I found a shady hostel that accepted cash and didn't require any form of identification. It offered a private room, so I took it immediately. The young lady that walked me to my room had more piercings than any one person should and looked as though she was strung out on something. Were I set up here permanently, I could sense she'd be my first customer. She fought with the key in the lock for a while and finally threw open the door to my room. To say that I was unimpressed is an understatement. The room reeked of urine and stale beer. Cigarette burns dotted every square inch of furniture. The twin bed sank down in the middle. Its legs were broken on one side and a stack of faded books propped it up. The floor was filthy and covered in what appeared to be rat feces. I looked at her in disbelief, but she just shrugged. I realized that at this point, my options were limited, and I'd better just keep my mouth shut and take the room. The last thing I wanted to do was make a scene and draw attention to myself in a place that appeared to be the definition of "off the beaten path."

I quickly took the key from her and locked myself in the room, grateful for a place to drop my things, but curious where I could do so without contaminating the last of my meager belongings. I made a few phone calls for any intel on whether the feds had been able to track me to Spain. My contact said he couldn't be sure, but he thought that they were still sniffing around Amsterdam. I breathed a sigh of relief and decided not to waste any more time in the squalor of my hostel room. I changed my clothes and headed out into the waning sunlight of Barcelona. The city was alive with activity. Couples strolled hand and hand down the sidewalk, friends sat chatting at café tables sharing tapas and wine, and everywhere I looked, people were smiling. It made my stomach churn to the point of nausea. Beyond the surface of contrived moments in time portrayed in cravenly planned selfies, I knew these phonies for the miserable people they really were. Needy, self-indulgent losers desperate to fill the voids in their lives by seeking a pathetic hit of dopamine in every "like" and "share" as they plunged themselves in debt to "find themselves" and be perceived as interesting. I hope they get dysentery from their pathetic little finger food and save the rest of us from having to witness their pathetic spectacle.

I decided to treat my sudden nausea with liquor, ducked into a dive bar, and ordered a double of whiskey. My Spanish is terrible and my Catalan is nonexistent, but the bartender got the point and gave me a generous pour. I threw back the glass of whisky, letting it burn a trail down my throat and making my eyes water. I dropped cash on the counter and headed back outside. My stomach growled fiercely so I grabbed some fried dough smothered in cinnamon and sugar from a stand. They called it a Churro, but I didn't care what it was called. I ate it in a few bites and evaluated my surroundings.

My hostel was located on a side street right off Las Ramblas. My friend hadn't let me down. The street was absolutely swarming with vendors and tourists strolling around, taking in the architecture, completely oblivious to their surroundings. I laughed to myself. This was just too easy. I started slowly. I followed a couple and watched as they stopped to browse at a jewelry booth. I picked up my pace and walked past them, reaching into the guy's pocket and quickly grabbing his wallet. He didn't move an inch. He was too engrossed in buying his girlfriend the perfect earrings to realize that I'd just lifted his wallet with his credit cards and all of his cash.

Chapter 49

<u>Hunter</u>

    Hunter rolled over in bed and groaned. His whole body ached. Muscles hurt that he didn't even know existed. He grunted as he tried to lift his arm up to rub his eyes. Climbing Multnomah Falls had been the ultimate challenge for his healing body. He was glad he'd done it and the sense of accomplishment he'd gained from it built his confidence, but today he was paying for it. He reached into his nightstand and fumbled around until he found some naproxen. He quickly swallowed a tablet and took a gulp of water. He didn't like taking medication for pain, but today was going to have to be an exception. He had to fight through his frustration when he remembered that he used to spend eight hours a day doing much more rigorous workouts and always bounced back the next day without any pain.
    He pushed the thought out of his mind. That was then. That was when Coach Sully was alive, and he was in peak physical condition. That was all before the bombing shattered the life he worked so hard to build. He felt a dark cloud descending but forced his mind to snap out of it. Dwelling on the past was useless. It wouldn't change anything. If he really wanted to get his life back, he was going to have to focus on today and think positively. He pulled out his laptop and looked at his schedule for the day. He had a physical therapy session in the afternoon, but his morning was clear. He had taken a few of his finals the week before, so his class schedule was relatively light. He decided it was time to send Kayla a message.
    Good Morning, Sunshine,

> *I'm sitting here in bed and finding it difficult to move. Uncle Jackson dragged me out on a hike yesterday. I had to climb up to the top of a massive waterfall. It was beautiful,*

but I'm paying for it today. My muscles feel like they're on fire, and it hurts to move. I decided to pass the time by writing a note to my favorite person. I hope you're safe. I worry about you, after all. I can't imagine what that crazy man is up to, but I sure hope he's keeping his distance. I imagine it must be terrifying to wonder where he's at and what he knows, but I know you are strong and well-equipped to handle this situation. Of course, it doesn't stop me from being concerned, but at least I know you can fend for yourself (unlike me who got whipped on a hiking trip yesterday).

Regardless, I was thinking that someday this whole thing is going to be over, and you're going to be able to get out of protective custody. That must make you happy! You'll be able to go back to your old life and your old friends. Of course, there is a selfish part of me who wishes you'd consider staying in the Pacific Northwest. I know that's a lot to ask and feel a little ridiculous even mentioning it, but if I've learned one thing from my parents' and Coach Sully's deaths, it's that you have to tell people what you're feeling because you never know when you'll get another chance.

Kayla, you're the only girl who's ever meant more to me than skiing (which is a little embarrassing to admit), but my point is that I've never met anyone like you. Now that I know you, I can't imagine going through my life without you. I'm telling you this because it's how I feel. I don't expect that you're going to make any promises, but I needed to say it. I know your life has been transient for many years. People have come and gone, and you've never been able to get attached because you always knew you might have to leave, but I want you to know that I'm not transient. I'm not just going to let you leave and forget about you. I'm in it for the long haul. I'll settle for emails until I can be with you in person again, no matter how long it takes. You mean the world to me. I'm thankful every day that you walked into my hospital room. Of course, if you decide to go back to your old life and forget about me when this is all over, I'll understand. It will make me sad, but I won't hold any grudges. I just don't want to go through my life knowing I didn't tell you how I truly felt. You're the most amazing person I've ever met. You're stronger than anyone I know, more beautiful than any women I've ever met, inside and out, and you light up every room you enter. You've given me the courage to get through my injuries and made me feel like a much better person than I actually am. My life is better because I met you, and I'll forever be grateful that our paths crossed.

Okay, I'm sorry if I made things weird, but I just had to write this. You're my world, Kayla, and I hope that you won't forget me when you get your freedom back.

Take care of yourself and be brave.

Always,
~Hunter

Chapter 50

Kayla

Kayla closed her laptop with tears streaming down her face. She couldn't believe what she'd just read. Hunter Erickson, *THE Hunter Erickson*, just wrote the most touching message she'd ever read. He was an amazing man, and she was in a state of disbelief that the email he'd written had been directed to her. Perhaps he'd meant to send it to someone else. She shook her head. It was a sincere email, and it was meant for *her*. She wished she could jump on the first plane out of Barcelona and surprise him, but she knew that was impossible. Agent Franklin was counting on her. As long as Kazamir was at large, freedom would continue to elude her. She'd made a commitment and needed to stick it out. She had to keep up the rouse of Karina Thibaut as long as necessary until Kazamir was apprehended. She just needed to think harder and remember more in order to give the feds the information they needed to bring him in. The sooner he was arrested, the sooner she'd get her freedom back.

She decided to give Agent Franklin a call.

"Good Morning, Frank," She said in a singsong voice.

"Kayla? To what do I owe this pleasure?"

"I'd like to do some shopping this afternoon. How would you feel about accompanying me to La Boqueria near Las Ramblas? I've been thinking a lot and might have remembered a few details about Kazamir that I hadn't thought to mention before."

"Kayla, can you tell me them over the phone?" Franklin was suddenly intrigued.

"Nope, I'll need to get out of the embassy to talk," Kayla responded with a smile. She was going to use every opportunity she could to get out and experience Barcelona while she was here.

"Alright, I'll pick you up at 1:00 PM. We'll only have an hour.

Is that enough time?"

"That's perfect," Kayla smiled. Any chance she had to escape the compound was a welcome reprieve.

"Okay, but Las Ramblas is a public area crowded with people. You have to promise me that you'll wear a large hat and sunglasses in order to disguise yourself."

She agreed, and Agent Franklin arrived at 1:00 PM sharp as promised. He jumped out as soon as the car stopped and jogged up to the front of the embassy. Kayla was waiting for him. He escorted her to the car and gave the driver directions to go to La Bouqueria. Kayla was thrilled. She had made a list of things she hoped to buy. As soon as she pulled her door shut, Agent Franklin turned to her.

"You mentioned that you remembered some details about Kazamir. What sort of details?" He asked her, eager to learn anything that might help track his nemesis down. He was getting tired of being away from his family and wanted to get this case wrapped up soon so he could go home.

"Well," Kayla chewed on her lower lip. "I remember something from the first night I saw him. I overheard a conversation he was having on the phone right before everything blew up in his face. He said "Salaam wa Aleikoum" into his cell phone. I couldn't tell what he was saying, but since I've been in Barcelona, I've heard the phrase a few times. I asked one of the people at the embassy what it meant, and they told me that it was the Moroccan way of saying hello. It seemed odd at the time that he was speaking another language. He must have been talking to someone from Morocco. It didn't seem important until I realized that Kazamir is on the run. I wonder if he might consider going to Morocco where he has a contact and can fly under the radar until things settle down."

Franklin looked at her, deep in thought. "Thanks for the lead. I don't know if it will get us very far, but it's certainly a possibility. We recently tracked him to Amsterdam, but all of our leads have turned into dead ends. It looks like he might have known someone on the inside and realized we were onto him. The ratty apartment he was renting was empty and scrubbed free of prints, and the people who bought drugs from him haven't seen him for a few days. We know he can't get back into the US, and I'm sure he won't stay in Europe. Morocco seems like a real possibility."

Just as Franklin finished his sentence, the driver pulled up to La Bouqueria. The huge market was full of colors and energy. Tourists milled about and vendors busily arranged an amazing variety of meats, cheeses, produce, and olives into enticing displays. Kayla eagerly jumped out of the sedan but slowed down when Franklin put his hand on her arm. "Stay close to me. There are a million pickpockets around here. Keep your hands on your purse, and pay attention to what's going on around you."

Kayla nodded her head. It was hard to concentrate on anything with the sights and sounds that greeted her as they entered the market. She stopped first at a display of olives. She'd never seen such a huge variety. There were all sorts of different colors, sizes, and shapes displayed in huge dishes. The vendor offered her a sample when she saw Kayla's interest. Kayla couldn't resist trying the big, black, fleshy olive she was offered. The vendor explained that the olives were Aceituna de Aragón, an especially green variety that turned black because they were left on the vines longer to ripen. They were popular to eat as appetizers or mixed into salads in the Catalonia region. Kayla let the flavor absorb onto her tongue, enjoying the salty flavor. She thanked the vendor for her time and then moved on to the next stand. Franklin followed her, but seemed uneasy and distracted by all the noise and people crowding around.

Kayla ignored his discomfort and made her way over to a stand selling fresh fruit juice. She ordered a delicious-looking strawberry juice in Spanish and paid. She was grateful that the little Spanish she knew was enough to understand how to order and pay for things. She sipped on the strawberry juice as she walked by a meat stand featuring its Jamón Ibérico. She had read it was popular in Portugal and Spain. It was a specialty type of cured ham from Black Iberian Pigs, which roamed freely and grazed on acorns. She tried a bite and immediately understood why it was so popular. Even Agent Franklin couldn't resist and eagerly ate the small piece the vendor offered him. Kayla smiled; she was certain he was having a good time in spite of himself.

Just as Kayla was about to purchase some Jamón Ibérico to take back to the embassy as a thank you for everyone's kindness, Franklin's cell phone started buzzing. He recognized the number and quickly explained it was a call he had to take. La Bouqueria was noisy, so he motioned that he'd be stepping out for just a few seconds. Kayla nodded and finished making her purchase. She was thankful she was finally experiencing Barcelona and was determined to make the most of her brief reprieve from the embassy.

Kayla carefully tucked her cured ham under her arm and turned around to take in the other stalls around her. The vast array of spices at the next stand mesmerized her. Hanging strands of dried peppers and garlic decorated the stall and huge bowls containing saffron, cumin, cinnamon, and turmeric sent an amazing scent wafting in her direction. As Kayla walked toward the stall, she felt a tug on her purse and reflexively tightened her grip. She spun around in time to see a man quickly dodge out of the way, and realized he was trying to snatch her purse. She was about to scream when their eyes locked for a moment. Kayla's heart stopped. The beady eyes staring back at her were penetrating and flashed pure evil. She felt her skin go cold when she realized this was not the first time she'd looked into those eyes. The eyes she was staring at were the eyes of a sociopathic killer.

After her initial shock, her body seemed to take over and go into survival mode. She clutched her purse and immediately ducked out of sight behind a stall selling an assortment of chocolate and candy. Her heart was pounding, and her skin felt clammy. She wondered if he'd recognized her and was grateful when she remembered she was wearing a stylish, black floppy hat over her sleek red hair and fashionable sunglasses that covered half her face. His devious eyes appeared lifeless and empty, so there was no way to be sure he hadn't recognized her but knew she looked nothing like the girl he'd seen in Chicago or the painter she'd been in Seattle. She peaked around a stack of truffles to see if he was still in the area. She scanned the endless faces in the market and honed in on him. He had his back to her and seemed to be searching the crowd.

    She needed to find Agent Franklin, but he'd be looking for her at the cured meat stall, and she couldn't risk returning if Kazamir had recognized her. She slowly inched to the next stall, trying to keep Kazamir in view, but keeping herself out of sight. She knew she should run, but seeing the man who had forced her to give up her life and everything she knew, not once, but twice, helped her to push her fear aside. She worked her way past the chocolate stall and crossed the aisle using baskets piled high with fruit to keep out of site. She was getting closer to Kazamir and could make out his clothing. He was wearing a generic t-shirt and blue jeans. Her eyes locked on his back pocket. There was a brochure, which seemed out of place because she knew he wasn't a tourist. She couldn't help herself and worked her way closer. He kept his back to her, and she ducked behind strands of dried peppers until she was close enough to make out the letters on the brochure. The words she could make out were "Barcelona Tangier Ferry". Suddenly it dawned on her; it was a ferry schedule. Kazamir must be looking to make some quick cash before he caught the next ferry to Tangier, Morocco. Just as everything started to make sense, he swung around, and she deftly ducked down under a display of nuts. From where she was hiding, she could just make out Kazamir swiping a wallet from the pocket of a man making a purchase. Before she had time to react, he disappeared. She lunged from her cover and took a step to follow him. Just as she was about to break into a full sprint, she felt a hand grip her arm firmly. She jumped at first before realizing it was Agent Franklin. He took one look at her wide, anxious eyes, and hustled her to a quiet corner.

    All she could manage to say in a breathless tone was, "Kazamir!" There were so many things spinning through her mind and so much she wanted to convey to Agent Franklin in the span of seconds. She didn't want Kazamir to get away and wanted to follow him, but she had to explain everything to Frank. There simply wasn't time.

Franklin looked confused. "Kazamir? Did you hear from him? What is this about?"

"He's here! He's at the market. I *saw* him. He tried to steal my purse, and I looked into his unmistakable eyes."

"Are you sure? Kayla, you haven't seen him in years, and he's totally changed his look since then. *Why* would someone like Kazamir be pick-pocketing here? He's a sociopath and a terrorist, not a petty thief."

"I'm absolutely sure, Frank. I don't want him to get away!" She tried to pull away.

"Hold on! You can't follow him, Kayla. If he knows that we know he's here, he'll run away, and we may never find him. Just hang on. Tell me everything you know, and we'll call in back-up."

Kayla took a breath knowing he was right. Trailing Kazamir would be dangerous for her. If he was aware the feds knew his location, he would disappear without a trace, just like he had so many other times. She took a deep breath and nodded. "Alright, but I need your help. He had a copy of the Barcelona/Tangier Ferry Schedule. I think he's heading to Morocco. We need to act quickly, or he'll disappear into Africa never to be heard from again."

Agent Franklin looked pensive. "Ironically, I just got a call from the central office. They had a witness report that Kazamir was spotted in Belgium and again near the border of France and Spain. According to reports, he was heading south through Spain, so the fact that you saw him makes a lot of sense. Let me make contact with the home office and call in back-up."

Kayla hated to leave when they were so close to the man who destroyed the life she had known and forced her into hiding, but she knew she had no choice. She allowed Agent Franklin to lead her to the black sedan that was waiting. They sat in silence on the drive back to the embassy. When they finally arrived, Franklin promised to call her as soon as there was more news. She thanked him and got out of the sedan, clutching her cured meat as if it were her lifeline, and made her way back into the embassy.

The diplomats who were lounging in the living area cheered when she entered carrying the Jamón Ibérico. She gave them a half-hearted grin and presented it to Marta. "It's my small way of saying thank you for being so kind," she said in her best French-Canadian accent. Then she politely excused herself and went upstairs, feeling like a prisoner in a very luxurious jail. If she left the premises, she would no longer be under WITSEC protection. She frowned pensively, then pulled out her computer and looked up the Barcelona/Tangier ferry schedule. She felt a surge of panic when she realized the ferry only left every few days and took nearly 32 hours to cross the Mediterranean Sea. According to the website, the most recent ferry had just left. If Kazamir was on it, there was no way they could reach him until after he landed in Tangier. She was sure that if he made it to Morocco, he would disappear forever in its vast expanses of winding alleyways and endless deserts.

She picked up her phone and called Agent Franklin right away. "Frank, he's probably already on the ferry! It's too late. The ferry just left!" she blurted out before Franklin could get a word in edgewise.

"I know that, Kayla. We're working on it. If he is on the ferry, there's nowhere he can go. We can arrest him when the boat docks in Tangier."

This made Kayla feel a little better.

"Kayla, we've got this. Just relax and try not to worry. We're doing everything in our power to bring him in, but things like this take time."

Kayla thanked him for his time and hung up. She didn't feel any better than she had before she'd called him. The only thing that could possibly make her feel better right now was Hunter. She thought about emailing him before remembering that he'd given her his cell phone number while he was in the hospital. She knew it went against her WITSEC contract to make phone calls without permission, but she was desperate, and WITSEC wasn't doing her much good. Under their watch, Kazamir had hunted her down in Seattle and now he'd spotted her in Barcelona. She dialed Hunter's number and held her breath when the phone started to ring.

"Hello," said a gruff voice on the other end of the line. Although it was afternoon for her, it was early morning for Hunter. He was not a morning person.

Kayla could tell she woke him up, so she kept her voice calm. "Hi Hunter, this is Kayla."

She gave him a moment to let it sink in. "Kayla? Kayla!" He was suddenly wide-awake and sitting bolt upright in bed.

"I know I'm not supposed to make any phone calls without permission, but I don't know who else to talk to right now." Her voice shook slightly as she spoke.

Hunter was alert and focused. "Kayla, start from the beginning and let me know how I can help."

Kayla took a deep breath and forced herself to speak slowly and clearly. "I'm in Barcelona. I know I shouldn't tell you, but I ran into Kazamir today, and I know he saw me. He didn't seem to piece it together right away, but he's going to figure it out. I'm pretty sure he's on a ferry to Tangier right now, so he'll be stuck on a boat for at least the next 30 hours and won't be able to come after me." She tried to keep herself on topic. "Like I said, I ran into him today. He tried to snatch my purse. When I caught his eye, I knew exactly who he was. A federal agent was with me at the time, but he stepped away for a second to take a phone call. Now that the feds know he saw me, I'm afraid they're going to move me again, and I just don't know if I can handle it. I don't want to stay in hiding for the rest of my life, and I'm afraid I'll have to if he makes it to Morocco. It will be easier for him to fly under the radar there, and the feds will never catch up to him. If he's never apprehended, I'll never get my freedom back."

It took Hunter a moment to process everything she was saying. "I'm so sorry, Kayla. I can't imagine how awful this whole ordeal has been for you. What can I do to help you?"

Kayla bit her lower lip in concentration. "I've got an idea. It's probably a crazy one, but I think it just might work." For the first time during the phone conversation, Hunter could actually hear hope and strength in her voice.

Chapter 51

<u>Me</u>

My pick-pocketing stint was demeaning. It occurred to me that I had been working my way down in the criminal world, but Las Ramblas was good to me. It's not that I couldn't do it or had no talent, I just wished I didn't have to return to what sustained me in my teens. Still, I had enough cash to bolster me until I got settled in Morocco. Most of the tourists I ripped off were idiots. They'd been so absorbed by the sights and sounds around them that they had no idea that I'd hit them until I was out of sight and on to my next victim. Now I'm safely onboard the ferry on my way to Tangier. I feel confident I'll be able to disappear into the crowds and alleys of the Medina, the old city center, for as long as I want until I decide to head to Marrakesh.

I picked up a caftan and hijab in Barcelona to use as a disguise when we arrive. No one seemed to pay me any heed as I sat at the onboard bar watching the rhythmic waves of the sea. I was feeling much more at ease than I had since leaving Amsterdam so abruptly.

I ordered the cheapest scotch available. Even though I had plenty of cash, I didn't want to blow it all at once. Also, I knew I couldn't get drunk and reek of alcohol when I got off the boat. No one would believe I was conservative enough to wear a hijab and caftan, yet also imbibe. Although I began to relax, something nagged at the back of my mind like a paper cut. I couldn't put my finger on it at first, but then mid-sip, the events melded in my mind. There had been one person who saw me when I tried to snatch her purse, and her face was burned into my retinas. The woman was purchasing an expensive cured meat at the Boqueria. She'd tightened her grip on her purse just as I tried to grab it. She looked directly at me. She must have known that I was attempting to rob her. Instead of yelling for the police, she just disappeared. I

Out of the Shadows

couldn't understand it. No one who was almost robbed would let the thief get away without consequence. Why didn't she say anything? Maybe she was a thief herself. It takes one to know one, after all. No, that couldn't be. She was dressed far too well to be a common thief. She was educated, too. I heard it in her voice. She spoke like someone who had an expensive education. Besides, she wouldn't be buying such an expensive piece of meat if she didn't have the money for it. If she was a thief, she would have just stolen it.

I sat sipping my scotch and replaying the events in my head. Her face had seemed vaguely familiar, but I didn't know anyone in Barcelona. All at once, the epiphany struck. She wasn't from Barcelona and that French Canadian accent faded in and out because it was *fake*. I pictured the face again, focusing on her eyes. I slammed my drink down. It was *Kayla*! She might have been wearing colored contacts and a lot of makeup, but I was sure it was her. Rage bubbled within me, and it was all I could do to not break the glass in my hands. She continued to haunt me, even across the ocean. I had managed to keep my pursuers behind me, but she surely recognized me and had told the feds that I was in Barcelona by now.

She had stolen my biggest score and the life I had earned. She put law enforcement on my trail for years. She stole my future and consumed my present. I just can't be rid of her. I quickly ordered another round of scotch and slammed it.

"Perfect, this is just perfect," I muttered to myself. What are the chances that Kayla, my nemesis, would spot me? I was hours from sneaking away undetected, but I had to reach for her purse. This is just unbelievably dumb luck. I shook my head and ordered another round, reasoning I had several hours for the booze to wear off. The alcohol was starting to work its magic. I could feel my brain quieting. I needed to focus and make a plan. I had no idea if the feds were swarming Barcelona in pursuit of me or if they had been tipped off that I was traveling to Morocco. Either way, I was going to have to be very careful. They were going to be sniffing around everywhere. My margin for error had depleted completely so my plan had to be perfect in thought and execution.

After much back and forth in my head, I congratulated myself because traveling to Tangier was a good strategy. I'd done a little research after all. Because of its location, Tangier had a long history of espionage and attracted a wide variety of criminals and international spies who had used it as a safe house. In addition, trains ran out of Tangier to Casablanca, Marrakesh, Fes, and several other cities, which offered an easy escape route.

There were downsides to traveling to Tangier as well. The most obvious being the language barrier. Other than casual greetings, I don't speak much Arabic and know minimal French. As a result, doing business was going to be tricky. I would have to rely on tourists or expats who spoke English or employ someone who could work as an intermediary for me. My contact in Marrakesh would be perfect. He knew the language and the customs. Given our history, becoming business partners would come naturally. I just hoped that the feds wouldn't be swarming the dock when we pulled into the Port of Tangier Ville.

I pulled out the Moroccan guidebook that I'd picked up in Barcelona. It was hard to find one written in English, but I'd managed to slip the store owner extra cash, and he'd produced what I needed within an hour. According to the guidebook, the ferry terminal where we would disembark was located at the entry of the Strait of Gibralter in the western most part of Tangier, between the bays of Cap Spartel and Cap Malabata. This was important information for me because if the feds had located me, I wouldn't have time to waste. They'd be sure to have eyes everywhere within several blocks of the terminal. They don't know exactly what I look like because I've drastically changed my appearance from my Chicago days, and I was wearing a ski mask in the footage they'd found of me at Mt. Baker. They'd only have Kayla's description to go off of. Degrading as it was, my plan was to dress in my caftan and hijab, which were traditional Moroccan women's garments that covered everything but the eyes. As long as I kept my hijab on and wore the cheap knock-off sunglasses I'd swiped from an ignorant vendor on Las Ramblas, I should be able to move undetected for a short period of time.

After another scotch and a thorough review of the guidebook, it looked like my best bet would be to disembark from the ferry, and go immediately to the train terminal. From there I could take the fast train to Marrakesh. I'd deal with Kayla after I felt confident I'd thrown everyone off my scent and things calmed. The faster I met my contact, the better. I needed sanctuary and didn't want to be wandering around the streets where I didn't speak the language branded as an outsider. It was imperative that I blended in because any attention drawn to myself increased my odds of being recognized, captured and incarcerated.

Thanks to Mt. Baker and Seattle, I'd be lucky if I didn't end up on death row. I shivered at the thought before forcing it into the background. I wished I could light up a joint, but knew that would get me kicked off the ferry in a heartbeat, so I settled for another scotch and staggered a bit on my way to a chair to sleep, hoping the next several hours would go by faster.

Chapter 52

<u>Hunter</u>

Hunter hung up the phone in a daze. He shook his head to make sure he hadn't been dreaming. The last thing he'd expected was a call from Kayla. The relief he felt from finally hearing her voice was quickly replaced by fear when he realized she was in danger. If Kazamir knew where she was, she'd have to keep moving with the WITSEC program. At this rate, he'd never get to see her again. Kazamir had ruined his life once by taking away his dreams and killing his coach, and he was about to ruin his life again by taking Kayla away from him. He was determined not to let that happen.

During their brief conversation, he and Kayla had devised a plan. The hard part was going to be convincing Uncle Jackson to go along with it. He knew he had his work cut out for him.

"No. No, no, no, no, *no*. Absolutely not," Uncle J was pacing back and forth shaking his head.

"I don't have a choice. She's in danger and doesn't have anyone else she can trust," Hunter countered back.

"This is ridiculous, Hunter! You just got your casts off and are finally walking again. You're not ready for a transatlantic flight. I don't care *how* much you love her. It's just not worth it." Jackson sounded exasperated.

"Look, I know it sounds crazy, but I promise I'll be careful. We'll have the protection of the feds, and I know my limits. I won't try anything crazy."

Uncle J started rubbing his temples. "Why *you*? You've already been through so much. Why do you want to put yourself in danger?"

"I lost my parents, my coach, and my career to terrorism. Now I'm about to lose the only girl I've ever loved to a terrorist. If I don't do something proactive to stop it this time, I won't be able to live with myself."

Hunter's argument seemed to hit home with Jackson. "I'll only agree if you call me every day and promise not to put yourself in unnecessary danger. You also have to keep up your PT exercises while you're gone."

Hunter breathed a sigh of relief. He'd known Uncle J would come around eventually. "Yes, absolutely. Thank you!"

"I suppose we'll need to buy you a plane ticket," Jackson said unenthusiastically.

"Yes, I need to leave on the first flight out. I'll start packing my bags. Will you drop me off at the airport?"

Jackson shrugged. "Do I have a choice?"

Hunter gave him a sideways smirk. "Not really."

Four hours later, Hunter's bags were packed, and Jackson was helping him carry his luggage into the airport. Hunter's suitcase was small. He'd only packed lightweight hiking pants and t-shirts. He figured he could buy anything else he needed when he arrived. The last-minute plane ticket hadn't been cheap, but the flight he needed had plenty of seats left, and he was able to get one with extra leg room. Although his body was healing, he still had to be careful during such a long flight.

He'd checked with his physical therapists before he left. Although they weren't thrilled he was making a transatlantic flight, they conceded. They said he would probably be okay as long as he kept his feet elevated and got up frequently to stretch so he didn't develop Deep Vein Thrombosis. They informed him a DVT was a blood clot that formed in the leg and could break free causing a stroke. Developing a DVT was not only life-threatening, but it was also incredibly painful and meant years of anticoagulant medications, frequent blood tests, and the threat of future clots. Hearing about the risks was all Hunter needed to make sure he took every precaution possible. He worked with the airline to get a seat that would allow him to elevate his feet and promised to get up every hour to stretch. He also agreed to drink plenty of water throughout the flight and avoid alcohol.

When he finally made it through ticketing, he turned to Jackson and thanked him for all he'd done. He promised to come home soon and agreed to call every day. He felt like a teenager negotiating to stay out past curfew, but he also understood Jackson's concerns. He was the only family Jackson had, and his uncle took his vow to look after him very seriously. After everything Jackson had given up, the last thing Hunter wanted was to cause him more stress, so he agreed to all the stipulations, embraced his uncle in a brief hug, and headed through security. It wasn't until he'd boarded the plane and was in the air that everything finally sank in. He was running on adrenaline and had avoided the reality of the situation until he was on the plane with only his thoughts to keep him company.

It seemed a little crazy that he was taking such a huge risk for a girl he barely knew, but after weeks of emails, he felt like he knew her better than any girl he'd ever dated. Of course, his feelings for Kayla weren't his only motivation for crossing the ocean. He also felt a strong need to see justice prevail and Kazamir put away for good. The man had killed his coach and caused death and destruction everywhere he went. According to the media, he was a sociopath whose grip on reality was slipping. No one knew what kind of destruction he would cause next. Hunter knew he would never be able to sleep well until Kazamir was locked up. After all, Kazamir wasn't the type of person who let things go. As long as he was free, there was a chance the lunatic would come after him again in order to finish the job he'd started at Mr. Baker. In addition, Kazamir had been stalking Kayla for years and continued to wreak havoc on every life she tried to create. The only way to end this was to end Kazamir. Hunter wasn't going to let fear or injuries stop him from ending his vicious reign of violence and terror.

Hunter's flight made a smooth landing in Newark, NJ. He had 45 minutes to cross the airport and board his next flight. He kept his promise to stay hydrated and bought a large bottle of water and a few pillows to prop up his feet. It took some searching, but he also found a book of common English to French translations. He wished he could speak Arabic, but knew it was out of the question. There was no way he could possibly learn the pronunciations in a nine-hour flight. He'd taken a few years of French in high school, so he settled on touching up on his French to get him by. He'd never been to Africa, so he'd also bought a book on Moroccan culture and was determined to learn everything he could before his plane landed in Tangier.

Chapter 53

Kayla

Kayla had a lot to accomplish in a short amount of time after she hung up the phone with Hunter. She knew WITSEC would have listened in on her call with Hunter and would contact her at any minute. Part of her agreement to receive protection from WITSEC was to follow their rules implicitly. She'd just broken one of their major stipulations, which was not to contact anyone outside of the agency without special permission and to *never* give up her location. She had followed all of their instructions carefully in the past, but things were different now. Kazamir was on his way to Tangier, and even though she didn't think he'd recognized her at Las Ramblas, she was sure he would eventually put two and two together. If he knew she was in Barcelona, he'd send someone after her.

She decided to call Agent Franklin and be up-front with him about her concerns. Franklin was not in a good mood when he picked up the phone.

"You know the rules, Kayla. You cannot communicate outside the agency. I heard every word you just said to your boyfriend. I can't believe you gave up your location. You know what this means, don't you? It means that you either have to be relocated or leave the program."

"I know that Frank, but I can't do this anymore. I saw Kazamir. He knows where I am, and I can't live like this forever."

"You *think* you saw Kazamir, Kayla, but it could have been anyone. None of us know what he looks like and even if we did, you were the only witness. We can't launch a full-fledged attack based on a hunch. I'm doing everything I can to get things moving at the agency, but these things take time."

"It was *him*, Frank. I saw his eyes. He might have changed his features with plastic surgery, but he can't change his eyes. He saw me, and it's only a matter of time before he sends someone after me. I can't spend the rest of my life in hiding. It's killing me. There's no permanence. I haven't communicated with my family or friends other than with brief emails for years and have no hope of falling in love, get married, or leading any sort of normal life because I have to disappear every time Kazamir tracks me down."

"I understand, Kayla, but there are no simple answers here."

"Come on, Frank. You and I both know that Kazamir is on a ferry heading to Tangier as we speak. In just under 30 hours, he'll disembark from the boat and disappear from your radar for good. He'll get involved in drug-dealing again, and will injure and kill countless more people while I wait around hoping he doesn't send one of his cronies to finish me off."

"Kayla, please. Be realistic..."

"I'm done being realistic, Frank. I'm done being scared. Most of all, I'm done watching other people die because of him. I'm leaving WITSEC, and I'm flying to Tangier. Now you can help me or you can fight me, but one way or another, Kazamir's reign of terror is going to end."

There was a pause at the other end of the line. "Give me one hour, Kayla. ONE hour. Please don't do anything irrational. I'll do what I can and get right back to you."

Kayla reluctantly agreed and hung up the phone. The next hour was the longest of her life. She'd never stood up to the agency or anyone for that matter. She'd always done absolutely everything she'd been told without question. This time it was different, though. This time she had more at stake. For the first time in her life, she had something to fight for. She had the promise of a relationship with Hunter and a real life. All she had to do was bring Kazamir into custody, and she and Hunter would both be free. Unfortunately, it was easier said than done. Kazamir was getting more desperate and reckless by the day. The crazier he got, the more of a wild card he was.

The ringing of her phone shook Kayla back into reality. She

answered immediately.

"Kayla, its Agent Franklin. The agency agreed to follow the lead. They don't want to let Kazamir slip through their fingers again. They're not happy, but they agreed to work with you. They'll allow you to fly to Tangier and will offer you protection, but you *have* to follow their instructions. You're our only hope for identifying him, so you must be very careful. If we lose you, we lose any hope of catching him."

Kayla breathed a sigh of relief. She would have gone to Morocco on her own, but knowing there would be federal agents there to back her up made her feel much better. The last thing she wanted to do was involve Hunter on a suicide mission.

"What about Hunter?" Kayla asked. "He's flying in to meet me."

"We can use him, too," Franklin promised. "Just remember, you're dealing with a sociopath. If he feels threatened in any way, he'll kill you and anyone else in sight. You have to take every precaution."

Kayla agreed and hung up the phone. She had very little time to get her things in order, which included changing her hair color, being outfitted in Moroccan clothing, and getting on a plane to Tangier. She didn't have time to reflect on what was happening. Years of being on the run had taken away her fear and replaced it with resilience.

Federal agents arrived as scheduled thirty minutes later. She did her best to act as though she knew them to avoid arousing suspicion in the embassy. One agent was responsible for outfitting her in a brightly printed djellaba and hijab to cover her head. The loose clothing was comfortable and left only her face exposed. Changing her hair color seemed unnecessary in light of the fact that she'd have her head covered, but the agency insisted on dying it black and trimming it into a sleek bob. She wasn't thrilled about it, but it was just hair after all. Next, they applied dark eye make-up with false eyelashes. Kayla barely recognized herself when she looked in the mirror at the sultry eyes staring back at her from underneath the traditional Moroccan clothing. The agents spent the remaining time reviewing everything she needed to know. They explained traditional Moroccan greetings and cultural norms to her in order to help her fit in. She found the culture fascinating. The Adhan, or call to prayer, rang through the city from the Mosques five times per day. In Morocco, there was no separation of Church and State. They were one and the same, and people pronounced their faith publicly five times per day. It was a totally different concept to her, but she listened and absorbed as much information as she could. Blending in was key to the mission. If she gave herself away too quickly, she would be putting Hunter's life and her own in danger.

"What about Hunter?" She asked the agents.

"He'll get a briefing as soon as he lands." They reassured her.

"Have you gotten anymore leads on Kazamir?" She asked hopefully.

"We haven't been able to confirm whether he's on the ferry to Tangier or not, but we have confirmed he's been in contact with a well-known criminal in Marrakesh. We've been tracing calls to his cell phone for a while and picked up a call from a burner phone being used in the Mediterranean. It appears the call was made from near the ferry's route. We believe Kazamir is planning to head to Marrakesh from Tangier as soon as the ferry lands."

Kayla nodded, relieved that they believed her suspicions were correct.

The agent briefing Kayla on the mission was done answering questions and spent the rest of the session drilling Kayla on the details of the plan. Kayla did her best to recite everything back and tried to stay as focused as possible, which was not easy considering the circumstances.

The agent abruptly ended their conversation. "You're ready, Kayla. A car will be waiting for you downstairs in fifteen minutes. Say goodbye to your friends at the embassy, and tell them you're going away to follow a lead for your next article. Tell them you aren't sure when you'll be back. You can tell them that you're going to a Muslim country, but don't tell them which one. Then get in the car and don't say a word to anyone. The driver will hand you a ticket and escort you to the airport. Go directly to security and find your gate. You'll look like you're alone, but there will be several undercover agents watching to make sure you arrive safety. Board your flight, but don't talk to anyone, not even the stewards or stewardesses. Don't accept anything to eat or drink. Do you understand?"

Kayla nodded and took a deep breath. She was starting to feel anxious but knew this was not the time to panic. She forced her voice to be steady. "Understood," She replied. She gave the agent a wry smile, gathered her things, and headed downstairs to bid her temporary friends at the embassy goodbye.

It was the middle of the day, so the embassy was fairly quiet. She found a few people in the lobby and thanked them for their hospitality. She gave the artwork she'd finished while in Barcelona to David and Marta as a thank you for all they had done for her.

She gave them both a hug and wiped tears from her eyes as she said goodbye. She had finally started exploring Barcelona and feeling comfortable in her new surroundings. Now, just like always, she was being forced to leave unexpectedly and venture into the unknown. Although she hoped it would get easier, it was still just as painful and frightening as it had been the first time when she'd had to leave Chicago.

When she saw a car with tinted windows pull up exactly fifteen minutes later, she excused herself and got into the backseat. Her stomach felt like it was in her throat, and she forced herself to take slow, even breaths. The driver said very little to her. He quietly loaded her bags into the trunk and started driving towards the airport. Kayla watched the sights of Barcelona go by and felt a twinge of regret that she wouldn't get to finish seeing the amazing works of Gaudí or watch a soccer game at Camp Nou Stadium.

As they approached the airport, the feelings of regret turned to excitement at the idea of seeing Hunter again. The last time she'd seen him, he was lying in a hospital bed coming to terms with his injuries and the loss of his coach. So much had changed since then. He was recovering faster than his doctors had predicted, and soon he would be meeting her in Morocco. They had shared so much over email for the past few months, and she wondered how she would feel when she saw him in person again. They always had so much to talk about over email, but she worried that seeing him in person might make things awkward. She decided the major issue was Kazamir, so her feelings for Hunter would have to be put on hold. As long as a deadly killer was on the loose, she was going to have to stay 100% focused on her mission.

When the driver pulled up at the airport, Kayla followed the instructions she'd been given and headed directly to check-in. She passed through security without any problems and made her way to her gate. She was careful not to talk to anyone and ate only the food the agents had sent with her in her carry-on. The airport was quiet, but she had an eerie feeling she was being watched as she sat at her gate, waiting for boarding. She hoped the feeling was just because she knew there were federal agents watching to make sure she was safe, but she also had a sick feeling in her stomach that someone more sinister was watching her every move.

She lowered her eyes and pretended to be engrossed in a magazine she'd brought with her, but couldn't shake the feeling. Relief flooded through her when they finally announced the start of boarding. She quickly got in line and scanned her ticket as she made her way outside. She stood on the curb with the others on her flight until a bus picked them up and drove them to a plane waiting nearby. The wind whipped her hair as she climbed the stairs and found her seat on the small aircraft. It was not a full flight, and she had an entire row to herself. She leaned her head back and closed her eyes. Her mind was racing, and she felt a sense of relief when the plane finally taxied down the runway and lifted off the ground. The sound of the engine lulled her to sleep, and she didn't open her eyes until the pilot announced they had begun their descent into Tangier. She turned her head and looked out the window just as the tip of Northern Africa came into view. The blue of the Mediterranean glistened below, and she could make out the Atlas Mountains rising in the background. The vibrant hues of the landscape were remarkable and for a brief moment, she felt like she was just a tourist rather than a woman on a mission to track down the man who had terrorized her life for the past three years. The reality of her mission returned as the plane landed, and her anxiety was replaced by determination.

Chapter 54

<u>Me</u>

I woke up to severe rocking and felt my stomach roll. I ran to the bathroom and dislodged the contents of my stomach. The wind has strengthened, and the sea grew listless while I slept. The waves had grown, and the ferry failed to negotiate through them with any sense of stability. I have always been prone to motion sickness and found myself suffering once again. My stomach reeled, and the boat pitched with the zenith and nadir of the waves. I could do little more than continue hugging the toilet in that disgusting bathroom cursing my luck. A plane would have been so much faster, but the risk was higher, so here I was on this pathetic ferry being tossed about like a ragdoll with no choice but to cling to my porcelain anchor and ride it out. In my pain, my thoughts returned to Kayla as the source of my misery. With enough time, I feel confident I can trace almost the entirety of my suffering to her. Once again, she mocks me, forcing me lower.

When my stomach was reduced to nothing more than bile, I decided to try to find my seat again. There were still 14 more hours before we would reach Tangier. I was miserable and certain I couldn't survive another hour in these conditions, but the weather finally relented and a nearby passenger offered me a scopolamine patch. I accepted it graciously and slapped it onto my skin. My nausea slowly started to subside and the scopolamine made me drowsy enough to sleep for another three hours. When I awoke, the sea was calm, and I was able to get back to business. I started by making a phone call to my contact, Kamal, in Marrakesh. Kamal and I have known each other for 15 years. We first met in Chicago when we were both still small-time.

Kamal grew up in Marrakesh. His parents split up when he was a teenager, and he moved to the states with his mother, who wanted to be closer to her family. He was bitter when I met him. He and his mother had moved to a rough neighborhood and life hadn't been kind to them. His mother struggled to pay the rent and put food on the table, and Kamal blamed his father for their hardship. Kamal hated seeing his mother working three jobs trying to provide for him, so he sought to help in any way he could. He made connections on the corners and began as a runner and lookout. He had a chip on his shoulder and a keen awareness of what went on around him at all times, which kept him alive and out of jail. He was tough and gave ground to no one. We met and formed a quick partnership. He was savvy enough to avoid getting busted and taught me a lot about dealing. Times were tough for us both back then, and we were determined to fight our way to the good life. Kamal experienced good fortune. He made some serious scratch in Chicago and cashed in while he was ahead. He even washed enough of the money to discretely take care of his mom. Finally, he moved back to Marrakesh, bought a huge house in the Medina, hired an army of servants, and now has a huge network of people working under him.

Life has treated us very differently, to say the least. While Kamal was living the good life, I was running from the authorities and scraping by. My life had become an embarrassment, and if I'm being honest, I resented Kamal for his success. I was desperate, though, and Kamal owed me. I'd taken a bullet for him back in Chicago. There'd been a drive-by shooting, and I'd pushed Kamal out of the way. A bullet hit me in the shoulder, and Kamal got by unscathed. Kamal never forgot it and was willing to do anything for me. Living in a desert in Northern Africa wasn't exactly my idea of paradise, but at this point, my friends were few and far between. I was out of options.

I had picked up a few burner phones at Kamal's suggestion. He was smart enough to know that the authorities were watching his every move. It was well known that Kamal was one of the wealthiest men in Marrakesh. There was plenty of speculation amongst the authorities as to where that money was coming from.

Out of the Shadows

The last thing he wanted was for me to come rolling into town and get him into trouble, so he'd taken it upon himself to give me careful instructions on how to dress and where to go. I hated being told what to do, but I didn't have much of a choice at the moment. I rolled my eyes and decided the only thing left to do was drink away the residual headache from the oncoming hangover and passing nausea and ordered another three fingers of scotch. Each searing gulp seemed to be my only escape from this purgatory. I could only close my eyes and wish it all to be a nightmare from which I would soon awaken.

Chapter 55

Hunter

    Hunter fastened his seatbelt when the pilot announced they were preparing for landing. The flight had gone smoothly, and he'd carefully followed his physical therapists' instructions. He watched as the Moroccan landscape came into view. He felt nauseous about what was about to happen but was also relieved that if everything went according to plan, the whole ordeal would be over soon. He'd been informed that an undercover agent would meet him after he deplaned and give him a disguise. He hoped it would be enough to prevent Kazamir from recognizing him. Kayla had reassured him she would be waiting for him outside of the airport in an unmarked car. He was excited to see her but knew that there wouldn't be much time for catching up. Time was of the essence, and Kazamir's ferry was due to arrive in just under two hours. They didn't have any time to spare.

    The pilot pulled off a smooth landing, and one by one the passengers deplaned and stepped onto the scorching runway. A bus was waiting in the oppressing heat and took them to the terminal. He kept his head down and walked towards baggage claim. It didn't take long for a man dressed in a black suit to fall into step beside him. "Don't say a word, just take this bag and head into the restroom to your right. Change as quickly as you can into the new clothes and place your old ones back in the bag, then exit the doors on the right just past baggage claim. Leave the bag behind. We'll take care of collecting your things." He thrust a black duffle bag into Hunter's hands and disappeared just as quickly as he'd arrived.

    Hunter followed his instructions and quickly changed into the caftan he found in the bag and wound a turban around his head to complete his disguise. The clothing felt odd, but he didn't have time to think about it. He stashed the jeans and t-shirt he'd worn on the flight in the duffle bag and headed out the doors just past baggage claim. Immediately, a black sedan pulled up to the curb in front of him and a door opened. He glimpsed a pair of dark eyes with long eyelashes peering out at him from under a hijab. It took him a minute to realize it was Kayla. She looked so different then the last time he'd seen her, but when a small smile touched the corners of her lips, he realized she was still the same woman who had stolen his heart over the past few months. He returned her smile, quickly climbed in, and closed the door behind him.

He wanted to kiss her so badly, but the driver was eyeing him closely through the rearview mirror, so he settled for putting his arm around her shoulders and giving her a kiss on the cheek. "How are you holding up?" He whispered softy in her ear.

She gave him a wry grin. "Better now that you're here. This all seems so surreal. I'll be glad when it's all over."

The driver cleared his throat and announced, "I'm taking you to a hotel where you'll meet with Agent Franklin and his team. They'll give you instructions on how to proceed."

There were so many things Hunter wanted to say to Kayla, but his attention was immediately drawn to the chaos outside his window. There were cars careening all over the place and pedestrians wandering into traffic. It was a disorganized mess, and he found himself tightening his grip on Kayla's shoulder.

The driver sensed his uneasiness and spoke up. "It's every man for himself out here. There are no real traffic rules; everyone just tries to avoid getting hit by everyone else"

Kayla and Hunter both breathed a sigh of relief when the driver finally pulled up to a hotel. A door attendant made his way over and opened the door. Kayla and Hunter both climbed out. "Go to room 2105 and knock three times."

Hunter nodded. They walked in silence to the elevator and breathed a sigh of relief when they climbed in and the door closed behind them. Hunter caught Kayla in a fierce embrace. She sighed into his kiss. She'd missed him so much and was still in disbelief that he had come all the way to Morocco for her. Hunter fumbled to punch in the 21st floor and groaned in frustration when the elevator dinged their arrival. Their stolen moment hadn't been long enough. When the elevator doors opened, they were greeted by a crowd of tourists impatiently waiting to get on. They carefully stepped off the elevator and avoided making eye contact with anyone. Then they headed to room 2105, and Hunter knocked three times. The door opened a crack, and someone motioned for them to enter.

The dimly lit room smelled of a combination of smoke and mint tea. Agent Franklin was sitting at a desk and two other agents were pacing back and forth. They seemed relieved that Kayla and Hunter had arrived, but looked apprehensive as well. They knew the stakes were high and one false move would allow Kazamir to sneak away and disappear for good. The American public was demanding justice. The longer he was at large, the more pressure they were feeling to arrest him and make him face the consequences of his actions.

One of the agents motioned for Hunter and Kayla to sit on the edge of the bed. He motioned for them to look at the opposite wall. The blank space was quickly filled with a large map from a projector, and he began explaining the plan. Hunter and Kayla listened carefully. The feds, who had done their research, spent the next 15 minutes explaining everything they needed to know.

Kayla felt overwhelmed as she tried to focus on what was being said. She was the only person in the room who could actually identify Kazamir since he had changed his looks so drastically after the Chicago incident and had been wearing a ski mask during the entire Mt. Baker attack. She had seen his face at the market in Barcelona and was the only one who could accurately identify Kazamir when he got off the ferry. She gave a careful description of what he looked like to the agents, and one of them sketched a picture of him that looked fairly accurate, but they still wanted her to be at the dock in order to confirm his identity.

She agreed to go on the condition that Hunter would

accompany her. She didn't want to face Kazamir alone. The agents reluctantly agreed and then explained that the ferry would be docking in 30 minutes, so there was no time to waste. They wired Kayla and Hunter with earpieces so they would be able to communicate with the team standing by. Finally, they instructed the duo to go back outside and get in the same sedan that had brought them. As they walked towards the elevator, Hunter took Kayla's hand and squeezed it. She squeezed back and felt her breath returning. She hadn't realized she'd been holding it throughout most of the meeting. She was scared to death but knew she would never have her life back unless she faced her fears and helped identify the man who haunted her nightmares.

  They obediently climbed into the waiting sedan, and it careened through traffic before finally pulling up to the harbor. Hunter and Kayla quickly slipped out and found their way to the ferry's landing. They hid behind a pillar that had a good view of the dock and waited. The tension and anxiety they both felt hung in the air, and time seemed to stand still. The ferry pulled in right on time and docked in what seemed like slow motion. After an interminable amount of time, passengers started shuffling off the boat carrying their luggage. Almost everyone was dressed in a loose-fitting caftan or djellaba and most of the women wore hijabs or colorful headscarves. Kayla started to feel frustration welling up as she scanned the passengers. Other than the tourists, almost all of the men were dressed in traditional Moroccan clothing. Identifying Kazamir should have been easy considering he was a foreigner in this mystical land. As the stream of passengers slowed to a trickle, there was still no sign of him. Her heart started racing, and she felt panic rising up in her throat. The entire plan was focused on identifying Kazamir as he disembarked. What if he had never boarded the ferry or found a way to escape in the middle of the Mediterranean? Had she been wrong about her hunch? Maybe her eyes had played tricks on her at La Bouqueria? She glanced at Hunter and couldn't squelch the feeling that she had let him down.

She could feel her freedom slipping away. She spoke into her headset, "There's no sign of him." She could hear the frustration in the agents' replies.

"Could he still be on the boat?" One of them asked.

Kayla looked around, but the crew was closing the gates. "I don't think so, but you could send someone to check just in case."

"We'll send one of the undercover guys to do a sweep of the ferry. Are you absolutely certain you didn't see him?"

Kayla bit her lower lip. "I didn't see him in the crowd, but he could have been wearing a disguise."

Hunter nodded and squeezed her hand before jumping in on the conversation "The only soul he knows in this country lives in Marrakesh. Let's go straight to the train station. There's a good chance that he's going to take a train to Marrakesh. He may let his guard down now that he thinks he's outsmarted us."

"Good idea," one agent responded. "We'll sweep the boat; you guys get to the train station and purchase tickets to Marrakesh. Be on the lookout for him."

Like magic, a car pulled up in front of them. They recognized their driver and climbed in. The car peeled away from the curb, and they made it to the train station in record time. When they arrived, Hunter and Kayla darted out into the throngs of people who were flooding the entrance.

"He must be leaving on the first train out," Hunter reasoned.

"There's the ticket counter!" Kayla pointed. "The next train leaves in five minutes. We don't have time to waste. We've got to get on that train."

"You watch for him, and I'll get tickets," Hunter called out as he hustled towards the ticket counter.

Kayla scanned the faces of the people shuffling past her. She felt like she was in a dream. Everyone seemed to look the same, and she didn't want to go too far for fear of losing Hunter. Just as she was about to give up, she saw something odd sticking out of a garbage can near one of the restrooms. Initially, she thought nothing of it, but soon she realized that someone had discarded a colorful caftan and headscarf, which seemed odd. She stepped closer and examined the clothing. On top of the pile, she saw the ferry schedule that had been sticking out of Kazamir's pocket at La Boqueria and an empty wallet that looked like the one she saw him swipe from a man just after he attempted to take her purse. As she stared at the pile, it dawned on her that Kazamir may have worn women's clothing as a disguise when he got off the ferry. The head covering was the perfect way for him to avoid detection. Once he'd made it to the train station, he must have deposited his disguise in the trash before boarding a train.

    She tugged on Hunter's arm and pointed at the trash bin as he paid for the tickets. "Kazamir's here. I think he dressed as a woman to sneak past us and threw away his disguise before he boarded the train. He must be on the train to Marrakesh."

    Hunter grabbed the two tickets he had just purchased and followed Kayla as she ran towards the platform. She was fast, and it was all he could do to force his healing body to keep pace with her. Their hearts started racing as the final boarding whistle filled the smoke-filled air. Their muscles ached and their lungs burned, but their determination propelled them.

    Kayla panted into her headpiece, "He must be on the train. Can any agents board and arrest him?"

    "Sorry Kayla, you're the closest one to the train, and it sounds like it's about to take off. Get onboard and try to find Kazamir without letting him see you. We'll have agents meet you at the first stop."

    Kayla grabbed Hunter's hand, and they jumped onto the nearest car, just as the doors were closing. Sweat was streaming down their faces, and they did their best to slow their breathing to avoid attracting attention. Kayla's heart was pounding in her chest so hard she was sure the other passengers would know something was amiss, but no one seemed to pay them any heed as they wandered down the aisle and took a seat.

She rested her head on Hunter's shoulder and closed her eyes. Things had not gone as planned. Kazamir should already have been in custody, and she and Hunter should have been able to start their lives together. She gave a soft sigh, realizing life rarely worked out as she'd hoped. She comforted herself with the knowledge that Hunter was with her, and there was still hope of finding Kazamir.

"What do we do now?" She whispered to Hunter.

He gave her a half-smile and kissed the top of her head. "We start checking each car and do our best to locate him."

"This is a big train! That could take hours." She whispered back.

"We'll need to be strategic. You're the only one who knows what he looks like, so we'll have to work our way from back to front." Hunter reasoned.

They were sitting in the last car on the train since it was the closest car to them when the final whistle blew. Kayla nodded. "That makes sense." She adjusted her hijab and put on a pair of sunglasses, hoping it would be enough of a disguise to prevent Kazamir from recognizing her. It was harder for Hunter to disguise himself since he was such a well-known sports figure, but he also pulled on a pair of sunglasses and did his best to look inconspicuous.

They started their search by scrutinizing each face in their train car. Most passengers were in the process of getting settled, and no one looked suspicious. They headed to the next car and realized it was a sleeper car. This posed a whole new challenge. It was harder to tell who was in the sleeper cars. Some men and women were sprawled across the seats with blankets and their faces covered from sight. Kayla let out a frustrated breath. "This is *not* going to be easy."

By the time the train made its first stop, they still hadn't had any success. Kayla and Hunter were notified that two federal agents were waiting and boarded as soon as the doors opened. They were undercover and would follow them from a safe distance during the search, which was reassuring but didn't make their job of finding

Kazamir any easier.

Kayla and Hunter pretended to be nonchalant as they entered each train car and casually walked down the aisles. Most people were engrossed in their cell phones or laptops or were sleeping. No one looked remotely like Kazamir. Time seemed to creep by at a snail's pace. There was very little airflow in the train, and the heat was sweltering. Kayla felt a mixture of exhaustion and frustration. Hunter was determined, and his encouragement kept her going. Each time the trained stopped, Kayla felt panicked. She knew Kazamir could get off at any point, which would make the entire effort worthless, but she knew they had no choice but to continue.

The federal agents stayed out of sight, but they both felt reassured knowing someone had their backs. They finally took a break when they reached a car with a small cafe. They both ordered coffee and a sandwich. The bread was stale, but they were both starving and fatigue was setting in. Kayla dumped three sugar packets into the sludge that passed as coffee. The food and boost of caffeine gave them renewed energy, and they continued the search. Faces started blurring together, and Kayla started to question whether or not she really did remember what Kazamir looked like. Maybe the image she had in her mind was just a figment of her imagination, and she'd already walked right past him. She could almost hear his laughter as he realized he'd escaped yet again. She shook her head, pushed the disturbing thought out of her mind, and continued. Eventually, an announcement came over the speakers that they were 20 minutes outside of Marrakesh. Her breath caught in her chest, and she looked at Hunter in desperation. He held up his hands to indicate that there were only ten cars left to search. She took a deep breath, and they pressed on.

The next four cars proved to be full of a youth soccer team. The only adults present were frazzled looking coaches who were desperately trying to quiet their players down. The car after that was a sleeper car, which made Kayla give a sigh of frustration. These were the hardest to search. They walked past three compartments that were filled with families. The next compartment had a man dressed in a caftan lying across the seats. His face was turned away from them. They looked on in silence until the man gave a loud snort, and turned towards them. Kayla stifled her disappointment when she realized that he looked nothing like Kazamir. Time was running out, and there were only a few cars left.

    A whistle sounded, and Kayla glanced out the window. Panic took hold as she realized the train was entering the tracks of the Marrakesh train station. She quickened her pace and frantically looked around. The train was slowing and people were starting to mobilize. Eventually, the motion stopped, and the train doors opened. She looked around desperately. They were just entering the final train car when she saw him. There was a man looking down and talking on his cell phone. He slipped off the train just as she caught a glimpse of his face. "That's him!" She spoke rapidly into her headpiece and described Kazamir's appearance and location to the federal agents who were standing by. She and Hunter rushed off the train and took off after him. They wove their way around a vast number of people all toting suitcases, garment bags, and in some cases, small children. It felt like they were in a maze of unfamiliar faces, surrounded by sights, sounds, and smells they'd never experienced. Stepping off the train felt like stepping into a dream world. The chaos and clatter around them were overwhelming. Kayla caught a glimpse of Kazamir as he and another man stepped out of the train station onto the street. She and Hunter narrowly missed a donkey with bags of goods hanging off his back. Hunter threw out an apology to the owner of the donkey as they darted around the animal in desperate pursuit. They were informed that federal agents were following them and were given permission to press on with their chase. Hunter watched helplessly as Kazamir ducked into a waiting car and slammed the door behind him. Tires squealed as the car took off. Kayla and Hunter followed suit and jumped into a waiting taxi.

    "Follow that car," Hunter urgently instructed the driver while pointing to Kazamir's escape vehicle. Then he added "Please" to soften the order. They breathed a sigh of relief when the driver understood English. His tires squealed as he veered out into traffic.

The driver expertly maneuvered around the donkey carts, taxi cabs, and pedestrians filling the streets. "Lane lines and traffic signs are merely a suggestion in Marrakesh," the driver laughed as he continued to weave around larger vehicles, narrowly avoiding an accident. "Welcome to my home!" He said jovially.

Kayla didn't exactly feel his enthusiasm. She was hanging on to her seat for dear life and praying they would make it to their destination in one piece. She received word that the agents were able to track their location with GPS and were following close behind them. Roads started to narrow as they entered the Medina, or old town. A large mosque rose above the city, and a loud horn-like sound reverberated off the buildings and filled the air with a mystical quality. She watched in fascination as people started walking toward the mosque from all directions.

The driver glanced at her from his rearview mirror. "Call to prayer," he said in his heavily accented voice. "It happens five times per day." Kayla nodded, amazed by what was unfolding before her. She snapped back to reality when the cab squealed around a corner. "They're slowing down," the driver pointed ahead to Kazamir's car.

He brought the car to an abrupt halt, and Hunter threw money towards him as they toppled out of the cab. The midday heat rose up and engulfed them like they'd just entered a sauna. The air felt thick, but they didn't have time to dwell on the heat. There was too much chaos going on around them to think clearly, and they narrowly missed being hit by a motorbike that came careening around the bend.

Hunter pointed up ahead as Kazamir ducked around a corner with another man dressed in a caftan. They hustled after them and quickly realized they were entering the souk, or large market area, filling endless alleyways throughout the Medina. They hustled past large displays of spices and breathed in the heavy smell of cinnamon, turmeric, and cumin. They rounded another corner, and Hunter scarcely avoided running into a large display of exotic fruits in all shapes and colors. Kazamir and his cohort were moving fast, but Hunter and Kayla were able to keep pace. They shook their heads at shopkeepers who were approaching them with jewelry, scarves, and handmade leather shoes. They rounded another corner, and the world suddenly opened up into the city's main public square, Jemaa el-Fnaa, which was filled with merchants, hawkers, and entertainers. Kayla stifled a scream when she spotted a row of snake charmers calmly handling their massive constrictors. She veered away from them and followed Hunter as he led the way past carts selling freshly squeezed orange juice and stands stacked high with bottles of argon oil. The heat was oppressive. She felt sweat trickling down her back. She took a deep breath and let out a cough. Smoke and the smell of horse manure filled her lungs. Just when she thought she couldn't take another breath, she saw Kazamir dodge down another narrow alleyway. She and Hunter were closing the gap. She felt a sense of relief as they escaped the chaos of the square and became engulfed in a quiet maze of alleyways again, but her relief didn't last long.

As the chase continued, she realized they were getting deeper and deeper into a maze. She felt disoriented and doubted she could find her way back out. They managed to catch occasional glimpses of their targets until they rounded a corner, and Hunter came to an abrupt stop. There was no one in the alley other than a few kids playing a game with bottle caps. The kids were laughing and carrying on as if nothing out of the ordinary was happening. One of them looked up when he heard Kayla let out a groan.

Hunter thought fast and approached the kid who was closest to him. The boy looked to be the youngest, but also seemed to be the most gregarious of the crew. "Did you see two men pass through here just a minute ago?"

The boy grinned and nodded. Hunter let out a sigh of relief. "Could you show me where they went?"

The boy smiled and held out his hand as if he was asking Hunter to pay him up front for his services.

Hunter reached into his pocket, but before he could produce any money, the oldest boy walked up and slapped the younger boy lightly on the shoulder. They exchanged some words in Arabic that Hunter didn't understand, but the little boy looked down and put his hand back in his pocket. "I'll show you," he said in surprisingly good English, "but my brother said I can't charge you."

Kayla giggled and tousled his hair. "Thank you."

Her smile seemed to be all the payment he needed. He motioned for them to follow him as he led them through an even narrower alley to a small wooden door. He motioned towards the door. "One of them lives here."

Kayla thanked him and gave him a hug. He blushed before running away.

"We're in front of Kazamir's hideout," she spoke into her headpiece and then waited for further instructions.

She looked at Hunter and explained, "The agents are tracking us with GPS right now. They should be here in two minutes. They want us to stay put until they arrive."

With nothing to do but wait, Hunter paused and gave her the kiss he'd been meaning to give her from the moment he'd seen her. She kissed him back with the same intensity. They finally broke apart when they heard footsteps approaching. Eight undercover agents rounded the corner. The first one showed them his badge. He instructed Kayla and Hunter to stay back with the agent who would be guarding the exit. They exchanged a glance and followed his instructions.

Hunter's expression was unreadable. His jaw clenched, and his eyes were trained on the entrance. He knew how much was at stake, and he didn't want Kayla to pick up on his apprehension. He gave Kayla's hand a reassuring squeeze that disguised his own uneasiness over what was about to happen. The agents did a quick survey of the area. There was no way to enter the compound quietly. The door was locked, and they were surrounded by walls. There were no windows facing the alley and no other entrance in sight. The only option was to blow the door open. Kazamir would know the second he heard the explosion that he'd been followed, and chaos would ensue. They watched in trepidation as the agents placed a device near the handle of the door and backed away. The click of a button would blow off the lock and grant the agents access to the hideout. Kayla held her breath and watched as the agent pressed his finger down on the remote.

Chapter 56

<u>Me</u>

You might think it's easy to dress as a woman in Morocco, but my feet were killing me after shoving them into those miserable shoes. I knew I should have stayed undercover, but the headscarf was suffocating and there was no way I was going to get anywhere in those shoes. I quickly changed in the train station bathroom and threw my costume into the nearest trash bin. I didn't see anyone suspicious when I disembarked the ferry and didn't notice a tail on the way to the station, so I think I'm in the clear.

It was all so easy. Kamal had tickets waiting for me at the train station. I was careful to go all the way to the end of the platform and board an empty train car in order to avoid as many people as possible. I found an empty cabin, took a few gulps of cheap whiskey from my flask and fell asleep, content that I'd evaded my pursuers again. The ride was hot and bumpy, but at least there was no sign of anyone who would give me trouble. The week since I'd left Amsterdam had been miserable. I was sick of being on the run. I was finally within reach of my salvation, my sanctuary. I knew Kamal would treat me like a brother when I arrived and spare no expense during my stay. I chuckled to myself as I pondered the duality of enjoying the comforts of Kamal's hospitality while knowing that I would have nothing and no one across the world where I'd become Public Enemy #1. While lesser men and women toiled searching for me, I was going to be hiding out in an old friend's riad, lounging by his pool and surrounded by servants willing to sate my every desire. A feeling of smugness began to eclipse my impatience to be finished running.

I still can't believe I attempted to rob the one person I've been trying to torment and kill for years. After all that time, to be so close and not even recognize her in the moment was humiliating. I couldn't even take a cheap, dime-store handbag from this woman without issue. Paranoia and anxiety wrestled for dominance within my mind and each threatened to boil away any sanity I had remaining. I finally reasoned that she couldn't have recognized me in the moment since I hadn't recognized her until hours later. Surely she wouldn't do anything about it either. She'd been paralyzed with fear for years and wouldn't dare take the initiative to challenge me. Even if she had, if they knew where I was and what I was doing, they would have tried to meet me in Tangier.

    The train slowed as we approached the station. My smile widened with each second. I was *finally* in Marrakesh. I gathered the few things I had and called Kamal. He answered on the first ring and confirmed he was waiting on the platform. I spotted him immediately and jumped off the train as soon as the door opened. We didn't waste time with pleasantries. That had never been his style. He wasn't the type who cared to spend more time than necessary in public, so I followed his lead. After a quick handshake, he led me to a waiting car, and we slid into the back seat. The car pulled away, and he started to fill me in. He owned a riad in the Medina where he did most of his business. He was overly cautious to begin with and the fact that his riad housed an excessive amount of drugs and countless women who worked in the world's oldest profession didn't allay his instincts. He informed me that we were going to have to take "the long way" back to his place. He didn't like the idea of being trailed, so we were going to have to weave our way through the Medina in order to lose any potential tails. I rolled my eyes but didn't protest. I was hungover and exhausted, but Kamal was willing to take me in despite the heat he was already under as well as what I may bring with me, so I knew I had no standing to complain.

    Eventually, the driver stopped the car and we climbed out. Kamal led me through a ridiculous maze. We wove our way through the winding alleyways of the Medina, narrowly missing horse muck, snake charmers, and henna artists. I was hardly able to keep pace.

Out of the Shadows

My breath felt labored, and I started to doubt that we would ever get anywhere in this madness. The chaos of the streets permeated the air, and my legs grew tired from the endless twists and turns. Finally, after I had convinced myself that Kamal was going to leave me to die in this maze, we rounded a corner and he gestured to a door. With the twist of a key, the door opened, and I swear I could hear angels singing from within. Before I knew it, we were out of the grimy, dim alleyway and had entered an insanely luxurious courtyard. A large pool was surrounded by pillars and benches covered in pillows, just as I had imagined. Platters piled high with mouthwatering food and a bar stocked with top-shelf liquor surrounded the pool. The heavy beat of Chaabi music filled the air. Scantily clad women lounged about, and I felt like I'd died and gone to heaven. It baffled me that the chaos and noise we'd just experienced in the outside world gave way to such a paradise. I smiled to myself. It was hard to believe that just days ago I'd been on the run in Europe. Now I was suddenly going to be treated like a king in Morocco. The moment overwhelmed me as I fell to my knees. Kamal said nothing but placed his hand on my shoulder and smiled as he pensively stared into the distance. Life was good.

Chapter 57

Hunter

Hunter ducked down and held Kayla close as the door exploded open. His one job was to make sure she stayed safe. No matter what happened in the next few minutes, he was determined to ensure that nothing happened to her. He hadn't been able to protect his coach during the Mt. Baker bombing, but this time things were going to be different. This time he was going to protect the person who was most important to him. They remained crouched in the alley, watching as the agents flew through the door with their guns raised. A combination of panic and anarchy ensued. He heard the agents yelling for everyone to get down. There was an infinite moment of silence. Suddenly screams broke out and gunfire followed. Hunter covered Kayla with his body and made sure she stayed out of the line of fire. They weren't able to see anything, but they heard shouts coming from the agents as they commanded everyone to get down.

"I'm scared," Kayla whispered.

"It'll be alright," Hunter spoke softly in her ear. "Kazamir doesn't have anywhere to go. The guards have the entrance blocked, and there's a helicopter just overhead that will get him if he makes it to the roof."

There was more silence followed by more gunfire.

Hunter could see some women dressed in flowing sheer skirts with veils over their faces being led out in handcuffs, but there was no sign of Kazamir.

There was another stretch of silence, and Hunter and Kayla could only imagine what was going on inside the premises.

Finally, agent Agent Franklin emerged through the door and motioned to Kayla. "We think we've got him."

Kayla let out a long breath she hadn't realized she'd been

holding.

"We'll need you to identify him. I'm sorry to ask you to do this, but I'll need you to come with me." He reluctantly motioned to Hunter, "He can come, too, but I'll warn you that it's not a pretty sight in there."

Hunter looked at Kayla, and she nodded for him to follow. Her eyes reflected the fear and apprehension she was feeling.

They stepped through the small wooden door and entered the riad. Hunter carefully looked around and took in the scene. Furniture was strewn everywhere. Platters of food had been flung over. Bullet holes were visible in some of the pillows and tapestries that bordered the courtyard. There was a body floating in the pool, turning the water from crystal clear to blood red. Kayla looked away, and Hunter pulled her in closer. As they walked, Franklin explained that the owner of the riad was a major drug dealer and longtime friend of Kazamir's. He'd been armed and had fired shots when the agents raided the riad. They'd had no choice but to fire back. Kazamir had used the commotion as a cover and ran up the stairs to the roof. He'd been attempting to jump to another building when the helicopter they'd called in for backup had shot him in the leg. The wound stalled him long enough for an agent to make it to the roof and place him under arrest. They were nearly certain it was Kazamir but needed Kayla to make a final identification.

They climbed the stairs to the second floor. The walls were tiled with colorful mosaics, and intricate lanterns lined the dark stairwell. In another time and place, she would have paused to admire the beauty of the riad, but they were there for one purpose only. After rounding another set of winding stairs, they emerged onto the rooftop. Hunter could make out a figure in the background. A mixture of anger and contempt filled him as he realized this was the man who was responsible for not only the death of his coach and the end of his skiing career but also the deaths of so many other innocent people. He looked down at Kayla and saw the same emotions reflected in her eyes.

"This will all be over soon, Kayla, and then we'll be free to start our life together."

Kayla smiled up at him, tears forming in the corner of her eyes. "It's about time."

Chapter 58

Kayla

As she stepped out of the staircase onto the open-air rooftop, Kayla could see the sun setting over the Atlas Mountains in the background. Shades of pink and reds filled the sky and light danced off the rooftops across the city of Marrakesh. The Mosque rose above the city and the sound of another call to prayer rang out, heavy and deep. Had circumstances been different, she would have stood in awe of the mystical scene that unfolded before her, but all she could think of now was the destruction Kazamir had caused wherever he'd gone. She could see him on the edge of the rooftop. He was huddled like a child surrounded by agents. His hands were cuffed behind his back, and he appeared to be in excruciating pain.

Kayla was grateful that Hunter was by her side. She squeezed his hand and looked up at him. He was one of the few people who could understand the contempt and loathing she felt for this man. She bravely walked with Agent Franklin and Hunter towards Kazamir. He looked up, and she recognized his blank and empty stare instantly. His cold, unfeeling eyes sent chills down her spine.

"That's him," she stated with absolute confidence. "I'd know those eyes anywhere."

"I'll end you and your boyfriend, you pathetic little whelp," he said, his voice full of rage, as he attempted to lunge towards her.

Kayla jumped back, and Hunter stepped in front of her.

The agents grabbed Kazamir and pulled him away. "That's all we need." They grabbed his arms and hauled him down the staircase. "Drink it in, Kazamir, because these were your last moments of freedom."

Kayla felt a weight lift off her shoulders as she watched them go. Kazamir was finally in custody and would never bother her again. She wouldn't have to keep running anymore. It was unbelievable. The weight of gratitude she felt was almost too much to process all at once. She wrapped her arms around Hunter's waist and squeezed. "Thank you," she said softly. He had been a big reason she'd had the courage to go after Kazamir. She didn't know how to fully express her gratitude to Hunter or Agent Franklin, but the sparkle in her eye and the sincerity in her voice conveyed the deep appreciation she felt.

"You're the one who finally brought Kazamir down, Kayla." Agent Franklin replied. "Without you, he'd still be at large, and his reign of terror and crime would continue." He paused. "My work here is done, so I'm going to catch the first flight back to the States and give you kids some privacy."

Kayla grinned at him and stood on her tiptoes to give him a hug. "Thanks for everything, Frank."

"It was nothing, Kayla," He blushed. "Just bake me some more of those chocolate chip cookies, and we'll call it even." With that, he left them in peace to watch the sunset over the Marrakesh skyline.

Kayla leaned into Hunter as the sun dropped behind the Atlas Mountains. The entire sky filled with shades of red as the last light of the sun drifted below the horizon. The silence that filled the air was a stark contrast to the chaos they had just witnessed. For the first time in years, Kayla felt a sense of total peace. She stretched up on her tiptoes and kissed Hunter long and hard. They'd both survived the worst, and they hadn't let it beat them down. Instead, it had brought them together.

Eventually, an agent climbed the stairs and cleared his throat, breaking the silence. "I'm sorry to interrupt, but Agent Franklin has arranged for your accommodations for the remainder of your time in Morocco. You'll need to stay in the country until all the paperwork is processed. We want to make sure you're comfortable during your stay." He gave them a card with the name of a driver and the name of a hotel, La Mamounia. Kayla recognized the name immediately.

"La Mamounia! Isn't that where Winston Churchill stayed whenever he traveled to Morocco?" Kayla asked.

"We trust you'll find the accommodations acceptable. Your driver will pick you up and take you anywhere you need to go while you're in Marrakesh. We'll need you to come down to the station at 8:00 AM tomorrow. You're free to do whatever you like for the evening." With that, he turned and left.

Kayla smiled. "Well, Mr. Erickson, how do you feel about going on a *real* date?"

Hunter grinned and took her hand. "I'd say it's about time! I've been waiting to take you out since the first day you came to visit me in the hospital."

They left the riad with an agent who led them expertly through the narrow, winding alleyways to a car that was waiting for them. The driver drove them straight to the most magnificent hotel either of them had ever seen. The lobby proudly displayed paintings done by Winston Churhill himself, and the expansive gardens were filled with flowers in every color imaginable. They dined that night outside on a patio surrounded by twinkling lights. The waiters brought out a bottle of champagne in a bucket of ice.

"To you," Hunter said, raising his glass. "The most beautiful women I've ever met, no matter what name or identity you happen to be using."

Kayla raised her glass, "To you, Hunter Erickson, for giving me the courage to finally end this crazy game of cat and mouse. Thank you for giving me back my future."

They clinked glasses and savored the dinner that followed. They agreed it was the most amazing meal of their lives. They were acutely aware that they were going to have to face reality and make decisions about their future soon, but the night was for celebrating. They knew that no matter what the future held, they would be in it together.

Jennifer & Barrett Gipp

Epilogue

Hunter and Kayla

Hunter and Kayla stayed in Marrakesh long enough to answer the endless questions from both the US and Moroccan Agents. The US agents were determined to make sure the case against Kazamir was airtight. They didn't want any errors in paperwork to allow him to slip through their fingers again. No matter how delusional or psychotic he was, there was no way he was ever going to walk free or harm another person. The days were long and the questions seemed never-ending, but eventually, Kayla and Hunter were told that they were free to go. The agents reassured them their flights home would arranged, and Kayla's belonging would be shipped from the Canadian Embassy in Barcelona back to the US.

The stress of the past few days had taken its toll on both of them, and they decided to stay in Marrakesh for a few extra days to recover. The peaceful gardens and pools at La Mamounia hotel were working wonders to calm both of their nerves. A combination of the savory Moroccan food, argon oil massages, and mint tea was exactly what they needed to block out the memory of what they'd seen during Kazamir's arrest. In addition, they wanted to take some time to explore the Yves Saint-Laurent's Majorelle Garden. The gardens appealed to Kayla, and she took endless photos so she could paint various scenes throughout the garden. She loved the vibrant blues of the buildings and bright primary colors of all the fountains and walkways. The lily pad-covered ponds and the variety of cacti and plants growing throughout the property inspired her. They ended up going back repeatedly in the late afternoon to escape the heat of the city and enjoy the shade of the dense foliage in the gardens. The extra time in Marrakesh also helped them plan for their future.

Kayla left behind her life in Seattle when was sent to Barcelona by the WITSEC program. Although she was excited to reunite with her family in Chicago, she didn't feel that she particularly belonged there anymore. She had grown to love living in the Pacific Northwest and wasn't in a hurry to move inland. After much thought and discussion, they both decided that Portland would be the perfect place for them to start their lives together. Hunter's physical therapists were there, and Kayla had already spent endless amounts of time painting scenes from Astoria and Cannon Beach for the Plaza Hotel. It seemed like Portland would be an easy fit for both of them.

 Hunter spent a lot of time thinking about his future. He was ready to be done leading the life of a professional skier. He used to love traveling the globe competing against the best of the best, but everything changed the day of the Mt. Baker Bombing when Coach Sullivan died, and his body was shattered. He no longer craved the thrill of the race and didn't want to live a life on the road anymore. He was nearly finished with his business degree and decided to use what he'd learned to continue making investments with the money he'd saved throughout his career and start a ski school.

 Both Hunter and Kayla had faced the demons of their pasts and were looking forward to beginning their future together.

 On their final night in Marrakesh, they took a sunset camel ride and witnessed the most intense sunset across the desert they'd ever experienced. Brilliant hues painted the mountains in the distance. The gorgeous scenery reminded them that despite the evil they'd both witnessed in their lives, life could still be incredibly beautiful. Later that night, they sat in the dark on the rooftop of their hotel watching the flickering light of the ornate, metal lanterns and sipping mint tea. They both knew that Kazamir was far away in a prison, plotting his revenge, but they also knew that justice would prevail, and he would never touch them or have any influence on their lives again. They went to bed that night feeling at peace with the world and hopeful for their future.

 The next morning, as their plane back to the US lifted off the ground; Hunter covered Kayla's hand with his own and kissed her forehead. "You're my world," he whispered.

She met his gaze with her eyes, and he saw all the promises of the future sparkling back at him.

Out of the Shadows: Discussion Questions

1. What is the significance of the title? Would you have given the book a different title?
2. Do you think the story was plot-based or character driven?
3. Which character did you relate to the most? What was it about them that you connected with?
4. If the book were being adapted into a movie, who would you want to see play what parts?
5. How did the characters change throughout the story? How did your opinion of them change?
6. What scene resonated most with you personally in either a positive or negative way? Why?
7. What was your favorite city featured in the story? Why?
8. How did you feel about the ending? What did you like, what did you not like, and what do you wish had been different?